MW01092547

Return to Sender

By Craig Johnson

The Longmire Series

The Cold Dish
Death Without Company
Kindness Goes Unpunished
Another Man's Moccasins
The Dark Horse
Junkyard Dogs
Hell Is Empty
As the Crow Flies
A Serpent's Tooth
Any Other Name
Dry Bones
An Obvious Fact
The Western Star
Depth of Winter
Land of Wolves
Next to Last Stand
Daughter of the Morning Star
Hell and Back
The Longmire Defense
First Frost

Also by Craig Johnson

Spirit of Steamboat (novella)
Wait for Signs (short stories)
The Highwayman (novella)
Tooth and Claw (novella)

Stand-alone E-stories

(Also available in *Wait for Signs*)
Christmas in Absaroka County
Divorce Horse
Messenger

Craig Johnson

Return to Sender

Viking

VIKING
An imprint of Penguin Random House LLC
1745 Broadway, New York, NY 10019
penguinrandomhouse.com

Set in Dante MT Std

LIBRARY OF CONGRESS CATALOGING-IN-PUBLICATION DATA
Names: Johnson, Craig, 1961- author.
Title: Return to sender / Craig Johnson.
Description: New York, NY : Viking, 2025.
Identifiers: LCCN 2024059988 (print) | LCCN 2024059989 (ebook) | ISBN 9780593830703 (hardcover) | ISBN 9780593830710 (ebook)
Subjects: LCSH: Longmire, Walt (Fictitious character)--Fiction. | Sheriffs--Fiction. | LCGFT: Detective and mystery fiction. | Western fiction. | Novels.
Classification: LCC PS3610.O325 R48 2025 (print) | LCC PS3610.O325 (ebook) | DDC 813/.6--dc23/eng/20241220
LC record available at https://lccn.loc.gov/2024059988
LC ebook record available at https://lccn.loc.gov/2024059989

Printed in the United States of America
1st Printing

The authorized representative in the EU for product safety and compliance is Penguin Random House Ireland, Morrison Chambers, 32 Nassau Street, Dublin D02 YH68, Ireland, https://eu-contact.penguin.ie.

For Andy Ramirez, my mailman

Neither snow nor rain nor heat nor gloom of night stays these couriers from the swift completion of their appointed rounds.

—Herodotus

ACKNOWLEDGMENTS

I wanted to be a mailman when I was a kid; it just seemed like such a wonderful job, bringing people letters and packages that they wanted—before I learned about bills.

I'm always looking for interesting stories that exemplify the unique area where I live, and when I read an article about a woman who had the longest postal route in the contiguous United States, over three hundred miles, I knew I had a story.

One of the things I love about Wyoming is that the vast distances consistently remind me of the power of nature versus the power of technology and how Mother Nature has a way of reminding us not to fool with her.

An area that epitomizes that aspect of Wyoming is the Red Desert in the south-central part of the state, which contains the largest living dune system in the United States. Go figure, huh? It's easy enough to just make things up for a story, but I'd much rather use the actual topography of the state, and where else could you find colorful names like Killpecker Sand Dunes?

Don't ask.

One of my favorite ways to explore the area is on this old dual-sport motorcycle I've got, which was instrumental in the Outlaw

Motorcycle Tour I used to ride across the Great Northwest in a five-thousand-mile loop. Next to walking or riding horseback, it's a pretty great way to get a read on a place, and I had a marvelous time doing it—other than a windblown night near the Boar's Tusk Monument in a rainstorm with a tarp partially tied over the bike and some of me.

Most of what I knew about the Red Desert before exploring it was the ice-cream stops at the Farson Mercantile or a beer at the Eden Saloon, where the beer isn't flat. But the thing I remember most was having lunch at Mitch's Cafe, where the owner-operator informed me that she was a fan of my books.

"Thanks."

Scribbling down my order, she glanced out at my motorcycle parked in the gravel lot and then looked back at me. "Watcha doin' down this way?"

"Researching another book."

"Where?"

Placing my helmet on the bench seat beside me, I threw a thumb over my shoulder to the vast, open area to the east. "Out in the Red Desert."

She studied me for a moment more. "Be careful. Strange things happen out there."

I knew I was in the right place.

"The mail runs like a river," my mailman, Andy, told me. And somebody's got to direct that river to keep it from exploding its banks. First in line for carrying the mail would be my agent, Gail "Going Postal" Hochman, followed by Marianne "First Class" Merola. Next, over at Penguin Random House, would be Brian "Special Delivery" Tart and his second in command, Jenn "Registered Mail" Houghton. My marching orders come from Sara "Letter Carrier" Delozier and Magdalena "Rural Delivery" Deniz. Jeep delivery drivers extraordinaire would be Michael "Stamp Book" Brown, Alex "Postcard" Cruz-

Jimenez, and Molly "Address Unknown" Fessenden. And who else but Eric "No Such Zone" Wechter and Francesca "Metered Mail" Drago could fill up the bag?

And last but far from least would be Judy "Valentine" Johnson, the mailperson who carries my heart.

1

"Nobody smiles anymore."

"Excuse me?"

"Have you noticed? Nobody smiles anymore." Mike adjusted himself in the tiny postal Jeep, setting his back against the passenger-side door as he sat on the floor beside Dog so no one would see him in the September early morning light. "Remember when we were growing up how you were taught that when you walked down the street and you met a stranger, that you smiled or said hello?" He sighed, staring at the plethora of mail and packages in the back as if it were a weight he could no longer bear. "People don't do that anymore."

Mike Thurman, my late wife's cousin, was in a bad mood, but that didn't mean he didn't have a point.

Mike had been having a tough month, so I tried to distract him just a bit, thinking of something to say while surveying the interior of the utility vehicle. "So, why do they call this model Jeep DJs?"

He grunted, swiping off his Seattle Mariners ball cap and rubbing his shaved head, then reaching over and scruffing the fur behind sleeping Dog's ear. "Dispatch Jeep."

"Oh."

"Also, they're two-wheel drive—smart for Wyoming, right?"

"Was she driving one of these?"

"No, there's no way you could fit all that mail in a 307-mile route in something like this. She had a hopped-up '68 Travelall that she drove." He shook his head, putting his cap back on and folding his hands in his lap. "She probably used up her entire paycheck putting gas in the thing." He nodded to the right. "Turquoise and white with all those hippie stickers in the back window. I think it was an old ambulance or . . ."

"Or what?"

"A hearse."

Neither of us wanted to dwell on that.

"I think it's for sale at the used car lot about a quarter mile down the main drag on Foothill Boulevard. That piece of shit boyfriend of hers, Benny, sold all her stuff about a month after she went missing."

"Don't you have to wait sixty days?"

"His name was on the title."

"Sweetwater County process the vehicle?"

He studied me with a raised eyebrow. "I'm a postal inspector, not a criminal investigator."

I glanced down at the heavy file folder in my hands. "Jeez, Mike, haven't you seen those TV shows, anybody can do this stuff."

"Yeah, right."

I gave up on trying to distract him. "So, what is it exactly that you want me to do?"

"Find her."

"Well, I can tell you from experience that that's not likely to happen."

"Because of the amount of time?"

"That, and the size of the area she was lost in." I shook my head. "Is there any way to narrow the search area?"

"I wish there was but it's as if she disappeared off the face of the earth somewhere in the Red Desert."

"Did you talk with the Sweetwater County Sheriff's Department?"

He nodded. "The primary investigator, Jake Moline."

"Never heard of him."

"Uturd, I think."

"Uturd . . . ?"

"From Utah, that's what they call 'em down here."

"Nice."

"Hey, I live in Colorado and shudder to think what you guys call us."

I slid the map he'd printed for me from the file folder and looked at the gigantic loop surrounding the Red Desert in the south-central area of my state. "So, you want me to pretend I'm a contract laborer and follow her route?"

"And just see what pops up, yeah."

"Pops up?"

He took a sip from his travel mug of coffee. "You're the king of pop-ups, you see things other people don't."

"And you don't think anybody will suspect that I'm law enforcement?"

"Nah, we get all kinds of people as contract rural carriers, especially the long routes that nobody wants." He chuckled. "Besides, you've got the fake ID and that nifty mountain-man beard."

I scratched the offending fur and then thumbed through the folder again, looking at the photo of the missing woman in her fifties. "Why do you suppose she did?"

"Did what?"

"Take one of the especially long routes, evidently one of the longest in the country."

He sat up a bit, looking around at the empty post office parking lot. "You know, she told me once that she liked to drive because it helped her to forget."

I stared at the photo of the dark-haired woman with the silver streak down the middle, one eye slightly errant and half-smiling with a note of wiseacre. "Forget what?"

"She never said, and I didn't ask."

I closed the folder. "You know, she could've just walked away."

"Not her."

"Why?"

"She was kooky, but she took things very seriously, at least some things." He shook his head. "How does it go? In neither sleet nor snow . . ."

"Neither snow nor rain nor heat nor gloom of night stays these couriers from the swift completion of their appointed rounds . . ." I watched as the first vehicle swept into the postal lot. "It's not official, you know."

"What?"

"The motto, it's not official."

He sipped his coffee some more. "The hell you say."

Stuffing the folder back in my satchel, I watched as a young woman got out of her vehicle in a Carhartt jacket and walked up the ramp to the back door of the facility, punching numbers into the keypad and then yanking the door open and going inside.

"That's Tess Anderson, she's the morning super and she'll be the one that shows you the ropes—she was pretty good friends with Blair."

"Was, huh?" I pulled the door handle and stepped out onto the smooth surface of the concrete, buttoning my old canvas hunting jacket and adjusting my hat. "When they built the James A. Farley post office in New York City, the architectural firm set the words in stone, and everybody assumed it was the creed of the postal service. Never adopted. It's from *The Persian Wars* by the Greek historian Herodotus. During the conflict between the Greeks and the Persians, 500 to 449 BCE, the Persians had a mounted messenger service, a really impressive one—so impressive in fact that Herodotus used those words."

"Well I'll be damned."

I gestured toward the beast next to Mike. "You'll look after my dog while I'm gone?"

"Sure."

"Greenies."

He looked up in confusion. "Excuse me?"

"We Wyomingites—we call Coloradans 'greenies.'"

"Why 'greenies'?"

"Your license plates are green." I shut the door and started off toward the ramp and the door with the keypad.

It was late September, but the high plains were already letting us know what was coming. Fall was on its way, and autumn looked like it was intending on making an entrance, stage left. I had the crucial beginnings of a serious relationship on my hands and a missing family member of my own, and here I was in Rock Springs with a burgeoning, if not falsified, career in delivering the United States mail.

Ignoring the keypad, I thumped a fist on the heavy metal door and waited.

The blonde's face appeared in the small window, peering at me through the cross-grid of wire within the glass, her voice muffled but strong. "Help you?"

"I'm the new gun for hire."

She stared at me. "Let's see some ID."

Instead, I opened the folder, pulling out the vita that the postal inspector had provided me with, plastering it against the glass and waiting. After a moment, the lock buzzed, and I pushed the door open and stepped inside. "Thanks, it's chilly out there."

She said nothing, taking the sheet from me. "Word from the high-ups in Colorado, huh?" I looked around at the overladen carts filled with letters, packing envelopes, and packages as she read the page and then handed it back to me, looking me over from head to scuffed-up boots. "I guess we'll just have to call you the Jolly Greenie Giant, huh?"

I didn't say anything as she walked away, indicating that I should follow her toward a bank of lockers that stood near a time clock and a large calendar. "You can have number thirteen. You superstitious?"

"Not particularly." I stared at the locker next to the assigned one for myself, covered in stickers with the name MCGOWAN written on a weathered piece of tape. "That the woman that went missing?"

She side-eyed me. "You know about that?"

"It was in all the papers, even down in Colorado."

"Yeah, well then you know why we're a little on edge concerning security these days." She started off. "C'mon, I'll show you your hut."

She led me to a large cubby near another wired window with banks of metal compartments that had stenciled names, at least a couple hundred of them.

Handing me a small device, she gestured toward a large, orange bin full of mail. "Here's your MDD, just use it to ID the pumpkin and the DPS tray, but when you go OTR you'll have to reread the ones in the CBU." She handed me a set of keys with a stylized peace-sign keychain and gestured toward the huge bins. "It runs like a river, the mail."

She started to go, but I called after her. "Hey . . . ?"

She turned toward me.

I held up the device. "What's an MDD?"

She stared at me for a long moment. "Oh my God."

"She's a beauty, huh?"

Standing before the vintage SUV made before there ever were

SUVs, I watched as a potbellied individual in his shirtsleeves approached, straightening his cowboy hat and rubbing his hands together.

"The heater works, and that's a blessing on a morning like this."

I noticed the silver crucifix pin stuck in his hat. "You in the blessing business?"

We shook hands. "Mister, I am in the business of moving rolling stock, and you've picked a winner here."

"Sixty-seven?"

He turned to introduce the vehicle like a long-lost lover. "This here is a 1968 International Travelall, panel model—has the big V-8 and the automatic transmission."

"Hearse or ambulance?"

He made a face. "Neither. She was used to deliver mail most recently. Heck, I know the fellow that bought her originally down in Salt Lake City back in '68."

"Who owned it more recently?"

He leaned in close, his breath cloaking the truth between us. "I'm not supposed to say because it gives a lot of people the willies, but you don't look like a Willy to me." He slapped my shoulder and then squeezed the muscle there. "No, not a Willy at all." He leaned in even closer. "It belonged to that mail lady that disappeared a couple of months back. Her boyfriend brought this fine vehicle in and sold her cheap. Seemed odd to me, but maybe he was just trying to get rid of all her stuff."

I walked around to the rear and read all the stickers and peace and love signs: WOODSTOCK, THE GRATEFUL DEAD, MAKE LOVE NOT WAR, STAY GROOVY, THE DOORS, FLOWER POWER, JEFFERSON AIRPLANE, THE AGE OF AQUARIUS. "What was he like?"

"The boyfriend? Oh, I'd rather not say." He looked back at the Travelall. "Are you in need of wheels, my good man?"

"How many miles?"

"About a quarter million, but she's rebuilt and a baby like this'll run an easy half million starting fresh." I gave him a look and he chuckled. "Well, maybe a third of a million miles?"

"How much, and don't say anything near a million."

He stuffed his hands into his pockets and considered the International. "An even five thousand?"

I looked at the glossy surface of the paint, and the good tread of the tires. "Four?"

He smiled and then walked around me to the front and lifted the hood, revealing a pristine engine compartment. "She's been well taken care of."

"Maybe, but she's a little on the high end of her lifespan."

He patted the fender. "Like fine wine."

"Forty-five hundred."

He fluttered his lips with an exhale. "I'll need to talk to my manager."

"You got the keys?"

He reached into his pocket and tossed them to me as he headed back toward the trailer at the center of the lot. "I'll be right back."

Opening the door, I climbed in and sat, slipping the key into the ignition and hitting the starter as the motor sprang to life and purred like a contented kitten. I gave a pat to the dash, then reached over and flipped down the glove box, but it was empty except for a folder and receipt for what were practically new tires. There were side pockets in the doors, but before I could get a look in them the car salesman was coming back.

He hung in the open window. "He's holding at five; the motor and transmission were rebuilt no more than a year ago and the tires are brand new."

I reached down and turned on the heat, splaying my fingers over the vent as the engine began heating up and exhaling warm air. Turning in the seat, I could see the slide-out cargo tray. "You're sure she wasn't either a hearse or an ambulance at one point in her lengthy career?"

"Positive. The mail carrier put that in herself."

"Did you know her?"

He looked puzzled. "Who?"

"The postal worker who owned it?"

He shook his head. "No, but I know the guy that did all the work; Sal Salvucci's shop over on the north side."

"You want to slap some dealer tags on it, and I'll go visit him?" He started to speak again but I'd already pulled out a wad of bills big enough to choke a horse, peeling off five grand and handing it to him. "Get the title and paperwork ready and I'll go over and talk to Sal."

He took the money, smiling. "Friend, you have yourself a deal."

The city of Rock Springs began its life split asunder by the railroad, the Lincoln Highway, and finally by I-80. Named for an actual rock spring, it's claim to fame was coal, commemorated in a vibrant illuminated red sign that welcomed all visitors near the railyard that used to straddle the highway itself.

Taking a right on my way to the mechanic's shop and under the highway, I spotted what I was looking for next door—one of those all-purpose fly-by-night electronics stores—and pulled in and parked at Flaming Gorge Vape.

The kid behind the counter with black hair and a number of piercings and tattoos looked up. "Help you?"

"Yep." I took a deep breath. "I, uh . . . I need to buy a phone."

The kid didn't seem to think it was a big deal, even if it was for me, and he gestured toward the case underneath him. "Are you looking for something with internet access, games, HD camera, social media, 4G, 5G?"

I cleared my throat, looking around at the vaping devices, incense, neon signs, airsoft guns, and electronic junk. "Um, I just want to make and receive calls."

He stared at me, speaking in the chopped cadence. "So. Just. Like. A phone?"

"Yep."

He studied me some more and then reached down and placed one on the glass between us.

I looked at the relatively simple device. "Is that a flip phone?"

"Yeah, but it's newer; they call it a JugBug, and it works and is real simple."

"Simple is good." I picked it up and studied it. "So, that's it?"

"Well, no, you have to buy it and then we sign you up for a cellular contract, either long term or monthly."

I flipped it open. "How much?"

"Twenty bucks for the phone and then twenty a month for the contract."

"Why so cheap?"

"It's refurbished or a trade-in; the people that buy those things generally die pretty quick."

"I'm assuming by natural causes?"

"Huh?"

I gestured with the device. "I mean the phone isn't killing them."

"No. Dude. They're just, like, old . . . and they die." He shrugged. "Believe me, nobody under sixty wants one of these things."

"Sounds perfect."

"You want the gray one here? Or I've got one in red?"

"I'll just take this one."

"The red one is easier to find if you lose it."

I pulled out my wallet and peeled off two twenties. "Here you go."

"I need a credit card."

"I don't have a credit card."

He stared at me some more. "What are you? Like, homeless?"

"No." I slid the bills across the counter. "I just don't have a credit card."

He leaned his pudgy body back on his stool, almost losing his balance. "I don't know, I've never done one with cash—I don't even know if they'll do that."

"Well, I'll tell you what. Do something ironic and call them up. I've got some business next door, which shouldn't take too long, and I'll be back in about twenty minutes. Then you can show me how to work that thing and, if not, I get my forty bucks back."

Pushing the door open, I stepped outside and into the fresh air, happy to escape the modern age. Glancing toward Salvucci's Rad Rides, I could see a man with a magnificent head of silver hair and a beard in worn blue coveralls, wiping his hands on a shop rag and walking around the Travelall, stopping to smile at all the stickers in the rear glass.

"Hey."

He looked up to see me. "You buy this?"

"I was thinking about it."

"It's a great truck, I redid it for the woman that owned it last."

"Blair McGowan?"

"Yeah. We pulled the 345, stroked and bored it and even found a four-barrel intake, and I made up a pair of custom headers for the thing. We ran a two-inch exhaust with flow-through mufflers, so she sounds good but not too loud."

"Nobody wants to listen to that for 307 miles."

He regarded me again with a hardened take. "No, they don't."

"When did all this work get done?"

He thought about it, tucking the rag in his back pocket. "I'd say we finished it about three months ago."

"Right before she went missing."

He took a moment to respond. "Uh-huh. Say, who are you?"

"Just a guy looking to buy a truck."

He placed his fists on his hips. "Well, you're asking way too many questions about Blair, and second, most people couldn't quote the exact mileage of her postal route. So, when you decide to play straight with me, maybe I'll answer your questions." With that, he turned and walked away and into his shop where the sound of metal on metal and pneumatic tools drowned out my thoughts.

I followed him inside and found him in what passed for an office where thick, grease-stained technical manuals lined the walls, threatening to collapse inward on top of us. There was also a faded Ferrari flag, a few trophies, and a number of black-and-white photos tacked on the wall. "You used to race?"

He tossed the papers he was reading onto his overcrowded desk and lowered his glasses. "I used to wrench for the guys that raced, yeah."

"Where?"

"Why do you ask? Does my East Coast accent upset your delicate western sensibilities?"

I chuckled, thinking about how much he sounded like my undersheriff. "No, it's just there aren't that many places to race Ferraris around these parts."

"New York State, Pennsylvania, Connecticut, Ohio . . . Road racing."

I continued to examine the photos. "Is that A. J. Foyt?"

"Okay, let's talk turkey, here." He sat forward in his chair, taking off his glasses and pointing an ear stem at me. "What's your connection to Blair?"

"Nothing, I'm just buying her truck and I'm curious."

He studied me for a moment. "Try again, and this is your last shot."

I took a deep breath, taking a few steps into his office to move a stack of motor manuals and sit in his guest chair. "All right, I've been hired by some folks to look into her disappearance. They think it just seems fishy."

"So, you're what, a private investigator or something like that?"

"Something like that."

"Well, your inklings are correct, because nobody puts that kind of work into a vehicle and then flies down to Rio."

"Any suspicions?"

He laughed. "A bunch of 'em, but whether any of 'em will hold water is another story."

"Tell me some."

He ran his fingers through his silver mane. "The boyfriend, for one. He's a real piece of work."

"What's his name?"

"Benny Schweppe."

"What's he do?"

"Works for a custom motorcycle fabrication shop on the south side, metal cutter and shaper operator—thinks he's a regular Picasso in pig iron."

"Anybody else?"

"Sure, anybody who has anything to do with that much-awaited Rock Springs Resource Management Plan, the Bureau of Land Management, Citizens for the Red Desert, the Wyoming Outdoor Council, the Greater Little Mountain Coalition, or half a dozen other organizations she pissed off."

"She was an activist?"

"Big time. I think she thought it was still 1968. She wanted to put a fence around the entire Red Desert and never let another human being go into the place."

"Anybody in particular she upset?"

"Oh, she got into a shouting match with Bill Higgins at one of those BLM hearings."

"That name sounds familiar . . ."

"He's the mouth for the Little Mountain Militia. Not that Blair was without her idiosyncrasies. You know she claimed to have been abducted by aliens; it was in all those oddball tabloids and a documentary thing on some idiot TV channel back in the '80s."

I stood up, shaking my head, and wandered toward the door. "Wow."

"You said it, brother. Anyway, for my money you're looking in the wrong place. I think she went missing out on the road."

I turned to look at him. "You mean the postal route itself?"

"I do."

"But her vehicle out there was found in the postal service parking lot."

"For my money, somebody abducted her and then drove that Travelall of hers back to the parking lot and dropped it off just to avoid suspicion."

"Isn't there a camera at the rear of that building?"

He raised his hands. "You tell me."

I stepped forward and extended a hand. "Thank you, Mister Salvucci. You've been a great deal of help."

I'd started to walk out when he called after me. "Hey, you gonna buy that International?"

"I believe I might."

"How much?"

"Five thousand."

"It's worth every penny of that. She said her father had one like this back in the '60s."

By the time I got to the parking lot, he was hanging in the doorway, calling after me some more. "I hope you find her; she was weird, but she was special, you know?"

"Why do you suppose she decided to take on the longest mail route in the lower forty-eight?"

"Prolly because somebody told her she couldn't—she was like that."

"How do I make a call?"

The kid from the Flaming Gorge whatnot shop held the phone out for me to see. "You just punch in the numbers and hit the green button. And to end the call you push the red one."

"What do I do to answer a call?"

He looked at me as if I'd just wandered off the farm, and in many ways I had. "You open it up. Hit the green button. Same . . . procedure."

I took the thing and looked at him. "We're good to go?"

"Yeah. Hey, can I ask you a question?"

"Maybe, try it and we'll see—keeping in mind that I may not be able to operate a cell phone, but I can field strip and reassemble a Colt 1911 semiautomatic in under forty seconds."

His face was all but blank. "Never . . . mind."

"See you on the trail." I pushed open the door and walked out, climbing into the International and heading back to the car dealership.

After getting the paperwork and temporary tags for the Travelall, I drove across town and along the railroad tracks on the appropriately named Blair Avenue before taking the cutoff into an expansive trailer park.

Cruising the loop, I stopped in front of McGowan's address and studied the small, well-kept yard and a postage-stamp-size deck that had only marginally been ruined by the couple of dismantled motorcycles in the driveway that I assumed belonged to the boyfriend. I didn't want to cast too much attention on myself, so I pulled down to the next turnoff, where I parked the truck and walked the short distance back to knock on the trailer door.

There was no answer, so I knocked again.

I'd just about thought of trying the knob when I looked at the next trailer over and saw the curtains being drawn shut.

Giving up, I started back toward the Travelall when a voice called out to me from next door. "Hello?"

I looked over to see an elderly woman, with an extravagant hairdo in a brassy red not seen in the natural world, standing on what passed for a porch, bundled up within a blanket over her shoulders, a bathrobe and slipper peeking out from underneath.

"Can I help you?"

I waved a hand and continued toward the truck. "No, ma'am, I'm just looking for someone."

"What are you doing driving Blair's truck?"

I stopped and looked back at her. "I think I just bought it."

"That's a shame. I was hoping she was back."

I turned and walked toward her, stopping at the small picket fence and the row of garbage cans between the trailers. "Did you know her well?"

"Well enough. How about you?"

"I'm afraid I didn't know her at all."

"Then why all the questions about somebody you didn't know?"

"I guess I'm just curious." I ducked my head in admonition and smiled. "That, and I'm the one who's taking over her postal route."

She studied my smile for a long while before rewarding me with one of her own. "Would you like a cup of coffee, Mister . . . ?"

"Walt. Just Walt."

She studied me a bit longer and then gestured for me to follow her into the trailer house where it was no warmer inside than out. Following my breath like a steam train overrunning its rails, I closed the door and watched as she pulled two mugs from a cabinet and set them on the worn Formica surface of a small breakfast nook along with a jar of freeze-dried instant Folgers and a single spoon. "I'm out of milk."

"Never use it, Ms. . . . ?"

"Frasier, Flossy Frasier."

I glanced around the trailer's crowded interior. "Flossy?"

She fanned a hand, pulling out a cigarette and lighting it. "My stage name. I was, um . . . I was a magician's assistant back in Reno, you know?"

"The kind that get cut in half?" It sounded a little dubious, but I went along with it. "Ms. Frasier, do you have any heat in this place?"

"Supposed to, but that wall unit pilot light keeps going off and I play hell trying to get it started." She put the kettle on and turned to face me. "Caught my hair on fire the last time."

"Would you like me to try?"

She smiled with a few missing teeth. "Mister, I thought you'd never ask."

After lighting the heater, I moved to the small bench seat and slid in across from her as she filled our mugs and stirred them both, continuing to smoke. "Blair used to keep it lit for me, but since she's been gone . . ."

"What do you think happened to her?"

"I think that no-good boyfriend of hers had something to do with it, whatever it was."

"Benny Schweppe?"

"Exactly."

"So, you don't think she just left?"

"No, I do not. Why would anybody think that?"

"How well did you know her?"

She sat back, looking out the window where I'd first seen her. "Well enough to ride the route with her a few times, just an aged Thelma and Louise."

"The 307-mile postal route?"

"Yes."

I lifted the mug and attempted to thaw my taste buds. "What was she like?"

"The kind of person I enjoy living next to—independent, truly independent in mind and spirit."

"I understand she was somewhat political?"

"She was definitely a child of the '60s." She sipped her coffee and stubbed out the butt in a clay ashtray that read OWL CLUB, EUREKA, NEVADA. "I mean she could be something of an activist, concerning things that were important to her."

"Like the Red Desert?"

She rested her mug back on the surface of the table and sat there staring at it. "Very much like the Red Desert. That was a personal cause of hers."

"So, you think it might've been political enemies?"

"Maybe, but she had more than her share of loose wing nuts out there on her route—people I wouldn't want to see every day, but she didn't back down from much."

"Any names you can give me?"

There was a sudden and tremendous crashing noise outside, and Flossy reached over to pull back the curtain. "Oh, shit . . ."

There was more noise as a voice bellowed from next door. "I told you not to put your trash in my cans, damn it!"

She let the curtain fall shut and then sat there with her hands clutched in her lap, shaking.

"Ms. Frasier?"

She slowly stood and then walked to open the door, stepping outside where the crashing noises continued. "I'm sorry, Mister Schweppe, but mine were full and I didn't think you would mind if I . . ."

The bellowing continued. "I pay for every one of these cans that they empty, and I'm not paying to have your trash hauled off! Do you hear me, you old bitch?"

I stood and walked through the front door and onto the small porch next to Flossy as the man in question, I assumed Benny Schweppe, dumped a full can of trash onto the elderly woman's lawn.

He was tall and stringy with a salt-and-pepper ponytail, and when he picked up another, I stepped off the porch and started across the lawn. "Hey, you don't have to do that, Mister Schweppe."

He finished emptying the can and threw it in the woman's yard. "I know you?"

"No."

"Who the hell are you, then?"

I took another few steps toward him and could make out the tattoos on his neck and even the three teardrops inked under one eye. "Just an interested party."

He reached under a hooded shirt jack for the waistband of his pants. "Back off, big man."

I continued toward him but raised my hands. "Hey, I'm not looking for trouble."

"Well, you're about to find it, motherfucker."

"Look, Benny . . ."

He yanked out what looked to be some kind of cheap semiautomatic and leveled it at my face.

I stopped and then cocked my head, looking at Ms. Frasier and then back at him. "Are you actually pulling a gun on me over purloined trash cans?"

He stared at me. "What the hell does 'purloined' mean?"

"Borrowed."

He frowned and gestured with the 9mm toward the Frasier woman. "I have told her to not put her trash in my cans and week after week she damn well does it again and again."

"Benny, have you been under a lot of emotional stress lately? It just kind of seems like you're overreacting a bit."

He swung the barrel back at me. "I said, do I know you, motherfucker?"

"Benny, there's a lady present."

He sneered. "She's a piece of shit, retired hooker from the Biggest Little City in the World who keeps using my trash cans, motherfucker."

"Benny . . ."

He shook the gun at me like it was a stick as his voice became even more shrill. "Stop using my name like you know me, goddamn it!"

It's a given that, in these types of situations, the first step is to get yourself out of the line of fire, which I did by stepping sideways and grabbing the gun's slide action with my left hand. Most people are afraid to do that for fear that if the gun fires it'll hurt your hand, but it won't. Then grabbing his hand at the rear of the gun with my right, I twisted up and back, forcing him to the ground as he began screaming. The problem was the low picket fence between us, but I was able to leverage the weapon from his hand and then toss it behind me into the dry and dead grass next door.

I looked back at Flossy to reassure the woman on the tiny porch with her hands covering her mouth, and when I turned back to Benny, he punched me in the chin.

It wasn't much of a punch, and I think he was shooting for my nose, but with the pain in his other hand where I'd come close to breaking his finger, his aim might've been off.

I've got a big chin, and his fist bounced off as he reached down, first clutching the one hand and then the other, screaming his favorite phrase some more. "Motherfucker!"

I'd just started to turn away when he made some kind of martial-arts noise and threw a boot up at me. He was off-balance from trying to nurse his fingers and it wasn't hard to catch the foot and flip him backward, where he fell onto the gravel driveway and started rocking back and forth. "You broke my finger! You broke my finger, motherfucker!"

I turned back to Ms. Frasier. "I should probably go."

Glancing around at the other trailers, she nervously lit another cigarette and nodded. "Maybe so."

I stepped over the part of fence broken in the scuffle to walk around him, but misjudged in that he drew himself up and charged at me. I tried to turn but wasn't fast enough, and he bounced off the sidearm at my hip and then fell onto one of the trash cans that littered the driveway.

Glancing back at Flossy, I shrugged. "You have to give him credit for persistence, huh?"

She folded her arms with a worried look, moving toward the door. "I guess."

I started to walk away again but this time one of the trashcan lids clipped me on the side of my head, knocking off my hat. I reached up and felt the blood where the thing had gotten me and then headed back for Benny. "All right, Captain America . . ."

He must've thrown it from his knees and then fell backward, and was now crab-walking away from me as I approached. Grabbing another lid, he whipped it at me like a Frisbee that whacked my knee and damn well hurt.

Scooping up the nearest can by the handle, I lifted it over him and then brought it crashing down; I thought it might contain him long enough for me to make discretion the better part of valor, but as soon as I started to let go, he began kicking me.

I held the can in place and then picked up one of the lids and began beating it against the can with him in it. "Can you hear me?"

"Fuck you!"

"I'm about done with you, but I want to make sure you understand that if you give Ms. Frasier here any trouble, I'm going to be back."

"Fuck you, and fuck her too!"

I beat on the can some more, only pausing to add, "Benny, I'm starting to lose patience with you . . ."

It was about then that a Sweetwater Sheriff's Department unit squealed to a stop at the end of the driveway and a very earnest and nervous-looking deputy threw open her door and leveled a .40 Glock at me from over the roof. "Sheriff's Department, I need you to drop the weapon!"

I gestured with the trash can lid. "You mean this?"

"Drop it!"

I did as she requested.

The deputy was reaching for her cuffs as I complied. "Now turn around and put your hands behind your head and lace your fingers."

I started to do as she ordered and turned, but then stopped, calling back over my shoulder. "It's at this point that I should probably tell you that I'm armed."

Flossy stared at me, incredulous. "You've got a gun?"

I shrugged and carefully pulled my coat back and unsnapped the .45 from the holster with two fingers, glancing back at the deputy.

Now she looked real nervous. "Just . . . Just toss it on the ground, there."

"I'm not tossing my vintage 1911 Colt on the gravel."

Flossy continued to stare at me. "You have a gun?"

I reached over and sat it on the up-sided bottom of the trash can as Schweppe's voice echoed from inside. "You have a gun?"

I placed my hands behind my head, lacing my fingers. "Shut up, Benny."

2

"What the hell, Walt?" Sweetwater County Sheriff John Grossnickle sat across the table from me in the interrogation room with his easy smile, shaking his head. He was young, in his second term, and in the right. "Did it ever occur to you to come in and introduce yourself—maybe tell us what the heck you're doing here?"

With the handcuffs somewhat limiting my dexterity, I fingered the bandage on the side of my head where the trash can had clipped me and where the deputy who had performed the arrest had patched me up. "I was getting to that."

"After you put one of the citizenry in a trash can and started playing the 1812 Overture?"

I dropped my hands in my lap. "It was more of an Art Blakey kind of paradiddle."

"Walt."

"I was just taking a look around and asking some questions before I came in and bothered you guys." I glanced at my manacles. "Are you going to uncuff me now, John?"

Grossnickle stood and walked around the table, sitting on the corner and looking at the two-way mirror on the wall. "Did you know that my county is the largest in the state?"

"I do know that."

"Did you know that it's the eighth largest in the country?"

"No, I didn't know that."

"I have over a hundred people in my department."

"I knew it was a big department."

"Well, let me tell you, what I don't need is one of my fellow sheriffs coming down here and rootin' and tootin', you catch my drift?"

"I do."

He reached down and unlocked the cuffs, tossing them on the table with a clatter. "All right, who are you working for?"

"Mike Thurman, the postal inspector out of Colorado."

He nodded. "Concerning the missing McGowan woman."

"Yep."

"And this Thurman fellow doesn't think we're up to the job?"

"He's family, the cousin of my late wife."

"So I can look forward to a bunch of federal agents swooping in here and looking over my shoulder?"

"Nope, just me."

"I almost prefer the federal agents." He stood and walked toward the door but then stopped, turning with his hands on his hips. "Schweppe wants to press charges, but the fact that he was brandishing a sidearm seems to undermine his claim that you assaulted him."

"Well, I kind of did, but only after he started brandishing."

"And then you started brandishing the trash can?"

"No, he brandished the trash cans first . . . at least the lids."

The easy smile returned, and he shook his head at the speckled tile floor of the interrogation room. "That's a lot of brandishing."

I stood, rubbing my wrists. "You can ask Ms. Frasier about the order of the brandishing."

"Flossy? She's got enough to contend with in this life." He knocked on the knobless door and it was opened, and he gestured for me to follow him across the hall where the nice young deputy handed me my badge wallet, sidearm, and my own cuffs from across a counter.

The brunette smiled a becoming smile. "Hi."

"Hi."

She shrugged, sticking out a hand. "Officer Rivera, sorry about all this."

I shook the hand. "Just doing your job."

She continued to smile at me. "I've had to arrest Benny three times, so I know where you're coming from."

"He's a unique personality."

Grossnickle pulled at my arm. "C'mon, if you're really nice to Jake Moline, the primary on this one, he might share his report and talk with you about the case."

I pushed the .45 into my holster. "So, no brandishing?"

"No, let's try and keep the brandishing to a minimum from here on out, shall we?"

He led me down the hall past the reception area to a small commissary where a balding, heavyset man in his forties sat at one of the tables, drinking a cup of coffee and thumbing through a folder.

He stood as we approached. "Sheriff Longmire, I've heard a great deal about you."

I glanced at Grossnickle. "None of it good as of late, I'm sure."

John ignored me and moved over to the machine on the counter. "I'm getting a cup, you want one?"

"Please." I looked around. "You got a bowling alley around here too?"

Moline slid the folder toward me. "Blair McGowan in toto."

I looked at it. "Kind of thin."

"Really thin."

"You want to just tell me the story?"

He laid an arm on the back of the chair next to him and looked at the ceiling, hooking an index finger in his collar and loosening his tie. "June ninth, McGowan reports to the post office for her daily run at four thirty a.m. She sorts the mail, loads it, and begins her route. All 307 miles of it. All the fine folks of Superior, Point of Rocks, Red Desert, Wamsutter, Lamont, Bairoil, Jeffrey City, Sweetwater Station, Kotey Place, Atlantic City, South Pass City, Farson, and Eden received their mail that day. The next morning, June tenth, her vehicle is parked in the post office employee parking lot with the keys hanging from the switch. No one pays much attention, figuring she must've run out to get a cup of coffee or a bite to eat, but the hours tick by and Blair is a no-show."

"Security footage?"

"You can see the vehicle pulling in but it's impossible to see who drove it." He sipped his coffee. "The postal folks called her house and woke up Benny, the walking skid mark, who I hear you attempted to can like he was Prince Albert, who tells them he hasn't seen her since the morning before and that he has no idea where she is."

"Does he have an alibi?"

Moline nodded. "Worked full shifts and overtime on both days, supposedly slept the rest but it's hard to believe he'd have time to do anything nefarious—besides the fact that he's about as useful as a pig roast at a bar mitzvah."

I opened the file, looking at the report. "I hear he can shape metal."

"He can run the machine that shapes metal, which means he's marginally smarter than it is."

I continued reading. "She was born in Riverside, California."

"Yeah, but after graduating from high school she ran off to San Francisco before spending thirty-five years in the valley near Fresno."

"She has a daughter?"

"Yeah, so far we haven't been able to pin her down, and from what I've gathered it wasn't a close relationship."

The sheriff returned, setting both coffees in front of us, and then sat down, facing his investigator. "What did she do in Fresno?"

"Worked for the hospital for the first fifteen years, then twenty with the postal service in California before she retired here."

I continued reading and found myself on the last page of the report with a lot of bizarre-looking information. "What's all this?"

"Links to the documentary they did with her on the alien abduction thing along with the tabloid stuff that made a big splash."

I raised my eyes to look at him.

"Yeah, I know. But there are some at-length interviews, and I thought they might shed some light on who she was and what might've happened to her."

I closed the file. "What are your thoughts?"

"I don't think she just walked away, I think there was something going on on that jumbo-size route of hers, or . . ."

I sipped my coffee. "Or what?"

"The aliens really got her this time."

"Who is this, and what the fuck have you done with Walt Longmire?"

"It's really me, honest." I cradled the cell phone in my ear trying not to talk too loudly in Fiesta Guadalajara, a restaurant comfortably nestled on the first floor of the Park Hotel complete with a plastic tropical forest. "How did you know it was me, anyhow?"

My undersheriff and betrothed continued. "Caller ID, your name came up—not that I really believe it's you, anyway."

I nursed my beer, then dipped a chip in some salsa as I waited for Mike Thurman to show up. "What's going on?"

"Ruby, Saizarbitoria, and I are cleaning out the evidence lockers because the sheriff hasn't done it since the Polk administration."

"Nixon."

"Whatever." I listened as she readjusted herself in her office chair. "So, are you through farting around down there or what?"

"No, I'm going to have to go out and run the route just to see what I'm up against."

"Why?"

"It's important to Mike, and he's family."

"How is that again?"

"Martha's cousin."

"Oh, right." I listened as Vic Moretti breathed and missed hearing it in person. "So, what, another couple of days?"

"For now." I read off the information I'd called her about. "Bree, short for Sabrina McGowan, that's the daughter, possibly somewhere near Fresno. See if you can come up with anything?"

"I heard you got arrested."

I spotted Mike and waved as he came in through the hotel lobby, but he didn't see me. "Momentarily."

"I heard you put somebody in a trash can?"

"How did you hear about that?"

"Ruby's friends with the dispatcher down there in Sweetwater County. Personally, I think the dispatchers have their own information syndicate going on."

I stood, waving again. "Miss me?"

"Not when you give me shitty jobs like this to do."

"I miss you."

"You should. I'll call you when I find the daughter."

I watched as Mike came over and sat opposite me, placing a small bag on the seat beside him and plucking a menu from the holder. A waitress approached and Mike pointed to my Pacifico, whereupon she immediately departed.

I continued my conversation with my slightly miffed staff. "You sound pretty confident."

"I am."

The phone went dead in my hand, and I held it in front of me, carefully punching the red button and closing it up. "Howdy, where's my dog?"

He studied the menu. "It's a phone, you don't have to handle it like a bomb disposal unit."

I gently placed it on the surface of the table. "It's my first one."

"Congratulations. I put your dog up in your room and fed him. Along with that rifle case." The waitress arrived with his beer as he turned to me. "Speaking of, what are you having?"

"Fajitas, beef."

He looked up at the waitress, scribbling away on her pad. "Same, but with chicken."

He lifted his beer in a toast. "What's in that case, it weighs a ton?"

"The Cheyenne Rifle of the Dead, a Sharps .45-70 that I was hoping to have appraised up in Cody at the Buffalo Bill Center of the West before heading home."

He nodded. "I heard you were arrested."

We tipped our longnecks and both took a slug. "What, is there a billboard?"

"Grossnickle called me."

"Checking up on me, is he?"

"I think he's one of those guys who check everything."

"Good man."

"So." He took another sip. "What have you got for me?"

"The general consensus on Blair McGowan is alien abduction."

He suddenly started. "Oh, shit, I brought this for you." He reached beside him, placing the bag on the table and slid it toward me. "I got you something."

I peered in the bag. "What is it?"

"A portable DVD player, but now that I see you have an actual phone, I could've just texted you the links."

"I don't think my phone can do that."

He studied the simple-looking device. "What can it do?"

"Make and receive calls."

"Oh brother." He slid the bag to me some more. "This DVD player—do you have any idea how hard these things are to find these days?"

"No."

"Well, they are, and lucky for you I had one in the top of my closet."

"Why do I need that?"

"It's got all the interviews Blair did about her alien abduction."

"And why do I need that?"

He shrugged. "I just thought you'd like to meet her?"

"Maybe not under those circumstances, but I'll give it a look. How does it work?"

"You plug it in and hit play."

"I think I can handle it."

We sipped our beers. "So, Tess Anderson is accompanying you on your route driving tomorrow morning?"

I nodded. "At least for the first leg on I-80."

"The Snow Chi Minh Trail."

I chuckled. "So they say."

After putting the Sharps in the hidden compartment of the International, I lay on my bed in the corner room of the fourth floor of the Park Hotel with Dog. I had to admit the place had seen better days, but there was no one else in the forty-some rooms and the grand old lady still had her charms with dark woodwork and transoms above the doors, and a private bathroom including a massive, claw-foot tub and hot and cold running water.

The hotel wasn't particularly open to the public, but Mike had secured me the room in the firm belief that I was in "deep cover," whatever that meant.

The Park was famous for a momentous party that took place on June 30, 1919, that was supposed to have been wrapped up by midnight, just under the wire of a new law called Prohibition. For all intents and purposes, the party had continued into the night and into the next morning. Not that Prohibition had done that well in Rock Springs after being implemented, as the great number of immigrants who worked in the surrounding mines owned vats for production of their own, personal imbibing. During Prohibition, a grand total of one hundred carloads of grapes were received in the greater civic limits of Rock Springs, and only a few years later the town made headlines across the country as "the wettest spot in the western United States" when a federal seizure with a US marshal and more than fifty deputies confiscated so much bootleg hooch that they had to use a special railroad car to remove it.

I reached for one of the cans of Rainier I'd purchased at the Cowboy Lounge below and took a swig, and then grabbed the DVD player and sat it on my lap. After plugging the thing in and hitting the play button as Mike had directed, I watched as the show started and the dated graphics and crappy techno music of *Mysteries from Beyond* began. After a moment of this, some cheesy-looking actor with very pale-blue eyes that had played some character in some show that was long since canceled appeared on the screen and did his best to convince me to sacrifice the next thirty minutes of my life to watching this C-grade TV show.

I really didn't have much choice in that it was a job and who knew, maybe Blair McGowan was up for an Emmy.

Showing a group of cows meandering in the blue light, the actor's voice extolled the alien abduction period in the '70s. "Boar's Tusk monument, near the Killpecker Sand Dunes—not the place you would think of when considering an alien abduction, but it was here that Blair McGowan first met Higgo One, an alien who had traveled billions of light-years."

First off, you can see the remnants of the volcanic explosion that had formed Boar's Tusk for miles, and second, Killpecker Sand Dunes is the largest area of dunes in the country and a pretty poor place to try and graze cattle.

They cut away to a woman I recognized as a younger Blair with all-dark hair and no skunk stripe who began talking about her experiences that fateful night. Why fateful? Because that was the kind of language they used in crappy C-grade TV shows.

"I was camping near the Boar's Tusk when I saw these orange streaks in the night sky, like shooting stars. But then they just hovered around the monument. I climbed out of my tent, but when I began approaching them, they just flew off. The next night, the lights returned and I went out, but this time the clam people stayed and allowed me to approach. They were very large, at least twelve feet tall, and they looked like giant clams with tentacle appendages and oversized eyes. They invited me into their spaceship, and I went in, where they had five cows."

I stared at the screen and then at Dog. "Cows. Why is it always cows?"

The young woman continued in an excited voice. "They asked me if I'd like to go for a ride in their ship, and I said yes. The trip was close to two hundred thousand light-years away but took only a moment. There was a large halo that glowed, and the ship attached itself to that, lowering us to the ground of their home planet. The main clam person introduced himself to me as Higgo One, and that he had a dire message for all of us here on planet Earth."

She had a nice voice and a pleasant demeanor, but she was obviously as nutty as a five-pound Claxton fruitcake.

I closed the DVD player and sat it on the nightstand and wondered what I was doing here. Still, the fact remained that she'd spent a lot of time and money fixing up her truck, and generally people don't do that and then decide to walk away—but then again, some do.

It's commonly known that the first seventy-two hours of a missing persons case are the most crucial, and every hour after that sees a significant drop in the chances of finding that person alive. Blair McGowan had been missing for almost four months—so, who was the real fruitcake here?

I wondered if Higgo One had a phone number; heck, I'd even spring for long distance.

There was a creaking noise out in the hallway, which was odd in that no one else was supposed to be in the upstairs part of the building. Dog raised his head, looking in that direction and confirming my suspicions.

Swinging my stocking feet to the floor, I stood and listened, holding a finger to my lips and indicating that he shouldn't bark as I lifted my .45 from the nightstand.

There was another creak of the floorboards, but it could've just been the old building settling, except for the odor of cigarette smoke. I turned the knob and clicked the door open as it slowly crept wide, like a tomb, running into something on the hinged side.

"Ouch."

I reached out and pulled the door toward me, finding Benny Schweppe on the other side, wearing a worn leather jacket and a do-rag, rubbing his nose, with a bent cigarette comically hanging from the corner of his mouth. "Say, you really did have a gun." He glanced down at the Colt hanging from my hand at my side. "You in 'Nam?"

"Yep."

He plucked the cigarette from his lips and attempted to straighten it. "Me too."

We stood there for a moment more and I was compelled to ask, "Can I help you?"

"No, but I was thinking maybe I could help you?"

"Really."

He rubbed his scalp underneath the headgear with skulls and crossbones printed on it. "You did a number on my head, and my finger still hurts." He held the bandaged digit out to me to examine. "I think it's sprained."

"You were being unreasonable."

"Yeah, yeah. Sorry about that."

"How's Ms. Frasier?"

"Who?"

"Flossy, the woman next door you were screaming at this morning?"

He stared at me blankly for a moment and then nodded, taking a drag on his cigarette. "Oh, yeah . . . I went over and apologized to her too."

We stood there in silence for a while as Dog, having grown curious, stuck his head through the doorway.

"Whoa . . ." Benny took a step back. "Whose sled dog?"

"Mine." I ruffled Dog's ear and was compelled to once again ask, "How is it you want to help me, Benny?"

"Oh, yeah . . . First, I need to know, I mean, why is it you're looking for Blair?"

"Who said I was looking for her?"

"A buddy of mine."

I leaned a shoulder against the door and studied him. "Benny, most relationships rely on a certain amount of honesty, and I get the feeling that you're not being completely forthcoming with me."

"Are you?"

I blinked in surprise. "Am I what?"

"Being forthwith, forthright, whatever . . . Honest, man, are you being honest with me?"

"Well, to a point."

He leaned in and I could smell the alcohol on his breath as he smiled. "Trevor Waggoner."

"Who is Trevor Waggoner?"

"He works at the head shop up on the north side."

I nodded, stuffing the Colt in my jeans. "The kid I bought the phone from?'

"Yeah, Flaming Gorge Vape, that's him—Trevor, I mean."

"I wondered how he knew to put my name in it so that it came up on caller ID. He looked me up?"

"Are you really a sheriff?"

"Yep. Now, how are you going to help me, Benny?"

"Um, first I have to be sure that you're not going to tell anybody I'm helping you."

"I think I can pretty much guarantee that, so long as you don't tell anybody about me," I folded my arms and waited.

"Sure. So, we're like, working on a case together, right? Like undercover."

"Sure."

"There were some people you've got to be careful with, and I'm thinking that they might've had something to do with Blair."

"With her going missing?"

"Um, yeah."

"Who?"

"Look, you can't tell anybody I told you any of this, okay?"

"Yep, that's the agreement." I waited another moment. "Hey, Benny, no offense, but I've got to get up really early in the morning to deliver the mail."

He glanced around again. "Zeno Carruthers."

"And who is Zeno Carruthers?"

"He's got this religion. The Order of the Red Gate. A cult, man."

"A cult."

"Yeah, they believe in these angels but they're really aliens and they're coming to Earth to take a special group of people away."

"Higgo One and the clam people?"

His eyes widened. "Are you one of them?"

"No, but I've seen the movie." I pushed off the facing of the door and hitched my thumbs in my belt. "And where do I find the church of Zeno Carruthers?"

"What movie? There's a movie?"

"Benny, let's concentrate here. Where do I find this cult?"

"That's just it, they move around in the Red Desert, you know?"

"Nomadic?"

"Huh?"

"Never mind. How did Blair get involved with them?"

"She delivered their mail."

"In the desert?"

"Yeah, they had a spot where she would deliver their stuff near the Crookston Ranch campground and another near Rock Cabin Dugway, under a rock."

"You're kidding."

"No, man, really. The rocks are painted with this fluorescent green paint." He pulled a few folded pieces of paper from his back pocket that looked to be parts of a quad map. "This is her map that shows exactly where they are, near the Leucite Hills and the Steamboat Rim. That's, like, their territory."

He handed me the sheets and I stared at them. "So, what makes you think these people might've taken Blair?"

"She was the first one to have anything to do with them a long time ago and when Carruthers made contact. They asked him to bring Blair with them."

"The aliens."

"The angel-like aliens, yeah. That's their theory—that angels and stuff are just extra-triennials."

"Terrestrials?"

"Huh?"

"Never mind. Where?"

"The Red Desert."

"So, the Order of the Red Gate folks are all going to fly off into space with the clam people?"

"Well, it's not clam people anymore but yeah, that's what they say, yeah."

I gestured with the partial maps. "Well, thanks for this."

"You gonna check it out tomorrow?"

I folded them and stuffed them in my pocket. "I may."

"So, like, you're gonna need some backup, right?"

"No, I'm thinking this early in the investigation, I can handle it myself."

"I can get off work."

"No, that's okay."

Benny nodded, taking another drag on his dogleg cigarette. "Don't underestimate Carruthers, man. He's bad news."

"Really?"

"Yeah, they say he killed a lot of people."

"How?"

"I don't know, he was a doctor or something."

"Malpractice?"

He thought about it. "Or maybe he just played one on TV."

I reached over and took the doorknob in my hand, indicating that the conversation was coming to a close. "You ever meet him, this Carruthers fellow?"

"Once. I gave Blair a ride on my bike to a meeting they were having up near Reliance Tipple and she didn't want to go alone."

"And?"

"He's a spooky fucker, man. He's a big guy with these really light-colored eyes; wears a robe and everything. He was an actor and did a lot of those religious study films, you know, for churches? I mean, he looks like God."

"How many people does he have out there with him in the desert?"

"I don't know, it varies . . . When we saw them that one time there were like forty of 'em, mostly older people."

I ushered Dog back with a leg and started to close the door. "Okay, well, I'll check it out."

"You sure you don't want me to come with you?"

I thought about what it would be like to be stuck in a vehicle with Benny Schweppe for 307 miles. "Nope, I've got Dog here."

I closed the door and waited as Benny retreated back down the hallway, and then moved to the window overlooking the street as I watched him exit the building before kicking his motorcycle to life and riding away under the red glow of the Rock Springs Coal sign.

Driving along on I-80, I tried to keep the vintage SUV between the lines, but with the constant wind and my yawning, it was possible we might end up in a ditch. "I think I've gotten to the age in life that when my alarm clock goes off earlier than four a.m., I think I'm having an aneurysm."

Tess Anderson finished petting Dog and then organized the trays in the back of the Travelall, turning back in the seat and reattaching her seat belt "You get used to it."

"Heaven forbid." I took the exit at Wamsutter and pulled into the empty parking lot of the Kum & Go there, cutting the motor. "You want a cup of coffee before we head off into the Big Empty?"

"I'll buy." She smiled. "I never turn down the Shoot & Scoot."

I smiled back.

"What?"

"I've got a friend who collects those. I'll have to tell her that one."

Leaving Dog inside, I got out and noticed the wind was gusting to the point that Tess couldn't get her door open. Gripping the handle, I pulled it as she pushed and then eased it shut after she got out and ran for the entrance before the wind took her to Cowdrey, Colorado.

Once inside, I followed her to the bank of coffee machines and watched as she picked out something fancy as I took the pot from the burner that looked as if it might've been there since the Crimean War.

"You don't seem like a postie."

I looked at her, placing the lid on my cup of black coffee. "No?"

"Not with those scars on your knuckles, that big one across your eye, and that part of your ear that's missing." She finished making admixtures to hers and capped her cup, turning toward the cash register at the front where it looked as if an altercation was going on between the young man behind the counter and a truck driver.

The driver leaned on the surface with both hands. "It took my card . . ."

The young man in the Kum & Go hat and apron backed away till he bumped into the counter behind him. "The machines can't do that, sir. You just push the card in and it tells you to pull it back out. Maybe you need to check it again?"

He looked back at us and then turned to the kid. "It ate my card."

"Sir, the machines on our pumps can't do that. The readers are manually operated, and they can't take your card."

He started to push off the counter and head for the door. "Fine, I'm leaving."

"Sir, you haven't paid for your gas."

He swiveled around, screaming at him. "It ate my card! How do you want me to pay, punk?"

Stepping to the side, I tilted my head till he noticed me. "Hey, you need to take it down a notch, please."

"And who the hell are you?"

"I'm a guy who's going to have been in two fights in two days, and I'm getting tired of it. Hey, maybe you dropped your card out there or something."

He stepped to the side, squaring off. "I didn't drop my card, and this is none of your business."

He was decently sized but not as big as me, though he was young and that counted for something. "Look, I don't want any trouble . . ."

"Then don't make any." Brushing by me, he pushed open the glass door and took a left, heading for his truck.

"That's the second time in two days that hasn't worked—I guess I'll start telling people I'm looking for trouble." With a glance at Tess, I started after him, calling back to the station attendant. "Call 9-1-1 and get the highway patrol out here."

Following him out, I hustled a bit in the wind, catching up with him as he darted through the pump island and started to open the door to his Kenworth. "Hey, hold up."

He paused and heaved a sigh of agitation before he turned and snatched a butterfly knife from his pocket, flipping it open and pointing it toward me.

I stopped, just out of reach as the wind buffeted us. "The HP's on the way . . ."

"Well, that's that much more of a reason for me to get out of here, huh?"

I shook my head at him. "Where are you going to go? That stretch of highway runs about four hundred miles, and you don't think they'll find you?"

"Just your word against mine."

"Two things." I held my coffee out to him.

He stared at me.

"Would you mind holding this for a second?"

Confused, he still took it, looking at me as if I were crazy.

Turning to my side, I pulled back my coat to expose my Colt. "First of all, don't bring a knife to a gunfight. And second?" I palmed my badge wallet, then flipped it open to reveal my six-point star. "They're going to believe me. Now, put the knife away and let's go inside and pay for the gas like none of this happened."

He stood there for a moment more and then folded the knife up and put it back in his pocket, embarrassed.

"Can I have my coffee?" He handed it back to me. "You have your card?"

"Yeah."

"C'mon, let's go."

Trudging back across the parking lot, I opened the door for him. "He found his card."

He gave it to the young man, who ran it as we waited, and then handed it back to him. "You're good to go."

"Thanks." He turned, not making eye contact with me. "Um, thank you too."

"You bet." I watched Tess set her cup on the counter and reach for her purse.

"On the house."

She looked up at the young man. "You're sure?"

He smiled. "Yeah, thank you."

I nodded and started out with Tess following and I held the door as she dodged in. I circled around the Travelall and wedged myself in. Placing the coffee on the dash, I started the vintage SUV and snapped on my seat belt as she studied me.

I pulled the thing in gear, then I grabbed my coffee and took a sip, noticing Tess staring at me. "What?"

"Did that guy pull a knife on you?"

I didn't say anything.

"I came out to help, but then saw him between the tractor and the trailer and it looked like he was holding a knife."

I let the brake off and we started moving. "Nah, probably just the credit card after he found it."

Driving north, we headed under the interstate highway and into the Red Desert proper on Crooks Gap Road as she took the lid off her coffee for a drink. "I called administration down in Denver and they say they've never heard of you."

I shrugged. "I kept a low profile."

"There was no record of you at all."

"Huh." I drank my own coffee as we climbed a bluff to an endless butte, the clouds racing overhead like a revolving ceiling.

"So, what did you do down there in the big city?"

"Kind of an enforcer; if people didn't use enough stamps or wrote the wrong zip code I'd go out and rough 'em up."

She nodded but said nothing as we drove along, periodically stopping and unloading mail in the rural boxes. We'd gotten to the Chilton Road cutoff when she leaned forward and spoke. "Stop."

I pulled the International to the side of the road and eased it to a halt.

She finished her coffee and got out, battling the wind as she walked toward a twelve-foot reflector pole where a fluorescent-green rock sat on the ground. Stooping, she glanced around, but as near as I could tell she didn't see anyone. She reached down and lifted the rock, and Dog and I watched as a piece of folded paper flew from underneath it and cartwheeled down the barrow ditch.

Racing after it, she was fortunate enough for it to catch on a stout piece of sagebrush and stick there long enough for her to retrieve it.

I watched as she unfolded the piece of paper, read the note, and then stuffed it in her coat pocket, the wind whipping her hair like her thinking, both of which I was sure were a maelstrom.

3

As we drove along on the county road, I allowed my eyes to wander toward her while she petted Dog. "So, are you going to tell me about that piece of paper you folded up and stuck in your coat pocket?"

"Just a note from an old friend."

I surveyed the desolate landscape. "What, they live around here?" She remained silent as I turned the wheel, and we headed north on a BLM road. "Say, have you ever heard of a group called the Order of the Red Gate?"

She stopped petting Dog and slumped against the passenger door, staring at me. "You're kidding, right?"

"What?"

"I thought you were normal."

"I am."

"People involved with that group are not normal."

"I'm not involved with them, I'm just curious since I'll be working in the area."

She gazed out the windshield. "Look, they used to be around here, but I haven't heard anything about them for some time, so if you're looking for them, I wouldn't have any idea where they'd be."

"I'm just curious. Somebody in town told me about them and I was just making conversation."

We drove along silently before she spoke again. "They started out in California, but then they were in Nevada, then somewhere else, and then here for a while—they seem to like deserts. Jeez, get on the internet if you want to know about those weirdos, they've done a half dozen documentaries on them."

"Like the one that Blair was on?"

"Oh, the *Mysteries from Beyond* crap?"

"Yeah, a friend loaned me a copy."

"No, that was long before the Red Gate horseshit, but I wouldn't be surprised if they got their ideas from Blair."

"Kind of odd, don't you think?"

"Odd isn't the word for it."

"So, was she?"

"What?"

"Odd."

"Well, yeah, I guess you'd have to say so." She laughed. "Anybody that says they ran off to the planet of the clam people with a half dozen cows must not be all there, if you know what I mean."

"I do."

"I get the feeling she didn't have a normal upbringing."

"Define 'normal.'"

"Touché."

We pulled up to another bank of mailboxes and began ferreting out the mail from behind the seat and slipping it in the metal boxes as Dog watered a sprig of something that looked as if it had been alive at some point. Once we'd finished, Tess moved to the side and stood there, looking at the shifting sand as it moved like a low and sparkling wave. "It stretches over a hundred miles; did you know that?"

"No."

"From Farson to the Ferris Mountains, it's the largest living sand dune in the United States." She turned to look at me. "Ever heard of the heavenly potholes here in the Red Desert?"

"Excuse me?"

"I grew up in Bairoil, which we'll be going through in a bit, and that's what my father used to call them, but Blair used to call them the ephemeral ponds." She looked back at the moving sand skittering in random patterns, swirling and making failing dust devils. "It's when the dune blows over and covers a snowbank in the winter, then the snow hardens into ice that's insulated so it thaws slowly in the spring and summer, making pockets of water. If you get stuck out here, they can save your life if you know where to find them."

"And how do you do that?"

"It's the little things; you follow the little things." She turned and started back toward the truck, walking past me and Dog, but then stopped. "Look, I don't know who you are, but I know you're not who you say you are. For now, I'm going to assume you're one of the good guys, but if I find out otherwise . . ."

"Then what?"

She paused as she climbed back in the Travelall. "I won't be buying you coffee anymore."

Established in 1916 by Charles Bair, Bairoil was named for the first oil well that transformed the sheepman into an oil baron. Hence the name, Bairoil. In 1924 the town petitioned for a post office and a year later got one. The first school was built in 1936 and electricity found its way there in 1952, while phone service arrived in 1970 with the addition of a landline—fortunately I had my nifty JugBug that miraculously appeared to have service. "When is the reception?"

There was a lot of static and a buzzing noise as I listened to the voice of the greatest legal mind of our time. "What? Over?"

I repositioned the phone in my ear. "When is the reception?"

"Yeah, it's really shitty reception wherever you are. Over."

"No, when *is* the reception?"

"Friday night. Hey, are you calling from a pay phone in Mongolia or something. Over?"

"It's a cell phone."

"I'm not on a cell phone. Over."

"No, I'm on a cell phone."

"A what? Over?"

"Will you stop doing that?" I practically shouted into the thing. "A cell phone."

"Whose?"

"Mine."

"Wait, you have a cell phone?"

"Yep."

"I've gotta tell you, it's a really shitty one."

"Well, I'm just starting."

My daughter, full-time smart-ass and the assistant attorney general for the State of Wyoming and potential future General of All Attorneys in the state, sighed. "Friday, which gives you two days to get to Cheyenne, over here on the other side of I-80."

"Where is it?"

"What?"

"Where is the reception?"

"At the state museum, you know where that is?"

"Actually, I do. Same building as the state archives."

"Very good. Cocktails are at six, food at seven, and speeches at eight."

"I'll try and make it." There was a pause, and I thought I'd lost her. "Hello?"

"I'm sorry, I thought you said you'd try and make it to your daughter's potential appointment as the AG of the State of Wyoming. Over?"

"I . . ."

"Because if you don't make it, I'm disowning you and changing my name. Over."

"Please stop doing that."

"And if you don't make it to the reception, I'm going to have your fiancée strangle you in your sleep. Over."

The phone went dead in my hand, or I lost her, which was totally possible. Over.

Tess joined me at the front of the International, parked by the chain-link fence that surrounded the old town hall, after filling the boxes in the long line beside the road and bringing a bowl over and setting it before Dog, who began lapping up the proffered water. "Trouble at home?"

"Daughter."

"Oh, real trouble."

"She's got a big promotion coming up."

"Down in Colorado?"

I closed the device and pocketed it. "That direction, yep."

"What does she do?"

"She's a lawyer."

She shook her head and discarded the water Dog hadn't drunk and then climbed in the passenger side as I slipped into my side, allowing Dog to climb in and closing the door behind us. She turned around in the seat, taking in what there was of the hundred-person town. "What?"

"I grew up here. I watched 'em close the school, try to close the post office, and even lose the one police officer we had."

"What are you trying to tell me?"

"You get a finer sense of things when people are trying to take things away from you all the time, and my fine senses tell me you're not going to be doing this job for very long."

I fired up the International and pulled out. "You never know."

"Uh-huh."

She didn't say anything for the next four stops, and I thought it was time I started a little fence-mending with some small talk as we parked in the mining settlement of Atlantic City, going through the trays and stuffing the sales brochures, letters, and bills in the rows of mailboxes. "First serial killer in the state."

She paused. "Excuse me?"

"Well, not here but just a little down the road in South Pass City."

She went back to filling the boxes.

"Back when they struck gold in the 1860s, there was a boom and there were saloons, a blacksmith shop, and the place swelled with at least a thousand miners and prospectors out to make a quick buck, but they weren't alone . . . A woman by the name of Polly Bartlett had an inn in South Pass City and was kind of cutthroat in competing with the other establishments, luring lodgers in with drink, sex, and the house specialty: arsenic steaks . . ."

She finally turned to look at me. "What?"

"South Pass City was a pretty rough town and most of the residents were either transient, footloose, or just passing through. There wasn't much law, no religion, and no way for these individuals to get in touch with family or friends, even if they were so inclined—it was kind of like being on the dark side of the moon."

"So, she started killing them?"

"Pretty quick, yep, bumped off twenty-two of 'em in one year alone."

"Did you just use the term 'bumped off'?"

Ignoring her, I continued. "She lured these guys in and then poisoned them, took everything they had, and then she and her father, Jim, would bury them outside a corral near her property.

"Twenty-two of them?"

"Yep, but she finally pushed her luck and poisoned the son of a wealthy mine owner, Bernard Fountain, and got the attention of Pinkerton's National Detective Agency, which discovered a thirteen-thousand-dollar reward for the Bartlett family. Polly and her father got wind of this and hightailed it for Oregon but were caught by an ex-lawman by the name of Ed Ford, whose brother had been killed by the Bartletts. Ford shot it out with Jim, killed him, and then took Polly prisoner, hauling her back to South Pass where they stuck her in a jail cell."

"I assume she was put on trial, pronounced guilty, and executed?"

"Well, she was executed. Otto Kalkhorst, a German-born superintendent of one of Fountain's mines—remember him, the mine owner whose son was poisoned?"

"Yeah."

"He went to a window outside Polly's cell that night and called her over to the window, where he shot her in the face point-blank with both barrels of a twelve-gauge coach gun."

"Yuck."

"Yep."

"So, was *he* put on trial, pronounced guilty, and executed?"

"Nope, wasn't even charged by Esther Morris, another Wyoming woman of celebrity status . . . She was the first female American justice of the peace."

She raised a fist. "Wyoming women: first to vote, first to hold office, and first to bump off twenty-two men."

"Did you just use the term 'bump off'?"

"That was for your benefit." She climbed back in the SUV. "C'mon, I'll let you buy me lunch in Farson."

We sat in Mitch's Cafe as she stirred her coffee in the Buffalo china mug. "First off, how do you know so much about local history if you're from Colorado?"

"Maybe I don't know as much about local history as I do about serial killers."

She stared at me and lifted her mug to take a swig. "That's unsettling."

I shrugged, taking the next to last bite of my cheeseburger and sip of iced tea. "It's a hobby."

She lowered her mug and stared into the swirling coffee. "You know, when I was a kid, I figured that whenever something really horrible happened in my life that somebody, somebody like you would step in and set things straight."

"Like me?"

"Don't interrupt." She took a deep breath. "Granted, you're a little older than I pictured and a little scarred up, but a big, handsome guy, maybe a little mysterious, who would suddenly appear and solve my problems."

"How'd that work out?"

"Not so good." She nudged the mug. "I've been married three times."

"It happens."

"You married?"

I thought about it. "It's complicated, but I think I'm engaged."

"You think?"

"Yep, but I was married before."

"Divorce?"

"No, she passed away . . . She passed away a number of years ago."

She picked up the mug again. "Why did you pause just now?"

"I seem to be stuck on her being gone for only five years, but it's been longer than that . . . ten I think."

She nodded and sipped her coffee. "How does this fiancée feel about that?"

"She likes taking chances."

"I bet she does." She smiled. "So, level with me: Are you really here to find Blair?"

"I'm here to deliver the mail . . ." I wiped my hand on a napkin and dropped it on my mostly empty plate. "But if I were here to help find Blair, the first thing I'd want to know is what was written on that piece of paper you found under the spray-painted rock."

She shook her head. "That's personal."

"Nothing to do with her?"

"No."

"Okay."

She stared at me. "Just 'okay,' that's it?"

"I'm not going to wrestle you to the ground and take it from you, if that's what you're asking."

She slid out from her side of the booth and stood. "Too bad—sounds like fun."

As she walked off toward the little girl's room a woman approached from behind the counter and slipped the check in front of me. "Here you go."

I peeled a few bills from my wallet, handing them to her. "So, are you Mitch?"

"My father, he started the place."

"Well, my compliments to the chef."

I wrapped up the last bite of cheeseburger in a napkin and stuffed it in my pocket as she took the plates off the table. She started back but stopped, toeing something on the floor. "This yours?"

I leaned out and could see something lying on the tile—the folded piece of paper that Tess had picked up out in the desert. "No, it's hers, I think, but I'll get it."

Walking over, I fetched the paper and returned to the booth with it in my hands, thinking that this is when a true investigator would've unfolded the thing and given it a careful read.

She'd said it was personal.

She'd said it had nothing to do with Blair.

I sat there for a moment more and then reached across the table and sat the note beside her mug.

After a moment the waitress came back and gave me my change, part of which I stacked in a tidy pile by my glass as Tess came back and sat on the edge of her side of the booth.

Reaching for her coffee, she noticed the folded piece of paper. "I guess you didn't have to wrestle me after all."

I nodded toward the waitress as she started off. "She found it on the floor."

She sipped her coffee. "She did, did she?"

"Yep."

"And you didn't read it."

"Nope, you said it was personal."

She shook her head, repocketing the note. "Tell me something, Jolly Greenie Giant, is everybody in Colorado as noble and upstanding as you?"

"Pretty much."

She studied me for a while longer. "Uh-huh." She stood again and started for the door. "C'mon, I want ice cream."

The Farson Merc was famous across the state for one thing: ice cream. The fact that Farson is positioned to be in the middle of hundreds of miles of nowhere helps to provide some mystique, but they do have a lengthy list of flavors.

"You gonna try it?"

The other thing they're famous for is the quad scoop, or the Big Cone, with enough ice cream to choke a hippopotamus.

I noted the different waffle cones and pointed to the smallest. "I'll have that one."

The young woman behind the counter smiled. "What flavor?"

I looked down at the myriad tubs behind the curved glass of the cooler. "Do you have vanilla?"

The smile faded. "We have five different vanillas."

"Um, just pick one?"

She dug out a half scoop and placed it in the cone, handing it over as Tess continued to study me. "Vanilla, really?"

I wrapped a paper napkin around the cone. "I like vanilla."

She ordered her own complex concoction, and we went outside to sit and eat our ice cream, the wind having died down. The original building had been an all-purpose school, townhall, boardinghouse, post office, and grocery store before it had burned in the forties, but because the structure had been brick, it was quickly rebuilt and served as a much-appreciated oasis not only for the locals but also weary tourists traveling to and from Yellowstone National Park.

All this knowledge I kept to myself.

Walking to the end of the wooden deck out front, we allowed Dog to join us as we sat at the picnic table and ate our ice cream in the warm, midday sun. "So, did Blair make this many stops on her daily route?"

"No."

"Then why are we?"

"We started early."

"Earlier than her?"

"Yes." She licked her cone and its variety of flavors. "I was trying to break you; I figured you'd either quit or tell me what the heck is going on."

"Funny, I was hoping that's what you'd tell me."

"Can I ask you a question?"

"Sure."

"You don't have to look so worried; it's a professional question."

"What profession?"

She ignored me and ate some more before asking, "How long do you have to wait before reporting someone as missing?"

"You don't."

"I thought you had to wait twenty-four hours?"

"Nope, contrary to popular belief there's no waiting period at all. As a matter of fact, with what they refer to as a 'critical missing person,' say with children or an adult over the age of sixty, the sooner the better."

She thought about it, turning her head and letting the slight breeze carry the swirls of blond hair from her face. "Okay, so say someone goes missing, an adult with their faculties intact. If you were to find that person, are you legally required to notify the authorities?"

"Yep, especially if there is an ongoing investigation as to the missing person's whereabouts."

She thought about that one. "And if the authorities were to find that person and discover that their actions were purely voluntary, would they still be required to disclose that person's location?"

"No, not without that person's permission. Filing a missing person report for an adult in this country doesn't entitle you the right to know where they are, only that they're alive and safe."

"What if it's a criminal situation?"

"I'm not sure what you mean."

"A suspicion of criminal activity involved with the missing person."

"Then it's a criminal offense and would involve law enforcement whether the missing person wanted it or not."

"I see."

I let that one settle and then added. "But that would have to do with the degree of criminal activity we're talking about." She nodded her head and continued licking her cone as I did the same with mine, trying to keep it out of my beard.

"What's the legal definition of kidnapping?"

"Unlawful restraint of a person's liberty by force or coercion wherein the person is taken to another location or concealed."

"What about that across state lines stuff you always hear in the movies?"

"Archaic reference, and no longer applies."

She was making amazing headway on her ice cream as I wiped the drip of vanilla from my hand with the paper napkin. "Okay, so if you really are undercover, then you're the worst undercover agent I've ever met."

I licked my cone some more in an attempt to keep from wearing it. "Met many?"

She smiled. "Look, if I'm going to help you you've got to tell me who the heck you are because I could be getting my friend into more trouble than she's already in, and I'm not willing to do that."

It was about that time that a large three-quarter ton Chevrolet pulled up in front of the Merc, a cloud of dust whipping away as a man in a black cowboy hat slid out and looked at me from behind his bushy white beard, followed by a tall woman with severe blue eyes and a brilliant smile close behind him.

Stopping short, he slapped a hand on the railing and shook his head at me. "Absaroka County Sheriff Walt Longmire, what the hell are you doing in Farson?"

I turned to look back at Tess, who, after a moment . . .

Predictably . . .

Exploded in laughter.

We waved bye to Bill Wiltse, the Fremont county sheriff, and his wife, Carol, the Wyoming state treasurer, as they licked their cones and backed their truck out northward. Sitting there quietly, I finally faced the music.

"You do this undercover stuff a lot?"

"It shows?"

"Kind of."

I wadded up my napkin and I tossed it into the nearest trash can with a nice wind-assisted curveball. "I had one other case up on the Powder River."

"How did that go?"

"About as well as this one so far."

She stood and I patted my leg for Dog to follow as we moved toward the OTR, or "Over the Road," bank of boxes near the Farson post office between Mitch's Cafe and the Merc. Dog sat in the shade of the International as we unloaded the cubbies and emptied them in the trays for delivery.

As Tess worked, she talked. "You really want to know about Blair?"

"Yep."

I held out a tray and she loaded the mail from the small lockers, careful to separate them into the few addressees left on the route. "There was this time three winters ago, you remember that winter?"

"I do."

"Well, there was a point where they shut down 287 and the majority of her route for twelve days. Blair would call those folks in

Bairoil—she had all their numbers—and would assure them that she was out here and come hell or the highway patrol she was going to get in there and get them their mail."

I filled one tray and sat it on the pullout, then picked up another, holding it out for Tess to complete.

"She finally borrowed a snowmobile from a guy who trailered her out as far as he could and then he set her down at the cutoff above Rawlins with a sled full of mail, food, and extra fuel. She took off and the weather was good, but you know how that crap is here in the state. Well, it started snowing and blowing and the temperature dropped a good forty degrees."

She grabbed more mail and sorted it as I stood there holding the tray.

"She'd called them and told them what time she thought she'd be there, and that time came and went. They built fires and sat there and waited for her and a couple of hours went by. They were just starting to think that they should head home, that she must've turned back and given up, when somebody spotted a figure out on the road on foot, dragging a sled."

She finished packing the tray and I placed it on the pullout, pushing it in and closing the door before turning to face her.

"The snowmobile had broken down and she disconnected the sled, pulling it herself for the last five miles."

"Gritty, huh?"

"Yeah, you could say that. She lost two toes on her left foot that day."

"I'll keep that in mind if I have to identify her."

She gave me a look and then climbed in the International as I let Dog in. I slid behind the wheel and fired it up. "Where to now?"

She glanced at the plastic digital watch on her wrist. "It's three o'clock and we have twenty-three more addressees to fulfill. The Eden Saloon is about four miles down the road and they have the coldest beer in Sweetwater County."

I hit the switch and the Travelall rumbled to life. "Sounds like the twenty-three addressees are waiting for their mail while we drink a beer."

She pointed through the windshield toward the open road. "To the saloon, James."

I drove the 4.3 miles to the Eden Saloon and we seated ourselves at the bar, whereupon a middle-aged man in a ball cap smiled and skidded two coasters in front of us. "Hi, Tess, what'll it be?"

"A Coors for me and whatever the Jolly Greenie Giant here drinks."

I lifted a finger. "Rainier."

He nodded and moved toward the coolers as she leaned in toward me. "I'm keeping up your alias so as to not blow your cover."

"Thanks."

The bartender returned and I noticed the Rainier was the Jubilee can, from last Christmas. "Fresh?"

"As the day is long." He pulled the tab, and I noticed there was a distinct lack of effervesce. "You from Colorado?"

I took a sip. "This beer is flat."

"So's most of Colorado, and my ex-wife." He started off. "Enjoy."

I reached over and tipped beverages with Tess as she tasted it herself and then sat her can down on the coaster. "All right, you know about me, now tell me about what's going on with Blair."

"One more question first: Who are you working for?"

"The postal inspector, Mike Thurman."

"Poppa Bear?"

"Is that what you guys call him?"

"We do. He's a great guy . . ."

"He is."

"So how did he get you involved in all this?"

"He's shirttail family to my late wife."

She nodded. "Was that him I saw hiding in the Jeep in the parking lot with you the morning you showed up?"

"Wow, can you make this any more embarrassing for me?"

She shrugged. "You're kind of noticeable for a guy trying to be undercover."

"Blair."

She looked down the bar to make sure the bartender was far enough away for her to not be heard. "First off, you didn't hear any of this from me, got it?"

"Got it."

"That group that you mentioned when I got the note, the Order of the Red Gate?"

"The cult that's going to fly off with Higgo One and the clam people to the planet far, far away?"

"Blair met a few of them out here in the Red Desert when she made arrangements with them to pick up and deliver mail."

"The fluorescent-green rocks."

"Yeah. Anyway, she's always making conversation with everybody, and she started talking to them . . ."

"They live out in the Red Desert?"

"Yeah, the name was different before but when they got here, they changed it to the Order of the Red Gate, the Red Gate being the Boar's Tusk formation out there in the Red Desert, get it?"

"Kind of."

"Anyway, they move around in tents and shit. Drives the Bureau of Land Management and the Forest Service crazy, but they got some people in the organization who are real old desert rat types who know all the hidden places out there so that whenever the feds are going to come in, they just disappear."

"I think Flossy mentioned something about going out there to meet them with her one time."

She stared at me quizzically. "Flossy?"

"The woman that lives next door to her in the trailer park on the outskirts of Rock Springs on the south side."

"That's a nice trailer park."

I nodded. "As trailer parks go, I have to agree."

"Flossy? Really?"

"Yep, she's kind of a piece of work. I went out there to take a look around and had a run-in with Blair's boyfriend, Benny Schweppe."

"Oh God, Benny?"

"Another piece of work, as pieces of work go."

"I'll say. Anyway, Blair got involved with these wackos and started this delivery system for them with the green rocks, and pretty soon she's talking about all this stuff they're involved with like it makes sense."

"Well, she was on that TV show all those years ago . . ."

She took a long, slow glug from her can. "I got the impression she was pressured into doing that."

"The whole alien thing?"

"Yeah."

"By who?"

"I don't know, but that's the vibe I got."

"So, you're thinking she's out there in the Red Desert with this cult?"

She nodded and sat her can back down. "It's the only thing that makes any sense, but if she's out there with them voluntarily I'm not so sure that there's any way to get her back."

"That's why you were asking all those questions about kidnapping and notification of the authorities?"

"Exactly. If she's out there, I wasn't sure what to do . . . At least up until now."

"What's that mean?"

"Look, I need help, and from where I'm sitting you look like you're it." She reached into her pocket and took out the folded note that she'd gotten from under the green rock and placed it on the bar between us, sliding it toward me with her fingertips as it began slowly unfolding itself as if it were alive.

I stared at it for a moment and then glanced at her profile before carefully unfolding the fast-food wrapper and reading the message scrawled in blood-red lipstick—SAVE ME.

4

After dropping Tess off back at the post office, I'd returned to the Red Desert and gazed at the Boar's Tusk sticking up out of the ground like a gigantic, hitchhiking thumb. "How could she just disappear?"

My deputy Santiago Saizarbitoria's voice sounded fatigued. "The guy from the FAA says the flight plan was filed but she never showed at her checkpoint in Iowa."

"What about radar, or something like that?"

"The plane is too small to be picked up by commercial tracking or the military."

"So, they're saying she just disappeared like Amelia Earhart?"

"Evidently."

"In the heartland of America?" I listened as Sancho breathed on the other end of the line, saying nothing. "That's ridiculous."

"I don't know what to tell you, Boss. I've got the investigator's number here, but he sure sounds like he's got a lot on his plate."

"She's a federal agent. What about the DOJ, are they trying to find her?"

"Yep, I talked to some guy by the name of AIC Blake Foster, and he's been put in charge of the search—he's actually in Iowa."

"Give me his number." I scribbled it down and sighed. "Seems like all I do is look for missing women lately."

"Hey, you're good at it."

"Thanks, Sancho. If you hear anything give me a call."

"What did you just say?"

"I said . . ."

"I know, I just enjoy hearing you say it."

The JugBug went dead in my hand, so I closed it and slipped it into my coat pocket. "And that's what I get for hiring comedians."

I stepped out of the small circle of stones indicating the one spot near the Boar's Tusk where, if you were lucky, you could get cell service. Tess Anderson had assured me she could run the route tomorrow morning, allowing me to poke around in the areas where the Order of the Red Gate had last been seen.

Dog trailed along with me as I walked back toward the Travelall, and I couldn't get over the feeling that I was being watched. I hadn't really seen anything, but there was an itch I didn't seem to have an ability to scratch, an itch I'd felt before.

As my backup lingered near one of the Forest Service signs, I watched as he took another step and then lifted his leg in civil disobedience, finishing, and then turning to look at me. "What? I bring you to all the nice places, don't I?"

Walking past him, I once again looked up at the volcanic remains of an ancient eruption dating back 2.5 million years, a four-hundred-foot lamproite feature that some say looks like a boar's tusk, others that it's fingers in a mitt, and others that it's just a rock. It's an important landmark for the people who passed through the high-desert region over the centuries, as it can be seen from a fair distance in every direction in a place where the flats and basins can start looking an awful lot alike.

"Hello."

I turned to see a thirty-something forest ranger walking up from the other side of the parking lot, regarding my sidekick. "I'm afraid your dog has to be on a leash."

I gazed around at the completely desolate landscape. "You're kidding, right?"

"I'm afraid not. It's federal law."

"I'll put him back in the truck."

"Look, as long as you don't tell anybody . . ." He adjusted his Smokey Bear hat, and I noticed the strong native features and the long, dark ponytail at his back. "It's okay, so long as we're the only ones here."

"This your post?"

"Yeah."

"Kind of lonely."

"My last one was the National Historical Park in Boston."

"A little busier?"

"Yeah." He regarded the northwest and the bruise-colored sky. "Looks like a storm blowing in. Good thing you've got that International. Had it long?"

"Nope, just bought it a couple of days ago."

He studied the vehicle. "Blair McGowan's?"

"Yep. You know her?"

He made a lopsided gesture with one shoulder. "She was my mailperson."

"You live out here?"

"Somebody has to . . . Actually, I volunteered for the duty." He nodded past me. "I've got a camper over at Killpecker Sand Dunes, near the campsite."

"Any idea what might've happened to her?"

"A few."

"Like what?"

He walked past me and stooped to pet Dog and then looked toward the frozen volcanic eruption. "She was hanging around with an odd crowd."

"Odd in what way?"

"Oh, some kind of cult that roams around here every once in a while."

"The Order of the Red Gate?"

"Yeah, that's it." He pointed toward the formation. "That look like a gate to you?"

I joined him at the edge of the gravel. "Not particularly, but it doesn't look like a boar's tusk, fingers, a mitten, or Mickey Mouse to me either."

"We call it 'The Parents.'"

I studied his profile as Dog circled around and sat on my foot. "Arapaho?"

He smiled, sticking out a hand. "Yeah, Rick Scout Traveler."

We shook. "You didn't care for Boston, so you came back here?"

He nodded and the smile faded. "Something I swore I'd never do, but this red dirt country, it gets under your skin," he gestured toward his Forest Service unit, parked a little away, "I'm about done for the day, and I've got a sixer of Rainier and some buffalo brats back at the camper I was going to grill up."

"Have you got two extra?"

The smile returned. "Beer or brats?"

"Brats." I scrubbed the back of the beast's ears. "Dog here isn't old enough to drink beer."

We sat at a picnic table underneath an awning that was attached to the camper, watching the late-afternoon storm clouds swallowing up the western skyline of the Wind River range. "Arapaho, Shoshone, Ute, Goshute, Paiute, Bannock, Lakota, and Cheyenne just to name a few—been here for tens of thousands of years."

I finished my last brat, handing the end to the monster at my side who wolfed the bite down without tasting it. "What's the attraction?"

He sat his own sandwich on his plate as he paused to think. "Trading routes, the longest ungulate migration in the country . . . The petroglyphs down near White Mountain mark it as a sacred place, so who's to say?" He picked up his can of Rainier and sipped, his eyes taking in the vastness of the land around us. "My father loved this place because it was odd, you know? Strange lands pushed up against each other with badlands, mountain ranges, isolated buttes, vast sand dunes, and open seas of sagebrush and juniper trees."

He paused as we both watched a small herd of elk skitter across a ridge to the east. "A showcase."

"Yeah." He breathed a laugh. "If aliens were going to visit us, they could do worse than to start here."

"Order of the Red Gate?"

He laughed. "Yeah, I've had to chase them off the thing a couple of times."

"What were they doing?"

"Heck if I know. Communing with the aliens, I guess." He shook his head at the memory. "Most of them are harmless, but there are a couple who are downright scary."

"The head guy, Carruthers?"

"No, kind of his second in command or security, a guy by the name of Freebee."

I took a swig of my beer. "Freebee?"

"Yeah, some hippie dude, but hippie like Charles Manson with a six-gun, if you know the type."

"I'm afraid I do."

He continued to nurse his beer. "And then there's another guy who never talks. Lowell Ommen I think they call him, really strange-looking guy, doesn't have any hair."

"You mean he shaves his head?"

"No, I mean no eyebrows, eyelashes, hair on his arms, nothing." He thought about it. "Actually, he could be from outer space."

"Sounds like an interesting group."

He shrugged. "I think most of them are harmless, you know, people in search of something, and Carruthers casts a wide net."

"How did Blair get connected, other than her previous connection with the whole alien thing?"

"You know, I talked to her about that, the TV show?"

"Yep?"

"She said it was bullshit, something she'd got conned into doing by her father."

"Her father?"

"Yeah, a real grifter. He convinced her that she could turn it into some real coin if she played along, but then things got serious, and the air force even sent a couple of guys to talk to her, so she shut it down."

I drained my beer as the wind picked up with the front moving in. "Are you telling me that Higgo One and the clam people aren't real?"

He laughed some more. "Yeah, I hate to be the one to break the news to you."

I sat my empty can down, but then feeling it attempting to fly away, crushed it and sat it on my empty plate. I looked out at the shifting patterns of the sand and I thought about Blair McGowan. "You know, I was going to ask you where it is this group hid, but after looking around I think I'd wonder how you found them."

He took the plates and detritus and stood, carrying them into the small camper and calling through the screen door. "It'd be hard!"

I stood, but waited for him to come back, sticking my hand out again. "Thanks for dinner, those are some great brats."

"Tribal, from the Arapaho herd."

We shook and I patted my leg as Dog joined me. "Do you think she's with them?"

"Blair? I don't know, but I hate to think it. I always thought she was smarter than that."

I nodded, moving toward the International. "Well, I guess we'll get out of here before the rain hits."

He pointed at the front differential. "I'd put that thing in four if I were you. These roads get greasy, and this looks like a downpour."

Locking the hubs, I opened the door for Dog and then climbed in after him, waving at Rick Scout Traveler and then backing out of his tiny camp as the first dollops of rain splattered on the windshield as if they'd dropped from a couple of thousand feet, which they probably had.

Threading my way along Chilton Road, I took the cutoff south on 17 toward the White Mountain Petroglyphs, hoping to get a look at them as I headed back toward Rock Springs, but unless I'd brought a scuba mask and snorkel, the chances were growing slim.

Rick had been right about the roads, and as the storm flexed its liquid muscles the surface became a muddy channel, the difficulty compounded by the '60s windshield wipers that kept the beat in Fab Four time but did little to clear the glass.

The headlights weren't much better, only providing a yellowish set of beams that pierced the darkness and torrential rain to the distance of about three car lengths.

I was lucky they did, however, because I could barely make out the figure in a cowboy hat who appeared from out of nowhere, cloaked in a full-length oilskin duster, walking in the middle of the road.

Locking up the brakes, I barely got the big International slowed to a stop as the individual, either unknowing or uncaring, continued to trudge ahead in the torrent as if I hadn't almost run him down.

I sat there for a moment, and then decided to tap my horn, at least to let him know I was there. I touched the button at the center of the steering wheel with the heel of my hand and listened as an air horn sounded from under the hood.

It wasn't very loud inside with the pelting of the rain on the sheet metal, but it must've been outside the car because the figure in the dripping cowboy hat and sopping duster turned to look at me. I could see he was carrying something that looked suspiciously like a gun-fighting rig under the knee-length garment as he stood there.

I was about to crack the window and yell at him when he started toward me, veering to the passenger side.

Pulling a hand from the poncho, he grasped the handle and pulled the door open and slid in, the long barrel of a six-shooter escaping from the poncho and aiming toward the floorboards as the rivulets of water rolled off him. His hand came up to push the hat back to reveal a remarkable face and head of plastered wet hair.

There is common imagery from the middle of the century of Jesus and that's what sat in the seat beside me. Dirty blond hair under a flat-brimmed hat and ferocious green eyes with a skin tone of golden brown only surfers and desert dwellers could achieve.

"When you pass through the waters, I will be with you; and when you pass through the rivers, they will not sweep over you. When you walk through the fire, you will not be burned; the flames will not set you ablaze."

He even talked like Jesus. "Isaiah 43:2, I believe."

"Chapter and verse." He smiled, and even his teeth were perfect except for a chip in the front right tooth. "You are a believer?"

"I *believe* I almost ran you over."

He laughed and ran his free hand over the dash of the International as if he'd never seen such a thing. "I didn't think anybody would be on the road this time of night, brother." He wiped the rain from his face and then extended the same hand. "Freebee."

We shook and I mused that one man's Jesus is another man's Charlie Manson. "Walt."

"Where are you headed, Walt?"

I nudged a chin out to the southwest. "I was hoping to swing by White Mountain and take a look at the petroglyphs, but we might wait for better weather conditions."

He looked perplexed. "We?"

I threw a thumb toward the rear, and Dog.

He hunched against the seat, looking in the back. "My lord, what is that?"

"Dog."

He continued to study the creature. "What breed is he?"

"There's a lot of conjecture on that . . ." I pulled the Travelall back in gear and started off in the deluge. "So, how about you—where to?"

He pointed through the windshield. "About a mile down here there's a cutoff to the left heading toward Cedar Canyon, if you don't mind dropping me off there?"

"Happy to." I looked down at the six-shooter. "Hunting?"

He smiled the ingratiating grin. "No, simply a pilgrim on the road to Damascus." He gestured with the old-fashioned weapon. "Liable to be beset upon at any turn."

Sawing the wheel, I attempted to keep us centered in the slippery luge track, the International wallowing like a beached whale. "I don't think there's much besetting going on out there tonight."

"One never knows." He reached a hand out to Dog, but a baritone growl escaped from the back, causing the man to pull his hand back quickly. "Your dog isn't very friendly."

"He takes awhile to warm up." I glanced at his profile and continued to struggle with the wheel. "Got a camp up there in Cedar Canyon?"

"Something like that."

"And this time of year, you're not hunting?"

"Oh, we're all hunting for something, are we not, brother?" He continued to gaze through the windshield like a man enraptured. "The highways are desolate, and the traveler has ceased. He has broken covenant; he has despised the cities and has no regard for man."

I nodded, raising my eyebrows for my own entertainment. "You're big on Isaiah."

Smiling again, he spoke in the singsong. "He speaketh to my soul."

I drove along a bit more before broaching the subject. "Say, have you ever heard of a group out here that goes by the name of the Order of the Red Gate?"

He didn't move, and the smile faded.

"The Order of the Red Gate, have you ever?"

"And why would you ask me about them?"

"I just figured that if you were out here you might've run into them?"

"No, no I haven't, but once again, brother, why do you ask?"

"I'm the new mailman for these parts and I'm still getting the lay of the land. I've gotten some correspondence for that group and all the address says is 'Red Desert,' so I'm not quite sure where to leave the mail. A woman I work with says that there are these rocks that are spray-painted green but I'm pretty sure that's not a US Postal Service–approved receptacle."

After a moment, he spoke softly. "You can give the mail to me."

"So, you do know where they are?"

"Sometimes." He continued to look out the windshield. "They move around, you see."

"Well, if you run into them tell them I've got their mail."

"As I said, you can give it to me."

"Well, pard, that's not how the postal service works, I'm a licensed courier for them and that means I have to deliver that mail to a registered address or to them personally." I glanced toward the back. "Besides, I don't have the mail with me at the moment."

He nodded to himself. "I see."

"If you run into them, tell them they can come into the post office in Rock Springs or just register with me where they'd like the mail delivered and I'll bring it out."

He nodded again and then pointed to the left, where an opening in the sagebrush revealed another two-track running into ours at an acute angle. "You can stop here."

I pulled out of the ruts and onto the level ground of the less-used roadway, watching as he pulled the handle and began climbing out and into the rain, but then stopped and leaned back in, what looked to be a .45 Colt single-action now in his hand. "What did you say your name was, brother?"

"Walt, and do you mind not pointing that Peacemaker at me?"

The smile crept onto his face ever so slowly. "Are you thinking I might shoot you, Walt?"

"I'm thinking that it happens by accident a lot of times."

Dog began rumbling in the back and his eyes shifted toward the monster before returning to mine. "Oh, if I was to shoot you it wouldn't be by accident."

"Are you threatening me, Freebee?"

"You ask a lot of questions for a mailman." He studied me a bit more. "And what's your full name, Walt?"

"Longmire. And what's your last name, Free or Bee?"

He stared at me for a moment more and then eased back, raising the barrel of the big Colt revolver before gently pushing the door closed, walking around the front, and starting off on the Cedar Canyon Road. I'd thought he was gone and I reached down to pull the truck back in gear when I noticed him, just out of eyesight, aiming the pistol at me again.

I sat there, looking back at him, making sure he knew I saw him, and then slowly pulled out, bouncing into the ruts and continuing south as Dog kept looking out the back and growling.

"I know how you feel."

Sweetwater County Sheriff John Grossnickle sat opposite me in the fancy commissary, sipping his coffee and shaking his head. "He pointed a pistol at you?"

I shrugged. "It was some pretty low-tech brandishing, yep."

He considered the situation. "First time we've ever had Jesus point a gun at anybody."

"Scout Traveler, the forest ranger, says he's more Manson than Messiah."

"Hmm . . ." The same female deputy, Officer Rivera, who had arrested me in the trash can altercation approached and handed John a file folder before flicking her big brown eyes at me. "How's your head?"

I smiled back, adjusting my hat and scratching my noggin. "Fine, how's yours?"

"Nobody's using it as a bongo."

I watched as she walked away.

"Say, aren't you engaged?"

I turned to look back at the younger man who was ignoring me and studying the folder. "Just looking at the menu. Besides, she's young enough to be my daughter."

At the mention of Cady, he looked up, smiling. "Hey, I hear we're all going to be working for your daughter now that Wally Fisk is out and Robert Lang is in."

"You've been talking to Joe Meyer?"

"Getting anything from Joe is like getting blood from a turnip, but I gather he's going to retire. Anyway, I've got my own friends in high places."

I lifted my cup and sipped my coffee, which I had to admit was pretty good. "Well, she's a potential nominee, which reminds me that I have to drive over to Cheyenne on Friday for a reception in her potential honor."

"What's the problem?"

"I don't know." I sat the cup back down. "To me, she's still twelve years old."

"She'd be a great AG, Walt." He laughed. "She comes from good stock."

"Thanks." I gestured toward the file he was holding. "Freebee?"

"Who does not come from such great stock, at least if he's the individual we think he is." He closed the file and placed it on the table, sliding it toward me. "Now, taking into consideration that all we have to go on is this singular name, like Cher, Madonna, Sting, Liberace . . ."

"Goofy, Sneezy, Dopy."

"Yeah, well, teenage Freebee Leland pops up in his native Oregon where he got into a fight with a guy in a bar in Burns and stabbed him with a knife, killing him, and then running off into the wilderness where it took authorities another month to catch him. He went to trial, but the eyewitnesses seemed to dry up and blow away by then, and the one who gave a deposition changed his mind and said the other guy started the altercation and had a gun, which was never found. Then the elusive Freebee turns up again in a missing persons case after he and a friend went camping in Crater Lake National Park and the friend just disappeared, never to be heard from again."

"So, he has an affinity for national parks."

John ignored me and continued. "Then he's involved with the abduction of a fourteen-year-old girl near Portland, but the parents, apparently under duress, refused to press charges." He took a breath and sat back in his bench seat. "Next, he was involved in the beating of a man in Studio City in Los Angeles and a vehicular aggravated assault in Bakersfield, where he noted his occupation as 'actor.' He was charged with robbery, which is a felony-only offense, and ended up doing sixteen months in North Kern State Prison. Evidently, while he was there he got religion, and there's no mention of him for a couple of years until he ups his game and gets charged with what the Securities and Exchange Commission refers to as affinity fraud, a Ponzi scheme he and some other guy, Ritt Ravitch, were running on elderly church members in and around Bakersfield. They were fraudulently raising close to five million dollars from at least fifty investors through unregistered security offerings."

"Sounds like he found more than religion in North Kern."

"Yeah, anyway, these people were all elderly, retired, and connected to this church he worked for, which went by the name Holy Trinity Empire, and he promised the old folks insider trading on tech companies in Silicon Valley, but this Ravitch guy just lost his ass in the market and used the rest of the money to buy expensive cars and take luxury trips on private jets . . . And get this, this Ravitch guy started this church three months after getting out of North Kern himself after being charged with mail fraud, false tax filings, and a dozen other financial crimes against greater humanity."

"Birds of a feather?"

Grossnickle drank some more coffee. "The question, of course, is why does this Freebee character get picked up by Ravitch? Muscle?"

"The character I met last night has a biblical quality to him."

"Table dressing?"

"Maybe, but he's dangerous." I tapped the file. "What about the other one, Lowell Ommen?"

"Nothing."

I stared at him. "Nothing?"

"There are a few Lowell Ommens out there in the greater populace, one of them an army medic, but none of them with remarkable criminal records—of course, it's possible it's an alias."

I sat back on my bench, trailing an arm across the seat and drumming my fingertips on the hard wood. "There was another one that Benny mentioned, Zeno something . . ." I thought about it. "Carruthers, Zeno Carruthers. Can you run him?"

"Sure." He lifted the file, plucking a pen from his pocket and jotting down the name. "You really think Blair is out there with these wackos?"

"So far, in that it's the only lead I've got."

"But no tangible evidence."

I pulled the scrap of paper from my pocket and laid it on the table between us. Sheriff Grossnickle leaned forward and read the two words scribbled in lipstick, his eyes coming back up to mine.

"And where did you get this?"

"Under a rock."

"You're kidding."

"Nope. I guess she was delivering mail to them by leaving it under these special green rocks out there in the Red Desert."

He folded his hands together, providing support for his chin. "Please tell me you're kidding."

"I wish I was. I was running the route yesterday with Tess Anderson and she knew about the rocks and found that one."

He studied the note. "So, she's there and wants out?"

"If that's her handwriting and her note."

"Then let's go round them up."

"That might be easier said than done."

"I've got people who know that territory like the back of their hand."

"I don't doubt that, but obviously they want to keep her for whatever they're doing and if we go charging in there, they might do something desperate."

"If it's her, then why do they want her that badly?"

"I don't know."

"So, what do you want to do?"

"I think the only way to do this is get in there and get the lay of the land before we do something massive."

"You could get killed doing this crap, Walt." He looked around. "There are a lot of places out there where you could bury a body and it would be awhile before we found it, if we ever did."

"Look, John, if you're trying to make me feel better . . ."

"I'm not."

"I gather that."

He leaned back with a thump. "Besides, I really don't want the potential attorney general for the State of Wyoming to have a blood vendetta out for me."

"Sabrina McGowan lives in Sacramento, and as near as I can tell she teaches primary school, is married, has two kids, including a newborn. She has no criminal record and is a fucking pilar of society."

I held the phone close to my ear, just enjoying the sound of her voice. "Is that last part your seal of approval?"

"Pretty much. We don't get to meet her kind in our line of work very often." I listened as she hummed a tune I didn't recognize, obviously involved with something else. "One point of interest: She didn't seem to want to stay on the phone for very long."

"Something?"

"Hell if I know; she's married, got two kids and a job . . ." She rustled some papers. "How's Dog doing? I miss him."

"You don't miss me?"

She continued humming. "In a different way."

"He tried to eat a guy, yesterday."

"No shit?"

"He was aiming a six-shooter at me."

She stopped humming. "Whoa, wait a minute. What?"

"The guy I was talking about, Freebee."

"He pointed a gun at you?"

"I left that part out?"

"Yes."

I cleared my throat; pretty sure I'd just made a mistake. "No big deal, he just had an antique, and it might've drifted in my direction . . ."

"I'm calling Henry."

I sighed. "No, you're not."

"Look, somebody's got to run the county but it's him or me, so who is it going to be?"

"I've got Dog, believe that's enough."

"If you get killed by some walking penis named Freebee it would reflect very badly on the department, you know that, right?"

"So if I'm going to be killed, what would be a good killer's name?"

"Victoria Moretti, asshole." She started humming again. "Hey, I'm supposed to remind you about this reception the higher-ups are having in Cheyenne on Friday."

"Yep, everybody in Wyoming keeps reminding me, but I'm kind of busy . . ."

"Look, if you really want to know how you're going to die, just don't show up for that reception on Friday, bub."

The phone went dead in my hand before I could ask what song she was humming.

I pocketed the thing and wondered if anybody said goodbye anymore, or did they just hang up like all the women in my life? Hopping down from the fender of the International, I wiped off the sheet metal of the now-clean vehicle and glanced at Dog as I started the engine and drove out of the carwash. "I think that's what we call a command performance."

Wheeling through town, I felt a pang of shame as I drove by the post office and headed out of town, going north on 191 and back to the roads I'd escaped last night. Thinking about how I was going to play it, I looked down at the bundle of useless mail Mike Thurman had been kind enough to throw together for me from the dead letter bin of the Rock Springs post office.

I said to Dog, "Just your average everyday mailman, right?"

He looked back at me in a way I think could be described as doubt.

The rain had stopped early that morning, and say what you want about the high desert, it soaked up water, and right fast. I rolled down the window and the smell of the rehydrated sage was as intoxicating as it always is, freshening the air to the point where your eyes watered.

Taking the Chilton Road cutoff, I wondered at how the landscape changed when there was light and you weren't drowning in a waterfall, marveling at the pinstripes of silver light that fought through thick, flannel clouds. The glow was horizontal and highlighted the bare landscape in a deep contrast, raising even the smallest detail.

The Cedar Canyon Road looked nothing like I'd remembered, but the Forest Service sign was there, and I took the turn, bumping along and climbing along a gully that held a surprising amount of water from last night's flooding. Buttes crowded the north side of the road, but the flats along the channel had spots where vegetation had taken hold, and I was surprised to find a couple of well-worn sagging wall tents clustered in a draw as if huddling together for communal heat.

There was an early '60s Blue Bird bus painted up like the Partridge Family gone to seed, and I could see a stack where a dwindling amount of smoke trickled out.

I stopped on the pullout next to the road and saw where they must've driven in, but I had serious doubts as to whether they'd get that bus out of there any time in the near future.

Cracking the door and getting out with the bogus bundle of mail, I lowered the window a bit and then shushed Dog and told him to stay before I closed the door and walked around the front.

The odd thing was that there didn't appear to be anybody around—no one milling or even looking out of the tent flaps or cracked and clouded bus windows.

Standing there at the turnout, I decided to follow the road up to the grade where they must've driven the conveyance and began walking toward the front of the bus. I'd just walked past the side door and was about to continue when the folding door opened, and I was once again confronted by Freebee sitting in the driver's seat, wearing a single rig and pistol aimed in my general direction.

"I thought I asked you not to point that thing at me?" Raising my hands in a comic fashion, I gave him a long look. "Forgive us our trespasses?"

"What is it you want, brother?"

I gestured with the mail in one of my raised hands. "Making a delivery; you said you wanted it last night."

He studied me a bit longer and then stood up from the driver's seat, leaving the lever of the door open and coming down the steps. "So, you come bearing gifts?"

I lowered my hands even though he kept the barrel of what I could now see in the light of day was the same Colt revolver he had pulled on me yesterday. "That a real Peacemaker?"

He nudged it sideways, giving it a look-see with a smile. "Yeah."

I nodded. "Well, I don't know about gifts. But it's mail, and I'm delivering it."

He stuck a hand out. "I'll take it."

I glanced around. "Say, are you the only one out here?"

"No, he's not."

I turned to see an older man accompanied by another odd-looking individual who also held another vintage pistol. Now, if Freebee looked like Jesus, the older man sure looked like the depictions of God that I'd seen since Bible school as a child. Tall, with shoulder-length ash-blond hair and a full beard that reached to his expansive chest, he was dressed in a long, flowing white robe, the patrician image only marginally diminished by the fact that he was wearing muck boots and smoking a cigar.

Smiling a brilliant grin, he extended a hand. "Zeno Carruthers. I understand you have some mail for us?"

5

I took the hand and we shook as the other man, a very thin, young individual with a bald head and no eyebrows underneath a beaten cowboy hat, drifted to my right. "You and your group are kind of hard to track down, Mister Carruthers."

He continued smiling and smoking his cigar as if he were on the red carpet instead of the Red Desert. "We like it that way, but you found us, didn't you?"

I nodded toward the other armed man behind me. "Well, I gave Mister Freebee a lift last night and that kind of limited the scope."

"Yes, Mister, uh . . . Freebee told me about that. Thank you for your kindness to one of our flock."

I handed him the stack of useless mail. "So, is this a religious organization, Mister Carruthers?"

He paused for a moment. "Can I offer you a cup of tea?"

"I'd love one, thanks."

He gestured for me to enter the bus, but first drew Freebee from it. "Speaking of our flock . . . Freebee, how about you and Lowell head up and check on them?"

"You don't want us to stick around?"

"No, I think it'll be best if you and brother Ommen check on the meditation session and stay there with them."

Freebee didn't appear to agree, but he and the hairless one left without another word and took a trail through the tents, disappearing into the juniper trees and the smaller canyon, the two of them in their cowboy garb looking like they were lost out of time.

"They mean well." Carruthers climbed the stairs of the bus as I followed.

"They're well armed."

He continued down the aisle to the back of the bus where a small woodburning stove sat with a kettle on it happily steaming away. Moving the kettle, he tossed the remains of the cigar into the stove. "Have a seat." He gestured toward one of the bus benches across from a wooden chair and I sat, watching as he took two coffee mugs from hooks on the ceiling and drew two tea bags from a small box. "I hope you don't take anything in it. We're limited in supplies as of late."

"Just something warm would be nice."

He added the boiling water and then handed one of the mugs to me and sat in the chair. "Careful, it's hot." He held his to his face and blew into it. "In answer to your comment about the weapons; we've had some instances where our people have been threatened."

"I'm sorry to hear that."

"It is a violent world and some of our members have leprosy, a stark reminder of the stigma and suffering associated with this dreadful disease." He reached into the inside of his robe and pulled out a leather case. "Forgive me, would you like a cigar?"

"No, thanks."

"Genuine Cohiba Robustos. Illegal, but I have a connection."

"No, thanks." I looked out toward where the two armed men had disappeared and turned back to Carruthers. "Pardon me for asking, but your acolyte there, he doesn't have any hair?"

"Acolyte?" He chuckled as he produced a brass cutter and trimmed the cigar. "You're very observant for a mailman, Mister . . . ?"

I sipped my tea. "Just Walt."

He cocked his head to one side and smiled. "Most people just assume that Lowell shaves his head."

"Then he must also shave his eyebrows and lashes."

"Alopecia areata universalis, a medical condition that involves the loss of all body hair. It's an autoimmune disorder where the person's immune system attacks the hair follicles. It's genetic, or so they believe, but has no other symptoms or effects on life expectancy." He pulled out a lighter and he puffed on the cigar, getting it lit and then exhaling a plume of smoke toward the ceiling. "I found him on the streets of Sacramento where he tried to rob me."

"And instead, you took him in?"

He sipped his tea and sat back in his chair. "We did."

"We?"

"The Order of the Red Gate. We're a religious organization not too different from many others aside from our belief that many of the tenants of all religions of the world come from alien contact."

"Aliens, like UFO aliens?"

"It's not as odd as you might think. There are segments of Scientology, the Church of Latter-Day Saints, the Nation of Islam to name only a few who believe that the angels and other celestial beings are indeed not from Earth. One difference is that we believe they move not only through celestial space but also time."

"Have you and your . . . your followers been here in the area long?"

"No, only for the last three months."

I took another sip of tea. "I was just wondering because one of our postal workers went missing around here somewhere, a woman by the name of Blair McGowan?"

He nodded absentmindedly, smoking his cigar. "I've heard that name, and some of our people have been asked about her."

"Do you know if she's with your group?"

He reached over and thumbed the stack on the seat next to him. "Do you have junk mail you need to deliver to her too?"

"Well, I know that the postal inspector of the state is looking for her and it'd be a feather in my cap if I was able to find her, so I'm just keeping an eye out while I'm over this way."

"Well, I can promise you that if we should run into her, we'll contact the authorities as quickly as humanly possible." He sipped his tea again and then sat the mug down on the stove to rewarm it. "I can assure you, Walt, that we're not out here abducting people."

"Well, I'm glad to hear that."

"We don't have much time before the alignment."

I studied the man, trying to get a read on him, unable to tell if he was genuine or if it was all just an act. "The alignment?"

"A celestial providence that portends the coming of the great transition of time and space, which is very close."

"You lost me there."

He smiled again, sadly this time, studying the cigar. ""I'm sorry. It would take more time than a cup of tea to explain." He slapped his knees in an indication that the meeting was over. "Can I interest you in some literature, Mister . . . ?"

"Longmire." I downed the rest of my tea and handed him the mug. "I'm always looking for a good read."

He stood, placing the mugs back on the hooks without washing them and started for the front of the bus where he paused and flipped open a cardboard box. He took out one of what looked to be dozens of paperback books.

Placing the cigar in his teeth, he handed me one. "I'm afraid that book is only available through a nominal donation of twenty dollars."

I pulled out my wallet and plucked a twenty from it and handed it to him. "Cheap at the price."

"I certainly hope so." He continued as I followed, and we stepped from the bus and onto solid ground.

I looked at the trail between the wall tents and juniper trees, but I still didn't see any sign of the congregation. "There must be a lot to meditate on."

"Yes."

I reached a hand out, shaking with him. "Mister Carruthers, if I were to have more correspondence for you and your group, is there any way I can reliably find you?"

Flicking the ash from the cigar, he smiled. "Not really, we move around, you see, searching for the temporal frequency which allows us to communicate with the otherworld."

"The aliens."

"Yes."

"I'm to understand that with my predecessor there was a system where the mail to your organization was left under painted rocks out here at different locations?"

"I believe that was experimented with, yes."

"It didn't work?"

"No, people would take the incoming mail and throw the outgoing mail in the trash."

"Obstruction of correspondence is a felony and a federal offense, if you'd like to press charges."

"No, we're not the type to press charges for something like that when there are far greater things going on in the near future."

I studied him for a moment. "Thanks for the book."

"Thanks for the twenty dollars. It'll be going to a good cause."

I nodded. "I bet flying saucer fuel is expensive."

"Scoff if you will, Walt . . ." He reached out and tapped the paperback with the wet end of the cigar. "But you might find a few answers in that little book."

"I'll try and keep an open mind, Mister Carruthers. Thank you for your help."

I walked back up the slope toward the International, trying to avoid the wetter parts of the two-track. I'd mostly made it when I slipped and caught myself. I pulled a bandanna from my pocket and I wiped off my hand and made it to the main road where I saw an older woman with flowing dark hair and a strong streak of silver standing by my truck, a hand reached into the partially open window to pet Dog.

"Most people wouldn't risk putting a hand in a vehicle with a creature like that inside."

She turned and looked at me, dressed in a hooded off-white robe similar to the one Carruthers had been wearing, along with a pair of muddy sandals. "What's his name?"

"Dog."

She continued petting the beast, scratching behind his ears the way he liked. "Creative."

I stopped a few steps away, wiping off some of the mud on the knee of my jeans. "I take it you're a part of this group down here?"

"How come your dog doesn't have a name?"

I straightened and leaned a hip against the fender. "Dog is his name."

"That's not a name."

"He likes it."

She pulled her hand away and he licked at it as she noticed the book in my hand. "Doing some reading?"

"It's fundamental."

She laughed, and it was silvery and melodic. "I remember those commercials from the '70s."

"It's still an organization, getting books in the hands of children."

"That how you got yours?"

"No, I think your leader has hopes of converting me."

She stepped back and looked at the Travelall. "Nice-looking vehicle."

"Thanks."

"Had it long?"

"Only a couple of days, now."

"I thought you were leaving." I turned to see Freebee and Lowell approaching from the common area where a large number of people in the hooded off-white robes were now watching us. Freebee stepped in the road, placing a hand on the butt of his Colt pistol like some half-assed gunslinger. "You can't get out this way, so you'll have to turn around, brother."

I smiled at him. "I'm working on it."

He looked at the woman. "You should get back down with our brethren, sister."

She stared at him for a moment and then started past me as I held out a hand, studying her muddy feet in the sandals. "I didn't catch your name."

She paused for a moment, but then Freebee took a step toward us. "The brethren don't use names; it's not allowed."

I faced him, placing the book on the hood of the truck. "And why is that?"

"It reinforces the collective for the good of the group."

I squared off with him; it wasn't going to be easy, but I figured it was time to make a statement. "Seems like there's a lot of reinforcing going on in this group."

As I figured he would, he took another step in, snatching the big revolver from the holster and pointing it toward my face, whereupon I raised both hands and did my best to look surprised even though I noticed he hadn't cocked the single-action.

It was going to be pretty much the same move I'd used on Benny at the trailer park and in numerous situations like it before, the difficulty being that the woman in the robe was standing behind me, not to mention Dog.

It was going to take a little more emphasis, as I didn't want the revolver pointing in their direction, cocked or uncocked, without them having the advantage of getting out of the line of fire. The trick was the timing and making sure that as I grabbed the action in my left, the striking blow to his wrist from my right came in almost immediately. The long-barreled revolver made it easier with the leverage I commanded as I twisted it back toward him, watching as his eyes got wider with the realization that he was likely to be the one who was going to get shot.

Generally, that's when they release their grip, and Freebee did just that as I snatched the thing away and stepped forward, bringing an elbow around and planting it alongside the temporal lobe of his head.

Watching him fall against the grille of the International, I spun the thing and stepped back, leveling it at Lowell, who stood there with his hand on his undrawn Smith & Wesson Russian Model.

The discount Jesus sputtered a bit and then rose up, nursing his head with a hand before reaching out with the other. "Give me my gun."

"Not a chance." I kept my eye on the other gunman. "Lowell, have you ever been shot from this close? Probably not, since you're still here." I gestured with the slightest nudge of Freebee's weapon. "Colt like this? Four-and-three-quarter-inch barrel, the gunfighter edition?" It was at this point that I cocked the big pistol. "At this range, and I'm assuming a 255-grain lead projectile, it's going to blow chunks of your heart out of your back. But if it hits bone, it'll turn them into secondary shrapnel, and you'll have a fist-size hole in you. That's unless my aim is off and I hit you in the lower abdomen, in which case you'll be shitting in a bag for the rest of your life. Then there's always that possibility that I'll go a little high, especially if you were the first to shoot, in which case I'll blow your head apart like an overripe pumpkin, or, worse yet, hit you in the neck and pretty much take your head completely off."

Freebee raised himself up, glancing back at Lowell and gesturing for him to not try it, finally turning back to me as Lowell did as he was told. "You sure seem to know a lot about this stuff for a mailman."

"I worked in some tough neighborhoods." I lowered my own weapon, and I turned to the woman. "I'm sorry, but are you sure you really want to be here?"

She swallowed and then looked away. "Yes." Calmly, she walked around me and between the two of them, continuing down the slope to the crowd below.

"You better go now."

I looked at Freebee, turning the pistol up and checking the base pin. I snatched it out, dumped it to one side, and pulled the cylinder, tossing it in differing directions before turning and throwing what was left to the would-be messiah.

I then glanced at Lowell. "Don't even think of pulling that Smith and Wesson, because if you do, I'm going to introduce you to *my* Colt, which I know even better."

I took the book off the hood, stepped back, and opened the door, slipping the keys from my pocket as I climbed in. I started the engine and pulled it into gear, swinging wide as I backed up to force them out of the way before continuing on down the road from whence I'd come.

Dog moved to the back, growling at the two antagonists as we drove along toward civilization. "They're lucky I didn't open the door, huh?"

I heard him approach, his hot breath on the back of my neck. "Hey, did you happen to notice that woman was missing two toes?"

He said nothing.

Navigating the ruts, I drove us out of the canyon. "Of course you did."

"So, you're sure it was her?"

I continued eating my burrito and thought about it, listening to the mariachi music at Fiesta Guadalajara. "Well, how many eight-toed women do you think are out there wandering around the Red Desert, Mike?"

"But it looked like her, from the photographs, I mean?"

"A little muddier and her hair was longer, but yep."

The Wyoming postal inspector went back to forking up his own burrito, deep in thought. "Then why didn't she come with you?"

"Well, she doesn't know me from Adam, and the other two had guns—maybe she was just trying to avoid a conflict." I took another bite and chewed. "Or . . ."

"Or what?"

"They've got leverage over her, or . . ." He stared at me and made a rolling gesture with one hand for me to continue. "Or she's drunk the Kool-Aid."

"Please don't say that, especially not in this context."

"Sorry."

He stared at me a moment longer with his forkful suspended somewhere between plate and mouth. "But it is possible."

"Yep."

He sat the bite back down without eating. "Did she seem crazy?"

I took a swig of my Rainier and ruminated on the woman I'd met in the canyon. "No, she actually didn't."

"So, was she under duress?"

"Like I said, there were two guys carrying guns."

"Right." He stared at the food on his plate. "So, the trick would be getting her away from them, where she could talk more freely."

"That's a thought." I sat my bottle of beer back on the table. "I wish we knew somebody who was closer to her, somebody who wouldn't be as threatening to the group as I've turned out to be."

"So, we'd need a second undercover person?"

"It's an option, but we wouldn't want to endanger anybody."

"Got anyone in mind?"

I sighed a very long and complex sigh. "The two people I'm thinking of are more dangerous than the Order of the Red Gate or me, combined."

"Who?"

"One is my fiancée."

"And the other?"

I laughed. "Oh, just the most interesting man in the world."

"Your friend Henry Standing Bear?"

I stared at him.

"Martha told me about him one time."

I scooped up some more burrito, taking a bite and chewing. "They're both kind of loose cannons."

He laughed. "That's what Martha used to say about you."

"I . . ." I chewed some more. "Am not a loose cannon."

"Says the guy that just swiped Freebee's Colt away from him and brushed his teeth with it."

"In retrospect, that might've not been the smartest thing to do, but I was just tired of him shoving it in my face."

"So what do we do now?"

"There's not a lot we can do if she doesn't want to be discovered, but there is the note we found under the rock."

"What if it wasn't her that wrote it?"

"Then we rescue somebody else."

"Walt."

"It's odd because she did make the effort of coming over to my truck and away from the others, which would lead me to believe that she wanted to talk, alone." I finished my food and pushed my plate away. "I'll head back out there tomorrow and see what we see. I'll make some excuse for tracking them down and then go from there."

"They're liable to shoot you on sight."

"Not if I tell them I'm thinking of joining up."

"You think you can pull that off?"

I took the book Carruthers had given me from the bench I was sitting on, placed it on the table, and then turned it and slid it toward the postal inspector. "I've just got to do some homework."

He looked at the amateurish cover. "You're really going to read that crap?"

"At least enough to sound like I'm genuinely interested."

He started leafing through it. "It doesn't have many pictures."

"No, but a few diagrams to show the trajectory of the aliens as they enter Earth's gravitational pull."

"Is it in any way scientific?"

"Not the term I would use, no."

"Is it at least well written?"

"Not the parts I've read so far."

"Good luck with that." He slid it to me. "What did you hear from Grossnickle on this Carruthers character?"

"Nothing, other than he was a character actor in a bunch of TV shows I've never heard of in the '80s and '90s. It's obviously an alias, so we're back to square one on him."

"What about the Order of the Red Gate?"

I sipped my beer. "They've got connections to a couple of other cultlike organizations, mostly in the southwest. One in particular was the Heaven's Gate group."

"I've heard of them." He thought about it. "Where are they now?"

"Dead. About forty of them committed mass suicide back in the '90s near San Diego." I sat my beer bottle back down, spinning the punt in the circle of condensation. "They supposedly believed that they themselves were aliens and were waiting for a spaceship that was trailing along in the tail of the Hale-Bopp comet. Evidently, they believed that when they killed themselves their souls would be transported from their bodies, or 'vehicles,' to the spaceship and take this long journey to heaven, or what they referred to as the 'Next Level.'"

"They killed themselves, all of them?"

"Yep."

"Do you think this group is planning on doing that?"

I continued to turn the bottle, thinking about it. "I'm not sure."

He pushed his plate away, having lost his appetite. "That's it, we're calling the cops."

"And what good will that do? Do you think they're going to admit to something like that—that their plan is to kill themselves? And even if it was, threatening suicide isn't illegal unless you seem incapable of making those types of decisions for yourself. No, they'll just backtrack and not admit it."

"What about the guys with the guns?"

"What about them? The only one that was threatened was me, and if I press charges then they're going to know who I am, and all this undercover stuff is going under the Grateful Dead bus they're driving."

He picked up the bottle and sipped his own beer, the lack of appetite not including alcohol. "So, you're going back out there by yourself?"

"I guess so."

"I don't think that's so smart."

"Well, I'm not exactly crazy about the idea, but look on the bright side." I reached out with the longneck of my beer as we toasted. "We found her."

Lying on my bed in the Park Hotel, I studied the cracks in the ceiling and snuggled my phone in the crook of my neck, listening to my second in command berate me. "If you don't make it to this reception, you're a dead man."

"I'm just going out there for a look-see tomorrow morning, then I'll jump in my new SUV and drive the three hundred miles to Cheyenne, I promise."

"What new SUV?"

"Actually, it was built in '68, but it's aged well." I thumbed through the pages of Carruthers's book. "Like me . . . Besides, I needed wheels."

"To deliver the mail."

"Exactly." Resting the book on my chest, I yawned. "Is Henry driving down too?"

"Yeah, I was going to get him a room at the Plains Hotel, but he says he doesn't need it."

I laughed. "What's her name?"

"Hell, if I know."

"I assume you've got a room at the Plains Hotel?"

"I have." She yawned. "Ruby and Lucian are staying with your daughter, so we all got the boot. I guess the future AG's place is going to be full."

"What's she doing with Lola?"

She shifted the phone in her ear. "I'm not privy to that information, but I can text her if you'd like."

"Nah, I was just going to offer to babysit if she needs it."

There was a pause. "She doesn't need it. What she does need is for you to be there showing your support for her, Sheriff of the Year."

"Is that an official title?"

"Not for long if you don't show up."

"You keep talking to me like that and I'm going to get my own room."

"Sure you are. Remember: Cocktails at six, dinner at seven at the state archives and museum. You got that, right?"

"I do."

"Don't come rolling in there at 5:45, okay? Get here in plenty of time for a shower, a clean change of clothes that are presentable, and possibly some whoopie."

"Is the whoopie last?"

"Probably not."

"What are 'presentable clothes'?"

"Cowboy dress—polished boots and a clean hat; jeans without holes, stains, or frays; a belt buckle smaller than a dinner plate; and a string or traditional tie."

"I don't have any of that with me."

"As I cast my gaze across the bedroom, I can see all those things hanging on your chair, ready to be packed up and brought to the state capital."

"Do you have clean underwear? My mother always told me to wear clean underwear in case I was in an accident."

"Yeah, you're about to get into an accident . . . You're going commando on this one, super cop." She yawned again. "How is Dog?"

I glanced at the foot of the bed where the beast was snoring. "How are you, monster?"

He lifted his bucket head to look at me and then immediately turned back at the sound of the floorboards creaking outside our door. The beast then looked at me again, preparing to bark, but I held a finger to my lips and all he did was turn his head back to the door like an Egyptian sentinel.

"Oh, he's sleepy, but he appears to be fine. Look, I know you're tired, so I'll let you go too?"

"Four o'clock would be a good time to be in Cheyenne tomorrow, hotshot."

"I'll try and be there."

"If you value your life, don't try—do."

"Got it." I listened as the phone went dead and then hit the red button and dropped the thing on the bed, lifting the book off my chest and once again carefully rolling over and easing up in my stocking feet. I slid my 1911 from the nightstand and stood there listening but heard nothing.

Glancing at Dog, I put the finger to my lips again and carefully made my way to the door, trying to hear the hallway outside, where there was another creaking noise in the hundred-year-old floor.

Figuring it was Benny again, I turned the glass knob and carefully pushed the door open as I'd done before, but perhaps a little softer in case he was standing behind it again.

The door swung wide to reveal the woman I'd met out in the Red Desert earlier in the day, now wearing boots, jeans, a flannel shirt, and an insulated jacket. "You know, for a deserted hotel, this place gets a lot of foot traffic."

She smiled, and the effect of the perfect teeth, bronzed skin, and silver skunk-streaked dark hair was impressive. "Howdy."

I lowered the gun to my side. "Blair McGowan, I presume?"

"Well, it ain't Doctor Livingstone fresh from Westminster Abbey." She pushed off the wall and walked past me and into the room where she was met by a wagging Dog, who remembered her from earlier in the day.

Giving a look up and down the hall, I stuffed the Colt into the back of my jeans, then closed the door but left it ajar. "Not his heart."

She sat on the bed, crossing her legs and petting Dog. "Excuse me?"

"Livingstone's body is buried in the abbey, but not his heart."

She looked around. "What, did I accidentally wander into the Christian Science Reading Room?"

I sat on the edge of the small desk, the only other furniture in the place. "How can I help you, Ms. McGowan?"

"Got anything to drink?"

"Tap water from the bathroom."

The smile faded just a touch. "I was looking for something with a little more kick?"

"You should try the tap water."

"I'll pass." She gestured toward my back. "You always sleep armed?"

I walked past her and leaned over the dorm refrigerator under the desk to pull out two Rainiers. "Not always, but as you've been witness to, I've had a few run-ins lately."

She pulled the tab on the can and took a swig, reaching over and picking up the book Carruthers had given me. "You must read a lot."

"I do."

"You haven't got the greatest of tastes." She tossed the paperback back on the bed and then propped herself up with her arms, taking another sip and then leaning back and studying me. "So, I hear you've got my old job?"

"I do, along with your truck."

Her eyes became sharp. "Benny had no right to sell it."

"Evidently his name was on the title, so when you went missing, he obtained ownership."

"How much did you pay?"

"Your friend Sal Salvucci over at Rad Rides says I got a bargain."

"How about the rest of my stuff?"

"I believe Benny sold all of that too."

"That piece of shit . . ."

I nodded. "That was my take the first time I met him and tried to put him in a trash can."

"He has that effect on people." She continued studying me. "Where'd you get that scar over your eye?"

"An old bird-watching accident."

"And that part of your ear that's missing?"

"I once had a hat that was too tight."

She actually laughed that same silvery laugh, heartfelt and honest. "Mister, I don't know what you are, but you ain't no mailman."

She then did something surprising. She pulled a snub-nose Smith & Wesson .38 revolver from under her jacket and placed it beside her. "These things are uncomfortable."

I shrugged. "You get used to it."

"I had planned on coming in here and roughing you up, you know, scaring you off a bit? But I don't think you scare easy." She sighed. "After this afternoon, I don't think you scare at all."

"I have my moments, like everybody else."

"That wasn't a postal move where you took that hogleg from Freebee."

"Nope."

She leaned forward, resting an elbow on a knee and cupping her chin, studying me like I was an item from the dead letter office. "Who are you?"

"A concerned citizen."

"Concerned about what?"

"You."

She turned her head, now looking at the revolver on the bed beside her. "Well, you can knock that off."

My turn to study her. "You don't want to be found?"

"Who's looking for me?"

"Mike Thurman, for one."

Her eyes softened and she smiled. "Good ole Mikey."

"The state postal inspector's concerned for your safety."

"Well, you can tell him I'm okay."

"Why don't you tell him yourself?"

"Because I'm involved with something, and you're interfering."

"Maybe if you tell me about it, it'll help me to understand."

She stood and walked around the bed to the other side of the room, where she parted the curtains and looked down on the switching yard to the right. "Look, no offense, but you don't need to understand because it's none of your business."

"It's kind of become my business."

"Why, because some people pointed guns at you? I'm pretty sure that's not the first time that's happened."

"No, but I get the feeling that something's going on out there, and that there might be people who don't really want to be part of it."

"And you're going to save them, huh?"

"I'm going to do what's right."

She dropped the curtain and looked at me. "'Right'?"

"It's a start."

She came back around the bed, giving Dog one last casual pet, and then she stuffed her .38 in her jeans before covering it with the coat. "Just to be clear, I'm not lost, and I don't want you looking for me."

I raised my hands like a magician making clear there was nothing up my sleeves. "How do your friends feel about that?"

"They're not my friends."

I got up from the desk and approached her with my hands on my hips. "Then who are they?"

"Kooks, that's what they are. Dangerous kooks."

She started for the door, but then stopped, studying the narrow planks of the aged floor. "Where did they bury the heart?"

"Excuse me?"

"Doctor Livingstone. If not in Westminster Abbey, where exactly did they bury his heart?"

"In Africa, near Chief Chitambo's village in Chipundu at the edge of the Bangweulu Swamps in Zambia under an mpundu tree."

She stared at me. "That's pretty specific."

"It's in all the books."

"That's the thing about books." She paused, nodding a moment more as she trailed the door closed behind her. "They don't ever forget where the hearts are buried."

6

There's a part of I-80—or, as the locals call it, the Snow Chi Minh Trail—that's spoken of as the Highway to Heaven that, when atmospheric conditions are right, gives the appearance as though the Interstate goes straight up into the heavens. But that wasn't the part that I was on. I was on the soul-leeching part that seems to go on forever; a life-eroding slab of concrete that tears the very hours from your life at an excruciatingly slow pace.

Or maybe that's just me.

The Highway to Heaven between Evanston and Lyman doesn't go to heaven but rather to the Bridger Valley, which is pretty nice.

So, maybe it was just me.

I was trying to be circumspect in my speed, but at about seventy miles an hour the trip was taking a little longer than expected, especially with my backup expressing his unhappiness with the journey's length by placing his paw on my shoulder every two minutes. "I know, but there's nothing I can do; it's a big state."

So, it wasn't just me.

"I can tell you the story of this road, if you'd like?" He didn't look particularly interested, but I decided to tell him about it anyway. "The old road was the Lincoln Highway that pretty much followed the Union Pacific railroad line that had been established almost a hundred miles earlier through the southern part of the state. The UP at one point considered using a shorter route but the local ranchers warned the railroad that if it did, the quote, unquote 'goddamn road'll be filled up with snow before you get it finished.'"

I glanced at Dog, and he appeared to be listening.

"The road that got replaced was the original Lincoln Highway, and there was a stretch the locals referred to as Blood Alley because of all the crashes that happened there. One of the more high-profile ones was in '57 when the *Jailhouse Rock* actress Judy Tyler and her husband were killed in a wreck a little ways up in Albany County."

Dog didn't look particularly moved.

"There was a lot of competition between the states for an east–west route for Eisenhower's new Interstate Highway System and our neighbor to the south, Colorado, really wanted to continue I-70 on to San Francisco or even Los Angeles."

An eighteen-wheeler whipped past us, barreling into the passing lane, and leaving us in the proverbial dust, followed by another, and another, and . . . Well, you get the point.

"Wyoming had an advantage in that the terrain was better suited for a highway than the peaks west of Denver. The major concern for I-80 was avoiding the extra twenty-one miles that the old route included. The federal government wanted the shorter route, the teamsters wanted the shorter route, and the bus lines wanted the shorter route, but that meant putting the new highway directly in the weather patterns of Elk Mountain," I gestured toward the very open road before us, "which we'll be reaching before long.

"There's a myth that Lady Bird Johnson was responsible for putting the road where it is. They say she was flying over the route in a helicopter during one of her visits and pointed a finger and said, "Put it there." But she didn't. It's possible people got the story confused with what was known as Lady Bird's Law, which was responsible for limiting billboards and beautifying the highways of America, but that had nothing to do with the I-80 route. If you check the official records, she flew from Billings to Jackson, then Salt Lake City to Green River, and then back to Grand Teton National Park—from none of which can you even remotely see Elk Mountain."

Finding something going even slower than me, I passed a vintage Volkswagen van with California plates as I continued my diatribe. "Jump to 1970 when they cut the ribbon in an opening ceremony for the brand-new interstate highway, and those same ranchers—and possibly the next generation—warned of the oncoming melee. Four days later, a winter storm swept in and buried the thing. Some people claimed that it'd been routed where it was to keep people out of the state, and I don't know but sometimes I think they might be right."

I thought about jacking my speed up but the opportunity of a speeding ticket might reflect badly on the father of the potential attorney general of the state. "Back in the '70s, before your time, there was a television show called *On the Road with Charles Kuralt* on CBS, and he called it the worst stretch of interstate in the nation. There's another rumor that a rock group, REO Speedwagon, wrote their song 'Ridin' the Storm Out' about getting stuck on this stretch of highway."

I noticed someone riding along beside me but ignored them. "It's also the first interstate highway with closure gates."

I got the sense the traveler to my left wasn't going to pass, so I glanced over to find a Wyoming Highway Patrol Tahoe riding along beside me. The driver, who I recognized, pulled back and slipped in behind me, hitting his lights as I dutifully drifted to the side of the road and parked.

I glared at Dog. "You were supposed to be on the lookout for those guys."

The poster boy for the Wyoming Highway Patrol exited his vehicle and walked up, bending down and peering in at us. "Where's the antique car show?"

"As opposed to the fire?"

Jim Thomas eyed the Travelall. "Nice-looking, but can't she go any faster than that?"

"I don't know, I was trying to not break the law." I slipped off my sunglasses. "What are you doing down here on the Snow Chi Minh Trail? I thought this was where you punished rookies?"

He shrugged. "The duty roster was low, so I volunteered. Besides, where else am I going to meet celebrities?"

"I was just telling Dog about Judy Tyler."

He looked past me, addressing the beast with a pet. "She was in an Elvis movie, *Jailhouse Rock*."

"Told you," I said to Dog.

"What brings you down here, Sheriff?"

"I'm trying to get to a reception in Cheyenne."

He straightened, his attention drawn to the highway ahead. "Is this the AG appointment for your daughter?"

I shook my head with a laugh. "Does everybody in the state know about this?"

"Pretty much." He checked his wristwatch. "What time do you have to be there?"

"Four?"

He shook his head. "You're not going to make it, unless . . ." He studied me a moment more, then suddenly started back toward his Tahoe.

I hung out the window, calling after him. "Unless what?"

He paused as he opened the door of the SUV. "Tuck in tight and try and keep up."

Watching Jim swing the Chevrolet onto the empty highway, I put the International in gear and hit the accelerator, trying to keep up as the speedometer began climbing to sixty, seventy, eighty, ninety, a hundred and finally maxed out at one hundred and twelve miles an hour.

I could see Thomas peering in the rearview mirror and slowing down a bit so I could keep up.

Skating along at over a hundred with a suspension and brakes from 1968, I glanced at Dog and smiled. "It's good to have friends in high places."

"Everything fits, I see."

"The boots are a little tight."

Victoria Moretti stood up on tiptoe and gave me a peck on the lips. "They're new, they'll stretch."

I surveyed the packed reception and then looked back at my undersheriff in boots, black jeans, a velvet blouse, and studded Double D leather jacket with fringe. "You got your hair trimmed."

She took in the crowd with her tarnished gold eyes. "I did, thanks for noticing."

"Where's the belle of the ball?"

"Over near the bar, with the rest of the hopefuls."

I looked over but couldn't see my daughter, finally giving up. "So, this party is for lobbying purposes?"

"No, from what I'm to understand the decisions have already been made, but it's just good manners to be on hand."

"Are they going to make some sort of formal announcements on posts?"

"I don't know, so just schmooze."

I sighed. "I'm not a good schmoozer."

"Fortunately for you, your blood brother is."

"Where's he?"

She pointed to where Henry Standing Bear was near a display of a Basque sheep wagon, saying something to Robert Lang. "Over there, talking with the new governor."

"Suck-up."

"Yeah." She tucked an arm in mine and ushered me toward the bar. "C'mon, let's make sure the potential future AG knows you're here."

"Looks like a pretty good turnout." Allowing myself to be shepherded, I smiled and nodded at folks who I knew and a bunch I didn't as we sidled up to the bar and Vic got me a beer to go with the dirty martini she paid for. "You know, power doesn't corrupt—it's fear that corrupts, or maybe the fear of losing power."

She sipped her drink. "That a review of the upcoming administration?"

"More of a warning, perhaps."

"What do you know about this guy, Lang?"

"He's the governor."

"That's it?"

"As far as I know." I felt a tapping at my back, and I turned seeing a recognizable redhead in a shimmering emerald-green dress and heels. "Howdy, punk."

"That's potential Attorney General Punk to you." Cady hugged my arm. "I didn't think you were going to make it."

"I wasn't until I got a hundred-mile-an-hour escort from Jim Thomas."

"Tell him I owe him one."

"I will." I glanced around as if attempting to see the toddler. "Where's my granddaughter?"

"Being sat at home by your fearless dispatcher, watching the mermaid movie for the 1,345th time and probably not noticing that we're not there."

"Ruby?"

"Yep, she decided that she could do me a better service in that capacity." She straightened the lapel on my tweed jacket. "This is new."

"How can you tell?"

"No moth holes."

I nodded toward Vic as she came around and handed me my beer and then tapped glasses with my daughter. "I dressed him."

Cady stepped back to study me. "Kind of a cross between an Ivy League English professor and a bouncer."

Vic nodded, joining her, and they both took my measure. "He looks better than he has in years. Now if we can just get him to shave off the beard."

Vic examined me. "I don't know, it's starting to grow on me . . . Like a fungus."

I nursed my beer and nodded at a few more people I quasi-knew. "Easy, I'm undercover."

My daughter looked at me as if I was watching some mermaid movie for the 1,345th time. "You're still doing that?"

"Well, probably not for very much longer."

"Find her?"

"I think she found me."

Cady leaned in to hear and to be heard over the crowd. "What's her name, the woman who went missing?"

"Blair McGowan, a postal worker from California."

Vic feigned shock. "A new plot development."

My daughter continued. "She showed up?"

"Kind of. She popped up at my hotel room after I bumped into her out there in the Red Desert."

Vic cocked her head and raised an eyebrow. "Tell me more."

"She told me to lay off—that she was fine, safe, and that my services were no longer needed."

"What'd your relative, the postal inspector, have to say about that?"

"I haven't told him yet, but there isn't much he can do about it. The law is pretty clear about this type of thing, and she made sure that I was aware of it."

Vic sipped her dirty martini as someone I didn't know came over and peeled Cady away from us. "So, case closed?"

"Maybe."

"Oh, I don't like the sound of that."

I shrugged. "There's a group out there in the Red Desert, a cult really . . ."

"You were saying."

"Some of them are a little violent."

Someone behind me caught her attention. "Violent?"

"Someone mention one of my hobbies?"

I turned toward the baritone and the face of my best friend in the world, the Cheyenne Nation. "Taking time for the common people?"

He nodded, his face half-hidden by a drape of dark hair, his black leather blazer a perfect fit. "Slumming now, actually."

"How's the gov?"

"Wanting to mount a task force on murdered and missing Indigenous peoples."

"You're going to start working for the government?"

"No, I have too much respect for myself . . ." He held out a hand, taking Vic's and allowing her to twirl, revealing her entire outfit. "Oh, my . . ."

"Well, you have to admit that his heart is in the right place."

"I do." He released my fiancée and looked back at me. "How is life in the Red Desert?"

"Odd."

He glanced around as Vic joined the conversation with Cady and the individual I didn't know. "You are not the first to say that."

"I ran into a friend of yours down there, Rick Scout Traveler?"

"I know his father, yes."

"Seems like a nice guy."

"I thought he was working somewhere in the east?"

"He was in Boston, but he came back. He says he got lonely for the desert."

"And he is not the first to say that, either." He reached past me as he smiled at the female bartender, who readily replaced his depleted gin and tonic, which I noticed he didn't pay for. "How goes the investigation?"

"At a screeching halt."

"Find the wayward postal worker?"

"Yep, and she told me to buzz off."

"Case closed?"

"Maybe."

"Do tell."

"Do you remember the Heaven's Gate group back in the nineties?"

He thought about it. "The mass suicide out in California?"

"Yep."

"The ones that wore matching tennis shoes?"

"That detail might've gotten by me . . . Anyway, I'm thinking this group might be a splinter of that one—kind of the same MO. Alien contact, clam people, being swept up and carried away to some planet or form of heaven . . ."

"Did you just say 'clam people'?"

"I did."

"That detail might have gotten by me."

"I'm not sure if the Heaven's Gate folks met the clam people, but anyway they seem to be running a kind of Ponzi scheme, getting people to invest or give them their money."

"And your jurisdiction in this is . . . ?"

"I'm pretty sure they're using force on these people."

"Have you spoken with any of them?"

"No, at least no one besides a woman named Blair McGowan."

"Then I do not see what you can do if no one has requested your assistance. Did this McGowan woman seem unstable or unhinged in any way?"

"Quite the opposite."

"Hmm . . ."

"Even more disturbing, huh?"

"Yes." He sipped his drink. "I still do not see how you can involve yourself."

I thought about it for a moment, both of us nodding our heads as I lifted my drink. "Cheers."

We drank and he leaned in closer. "On another note, the governor would like to speak with you, privately."

I stared at him. "The governor?"

"Yes."

"Why?"

"He did not say."

I glanced behind the Bear to where Lang was conversing with a large man who looked over his shoulder at me and then began moving our way along with another man dressed almost identically. "Uh-oh . . ."

Henry turned as we met the two sizable individuals in matching gray suits, greeting them by raising a hand. "Pēhē 'lorana, kōua ta'atoa?"

The Bobs stopped in their tracks, looking at each other and then back at the Cheyenne Nation, Bob Delude the first to speak with a squint. "What the hell, Bear?'

Henry spoke out of the side of his mouth toward me. "Rapa Nui."

The two large men looked at him and then back to me again. "I think my friend here just spoke to you in the language of Easter Island."

Bob Delozier looked at Bob Delude and then back to me. "Mind if I ask why?"

"I think he is intimating that the two of you in your gray suits look like the moai, or monolithic statues on that island in eastern Polynesia."

Bob thought about it. "Are they handsome?"

"What?"

The other Bob chimed in. "The statues."

"Absolutely."

They both smiled. "C'mon, the governor wants to talk to you."

"What, I'm being summoned?"

Bob reached out and patted my shoulder, pulling me with them. "Just a friendly chat."

I looked back at Henry as the two women in my life joined to watch the Bobs haul me away. "Hey, if they rub me out, make sure you topple them over, okay?"

He waved, smiling. "Ka oho riva-riva."

The Bobs steered me toward the suited man entertaining a group near the sheepherder's wagon. We paused as he finished a story and the small crowd burst into laughter. He glanced my way and nodded. After chatting them up a bit more, he took his leave and ducked through an opening, gesturing for the three of us to follow into a secluded area with a number of artifacts from the state's past.

After I entered, I noticed that the Bobs stayed at the only entrance and stood to ostensibly block it like, well . . . like two giant statues from Easter Island.

The governor sat on a bench and gestured for me to join him. "Have a seat. I don't know about you, but I can only stand so long at these things."

I sat and extended a hand. "Walt Longmire."

"Oh, I know who you are." We shook. "Robert Lang."

"Another Bob?"

"Yeah, I think I'll stick with Robert just to save confusion." He grinned an easy smile, emphasized by his Teddy Roosevelt mustache and glasses. "I'm glad they didn't have to rough you up."

I glanced at the backs of the twin giants. "Eh, we go way back."

He nodded. "It's nice to meet you, I've got a few things I'd like to discuss."

"Sure."

"One is Maxim Sidorov." He took a moment to arrange his thoughts and then smiled again. "I believe you've made his acquaintance?"

I thought about the Soviet spook whom I'd met. "He tried to kill me a few months ago, but I don't think it was personal."

"Well, he's turned state's evidence and provided the Department of Justice with an awful lot of alarming information concerning the altercation at your grandfather's ranch."

"Altercation, huh?" I shook my head. "Is that what we're calling it?"

He nodded. "We had hopes of clearing Tom Rondelle's name, but that's looking less and less likely."

"His wife tried to enlist me against the Regis family."

"They appear to have become a force to be reckoned with, here in the state."

"So, why are you bringing up Sidorov?"

"He's here."

I looked around, somewhat surprised. "At the reception?"

He smiled. "No, here in the city with an ankle bracelet, or so I'm told. As I said, he's been extraordinarily cooperative with the authorities and hasn't shown any signs of continued criminal behavior, but . . ."

"But?"

"He did try to kill you, and if there was someone like that in my proximity, I'd want to be aware of it."

"Thanks."

"I don't think he'll seek you out or anything, but I thought you should know." He reached out and popped a fist into my shoulder. "Hey, I'm thinking of appointing a certain young woman as the attorney general for the state—would you have any problem with that?"

"Do you mind if I ask in what spirit this question is asked?"

He laughed a heartfelt chuckle. "I've got daughters."

"And?"

"I'm not sure if I could work for them."

"Well, the relationship between the sheriff of the least populated county and the highest law enforcement official in the state is pretty wide and, in all honesty, I don't think we'd be working that closely with one another."

"You've had a pretty close working relationship with Joe Meyer over the years."

I shrugged. "That's different, I've known Joe a long time."

He continued smiling, his features not changing one iota. "You've known your daughter for a long time."

"Not in a professional sense. Besides, the state was smaller back in the day." I cleared my throat and looked at my new boots. "But you're not asking this on my behalf, are you?"

He laughed. "Just the sheriff of the least populated county in the state, huh? They warned me about you, that you'd likely try the 'shucks, I'm just an old cowboy' routine on me till we got to know each other a little better."

I studied him.

"No, no, I'm not engaging in this conversation for your benefit." The smile faded, but his eyes stayed sharp. "You cut a pretty wide swath in Wyoming."

"Is that meant as a compliment?"

"It is, but I'm just thinking about the exact size of that shadow that you cast and what kind of shade it might throw on a newly appointed attorney general who's attempting to prove herself."

"I would never stand in the way of Cady or her career."

"I'm aware of that on a conscious level." He stood and walked toward the opposite wall where a gigantic and ornate silver tea service sat, a remnant of the USS *Wyoming*. "They tell me that you've been pondering retirement."

I let the dust settle on that statement before responding. "For about thirty years now."

He looked at me. "How about I make you a deal?"

"So this is a political meeting?"

He laughed again and then crossed his arms, looking down at me. "You retire after this tenure, and I'll appoint your daughter."

I stared at him, letting even more dust settle. "And if I don't?"

"I'll have to think about it, if that's the case."

I started to speak, but then swallowed my words and said something else. "Governor Lang, I don't object to the idea of retiring, but I'd just as soon it be my idea."

"It would be, but the timing would smooth the way for my new AG, which is really what I'm after."

"How about I go get her and let her be party to this conversation?"

He really laughed at that one. "I'm not so sure that's such a great idea."

"Mister Governor, Cady and I don't keep secrets from each other, and you're putting me in a very uncomfortable position."

"That was not my intention." He stuffed his hands in his pockets and approached me. "It's just that I've been giving this problem a lot of thought, and this seemed to be the easiest answer to our dilemma."

"What if there is no dilemma?"

"Sheriff . . . Can I call you Walt?"

"Can I call you Bob?"

He gave me a quick look and then continued. "Walt, it's difficult enough for a woman to attain this position, let alone receive the kind of respect she deserves, and . . ." He glanced at the backs of the Bobs. "If, as I was led to believe, you are considering retirement, the timing couldn't be better."

I stood and sighed like a locomotive coming to rest.

"Look, if I've presented this in a somewhat clumsy manner, I apologize." He dipped his head to look under the brim of my hat. "My only concern here is Cady."

"I appreciate that."

"Well, give it some thought, and let me know what decision you come to?"

"I'll do that."

He patted my shoulder and then made his way out between the Bobs as if passing between a set of buildings.

I stood there thinking about what Lang had said and about what it meant not only to me but to Cady. With another sigh, I headed out, pulling up between the Bobs and just standing there between them for a moment. "Shitbirds, the both of you."

Bob Delozier spoke up quickly. "Hold on, there . . ."

Then Bob Delude joined in. "All we said was that you'd mentioned retiring, which you have numerous times."

"I repeat, shitbirds."

"Now, Walt . . ."

"Did you know that was what he wanted to talk to me about?"

Bob hemmed. "Well . . ."

Bob hawed. "Kind of."

I walked off, leaving the two skyscrapers sputtering.

"What the hell was all that about?" Lucian Connally sat behind the velvet ropes on a steamer trunk that I was pretty sure was part of the Basque sheepherder's display, a boot propped up on a sign explaining the life-size diorama.

"I don't think you're supposed to be sitting in there on that thing."

"Why the hell not?" He tapped his cane on the lid. "It's a hundred years old; I figure it can hold me. Besides, there isn't anywhere else for a one-legged veteran to sit."

"I happen to know you didn't lose your leg in the war."

"The hell I didn't, those Basquo bootleggers up on Jim Creek comprised a new front all to themselves."

"You're supposed to be mingling."

The old sheriff tipped his hat back. "In case you have failed to notice over the years, I don't mingle."

I stood there looking at him and could've sworn that he was part of the display—except he kept talking. "Might be for the best."

He pointed his cane toward where the Bobs had decided to vacate the vicinity, skirting along the wall and away from us. "Say, where are the Bobbsey Twins going?"

"Avoiding me."

"And, pray tell, why is that?"

"Nothing. One of those characters I had a run in with at my grandfather's place a few months back flipped and is now under protective custody here in Cheyenne."

His dark eyes narrowed. "Something we need to be worried about?"

"I don't think so."

He barked a laugh. "You never think so."

"I'm a trusting sort."

"Uh-huh." He reached his cane out. "Here, help an old man out of this exhibit before they hang a plaque on me."

I took the end of his cane and pulled him up, steadying him by his elbow as he stepped over the classy barricade. "What would it say, this plaque?"

"Nothing complimentary." He lifted his prosthetic leg over the ropes as he lowered his cane. I followed him as we started back toward the larger room where a band was now playing, and I could see Cady dancing with the Bear. "That's all you and the gov talked about?"

I watched my family members enjoying themselves and then asked. "Lucian, how did you know it was time to hang up your star?"

"You came along."

"No, seriously."

"I am being serious." He stopped and turned to look at me. "When I saw the county would be in good hands, I stepped down and never had a second thought."

"I don't think I have that luxury. Saizarbitoria isn't ready, and the voters won't elect Vic."

He smiled. "Maybe if you gag her."

I leaned against one of the partitions. "Besides, if I retire, I think she's going to call it quits too."

"And you two will run off to New Mexico and live happily ever after?"

"Maybe."

"Is that what's got you thinking about all this—getting married?"

"I guess."

"Or was that something you and the gov were also discussing?"

A waiter passed by balancing a tray with canapés, and I reached out and took two, handing one to my old mentor. "Lucian, do you think there would be trouble between Cady and me if she got this AG position?"

He popped the thing in his mouth and chewed. "Sure, there will be. How often do you think I concerned myself with what Joe Meyer thought back when I was on the job?"

I chewed on my own. "Not much."

"That could be the understatement of the century. Hell, how many dealings did you have with Joe since you took over the job?"

"Not many other than a few times he tried to warn me off."

"And did you listen?"

"Not much."

"Well, there you go—when's the last time you listened to your daughter, even when you should have?"

"Not much."

He fished in the pockets of his jacket, pulling out his briarwood pipe and the beaded Cheyenne tobacco pouch. Hooking a finger in, he pulled a plug of his personal blend that Hugh over at the Hitching Post made up for him on a regular basis. "Personally, I don't see how things have changed all that much."

"I don't think you're supposed to smoke in here."

He thumbed the bowl full and then struck a match, puffing on the stem of the polished wood until it caught, a billow of smoke rising around his face as he pulled back and became philosophical about the whole thing. "The two of you will find a way to accommodate your father-daughter relationship, and there might be a few times when it'll take a back seat to your sheriff-attorney general relationship, but you'll find a way to navigate your way through all the pitfalls."

"Lucian, you can't smoke in here."

He glanced up at me with a singular mahogany iris through the wisps of smoke, shaking his head at me. "And in case you have also failed to notice over the years, I tend to do things I'm not supposed to in places I'm not supposed to be."

The waiter came back through, continuing to balance the tray. I took another canapé in hopes that it might keep him from noticing that the old sheriff was aflame. All for naught, in that the next thing he did was lean in toward Lucian and hiss, "You're not allowed to smoke in here, sir."

The old sheriff squinted at the waiter with a quick puff on the pipe. "Yep? Well, youngster, how 'bout you go piss up a rope?"

7

The old sheriff reached down and rubbed between Dog's ears as the beast rested his bucket-size head on Lucian's prosthetic knee. "We didn't get kicked out of the state museum."

"Yep, Lucian, we did."

"If you two don't quiet down you're going to wake Lola and then we're going to have some real trouble." Ruby sat back in the kitchen chair, drinking a glass of wine, something I'd rarely witnessed and a sure sign it hadn't been an easy evening.

I sat my beer down on the kitchen table of my daughter's apartment and studied my dispatcher. "How was the 1,345th viewing of the mermaid movie?"

"I can recite the entire film verbatim, if you'd like."

"Spare me." I drank my beer as the greatest legal mind of our time entered wearing her bathrobe and fluffy slippers. "Had enough of the high heels and skimpy dress?"

Pulling a carton from the refrigerator, I watched as she slugged down some orange juice from the container and then snipped back at me, "It wasn't skimpy."

"It looked great, kiddo." I glanced at the other two musketeers and then back at her. "Everything okay?"

She closed the fridge, leaning against it with her arms folded, still holding the juice. "I guess I'm disappointed. I figured Lang was going to make the announcements tonight."

Ruby reached out and squeezed Cady's elbow. "Maybe things just got busy, and they ran out of time."

"Time being the issue here—he's got to get his cabinet set so that they can get to work on the transition, and the gubernatorial clock is ticking."

Lucian looked at me. "You talked with this Lang fella for a pretty long time back there. What'd he have to say?"

Cady shot me a look. "You spoke with him?"

I glared at the old sheriff for an instant and then turned back to my daughter. "Yep, mostly we talked about Maxim Sidorov turning state's evidence and working with the DOJ. I guess he's an enforced guest of the state here in Cheyenne, and he just wanted to let me know that he was here."

She came around the table and sat next to me. "And . . . ?"

"He wanted to know if I thought we could work together."

She sat back in her chair with a laugh. "We've been working together my whole life, why would he think that we couldn't?"

"I think he's just concerned with the effect that having me as a sheriff and you as the AG might reflect on you."

"In what way?"

"I'm not sure—nepotism, favoritism, partiality, bias . . ."

She sat the orange juice on the table like a bottle of whiskey, leaning forward. "That's bullshit. I'm being put forward for this job because I work hard and I'm very good at what I do."

I raised my hands in absolution. "I know that. We all know that. But there's always going to be talk, especially in the political arena."

"Let 'em."

"You don't think that'll hamper your ability to do the job?"

"No."

"Well then . . ." I dropped my hands and smiled at her. "There you go."

"What's that supposed to mean?"

I sighed and considered my next words very carefully. "I've been thinking about retiring."

"Oh, horseshit." Lucian pushed off and stood. "I've heard this song, chapter and verse. I'm going to bed, and I'm assuming I'm in the guestroom?"

Cady glanced at him. "Ruby's in the guestroom, you get the sofa in the living room, old man. There's a pillow and a couple of blankets. And don't be wandering around the place in your underwear in the morning, I've got enough to explain to my daughter."

"I'm going to bed too." Ruby yawned and also stood, addressing me. "Do you have any idea when Vic is planning on swinging by and picking us up for the long haul back home?"

"No, but when I get back to the hotel, I'll ask her and let you know."

She paused and then came around the table, kissing my daughter on the top of her perfumed head. "Are you sure you really want to work with this guy, sweetheart?"

She studied me. "I don't know, maybe I can whip him into shape."

"Good luck with that. I haven't had much." Ruby kissed her crown again and then disappeared, leaving the three of us in the kitchen alone as Dog curled around Cady's slippers like a domesticated grizzly.

"What did you do?"

I sipped my beer to just give me an instant of thought, the results less than compelling. "I don't know what you're talking about."

"What kind of deal did you make with Lang?"

I sat there, silent for far too long. "I . . . I didn't make any deal."

"What does he want?"

"Me. Gone."

"I knew it."

I reached out for her hand. "He's just concerned that you might not be taken seriously . . ."

She pulled her hand away. "How about the two of you let me worry about that, huh?"

"I don't think . . ."

"The hell with it, I'll withdraw."

"Cady, you can't do that."

"You watch me."

I scooted my chair in. "Look, I've been thinking about retiring for years, maybe this is a sign that it's time."

"Don't give me that crap."

"Cady."

"You think I want to be the one pushing you into retirement—how do you think that's going to reflect on me? How do you think that's going to make me feel? I don't want the cruddy job that badly. Okay?"

I reached out and took her hand as she tried to pull away but finally gave up. "You'll be a great attorney general."

"And you've been the greatest sheriff the state has ever had."

"'Had' being the operative term here." I saw tears welling in her eyes. "I don't want my position as sheriff any longer than it wants me. I don't want to be wandering around behind this badge just filling out a uniform." I squeezed her hand. "Maybe it really is a sign."

"Will you please stop saying that? You sound like Lonnie Little Bird."

"Um-hmm, yes, it is so."

She stifled a sob and clutched my arm, her head on my shoulder. "I'll tell Lang I'm removing myself from consideration."

"No, you're not—of all the things that are going to happen, that's not one of them."

"I—"

"No, if you do that then I'm going to retire right here, right now on the spot." I pushed her back and lifted her chin as Dog sat up and looked at us. "Now that we both know the score we can try and navigate this thing, and I'm sure that between the two of us we'll figure it out." I smiled at her, pushing some of the hair from her face as she reached out and stroked Dog's head. "Otherwise, we're both out of a job and Lola has to support us, and I don't think there's that much of a market for watching the mermaid movie 1,345 times."

There was an odd noise as I drove over to the Plains Hotel, a noise I'd never heard before. Figuring it must've been something on the old SUV, I kept driving, only to hear it again as I pulled the International to a stop in the parking lot.

I listened to the chirping sound and thought about how it sounded different from any noise the Travelall could've been making—more modern, more electronic. It was about then that I felt a vibration in my pocket and pulled out the JugBug, looking at the device. There was a number on the screen with a 202 area code, one I didn't recognize . . . but that was nothing new in that I didn't recognize anybody's number on the planet.

Looking at the thing, I wondered what you did to call whoever it was back.

I climbed out of the International and walked around the block, entering the lobby of the grand hotel, flipping the phone open, and staring at the number. Taking a shot, I just hit the green button for CALL.

I held it to my ear and listened to it ring, whereupon somebody answered with a very recognizable accent. "Hello, and to who am I to speaking?"

Shaking my head, I met the eye of the guy at the front desk and waved him off. "Do you mind if I ask how you got this number?"

He laughed. "Sheriff, this what I am doing my whole life. It is your very lack of technology that makes it easier for to track you down."

I stood there at the front desk, leaning on the counter. "How can I help you, Mister Sidorov?"

"I would like to speak with you, if is possible?"

"Well, I'm kind of pressed for time."

"You are available of the now?"

I quickly made sense of the word salad. "Right now?"

"Yes." He laughed and there was an echo in the phone. "Look to your left?"

I did as he said.

"Yes, now up?"

Glancing into the mezzanine I could see a thickset man with wild hair and an eyepatch, toasting me with a clear-looking liquid. Setting his phone down, he waved for me to join him, gesturing toward the marble staircase in the corner between us.

I mounted the steps and came out above where he sat at one of the two-tops with a Poloz 9mm pistol residing at his elbow. "Come. You sit, and we drink." He nudged a small glass my way, explaining. "The bartender, he goes off of the duty at midnight, so I purchase entire bottle and borrow the two glasses."

"You get the semiautomatic from him too?"

He grunted a laugh and winked. "No, gun was procured through different channel."

I sat opposite him, turning off my phone and pocketing it, figuring I've had enough calls for one night. "You knew I was here?"

Pouring me one, he then decanted himself a shot. "Sheriff, I recognize you best me but do not underestimate."

I considered the glass. "What is it?"

"Polugar, rye vodka, you probably not have." He held his glass up and I lifted mine, tipping the rim to his as he looked over them at me with the one eye. "You like patch?"

"It's very roguish."

"Roguish." He laughed again. "Thank you. I think is compliment?"

"Pirate-like . . . Sure."

"I was going to replace eye with glass one, but I think, why? Cannot see out of, so is for others—I decide eyepatch is more honest, yes?"

We drank, and I set my glass back on the table. "How can I help you, Mister Sidorov?"

"More is I to help you."

"And how can you do that?"

He poured himself another, and then mine. "The woman, Ruthless?"

"Ruth One Heart."

"Da, they not find her."

I studied him. "And you can?"

"Is what I do, Sheriff."

"So, what is it you're proposing?"

"I have make deal with your Department of the Justice and State but they do not give me mobility in what I do." He lifted his leg, revealing the ankle monitor above his motorcycle boot. "Perhaps if you put in word of good, you allow me help you finding of her?"

"I take it this isn't something I can do on my own?"

"No, as I have said before you are very above pay grade." He lowered his leg and picked up the small glass. "I know people you are against; I know their resources and capability. You need the help."

"You'll excuse me if I say that's not the most comforting of assurances. In that the last time I saw you, you were trying to kill me."

"Sheriff, if I were to trying kill truly you, we would not be having conversation now." He sipped his diminutive drink. "They will be of contact to you, to arrange return of her or allowing of you to retrieve her. I will be of advise to you to tell you what to do, or more of the importance what not of to do."

"So, in an advisory capacity."

"Yes, but then there will be the action and that is of where you need of me the most."

"So, the Regis family or their associates have her?"

"I am to believe, yes."

"And she's alive?"

"I am to believe, but there is no guarantee of this."

"And why is it you would want to help me?"

He settled into his chair, relaxing with the thought. "To settle score with Regis family, they no pay me for previous job."

"That job being me?"

"You." He shrugged. "They also leave me to dangle."

I gestured toward the 9mm on the table. "And what is that for?"

"I was not sure of response to offer. Is Wild West, yes?"

"Yep."

"Besides, I am not wanting to underestimate you again. Have only one eye left."

It was about then that he felt the muzzle of a Glock 19 pressed against the back of his head. "That would be wise of you." I carefully reached out and slid the Russian 9mm away from his grasp. "Mister Sidorov, allow me to introduce my undersheriff, Victoria 'the Terror' Moretti."

She gathered her luxury robe as she slid to one side and sat on the chair across the aisle, holding her Glock pointed directly at him. "What's up, Rasputin?"

He half-smiled, nodding to himself as he turned his head and studied her. "She is even more beautifulness in person, yes?"

"Flattery will get you to Siberia." She glanced at me. "What's he want?"

"He says he can find Ruth One Heart."

"Zat so, comrade?" She glanced back at him, covering her legs with the robe as he attempted to study her. "Well, why don't you just tell us, and we'll take care of it?"

"Not quite so simple."

"He says the Regis family is involved—that they took her, and he can help us get her back."

"Generous of him."

I picked up the Poloz and dropped the mag, thumbing off the 9mm rounds onto the table between us. "Yep, there's only one problem."

He turned to look at me as the bullets rolled around on the surface of the table between the glasses and the bottle. "And this is?"

"I don't trust you."

He smiled the lopsided grin again and I had to admit it was a good one. "Not even little bit?"

"Nope." I swept the rounds into my coat pocket and sat back in my chair, replacing the magazine and tossing it on the table before watching it slide toward him. "So, I take it you don't know exactly where she is?"

"No, but can make it business to find out." He shrugged. "After they learn that I make contact with you, they be of more motivation to hire again."

"Why don't they just contact me themselves?"

"They will eventually, but they prefer to use intermediary."

"Why?"

"Because are afraid of you."

I made a face. "And you're not?"

"No."

"Why?"

"Because I have met you and am only one left alive or not in maximum security prison, they are of thinking you are one who is ruthless."

"And you don't?"

"No, you are many of things, Sheriff, but ruthless you are not."

"Some people would argue that point."

He smiled the grin yet again, glancing at Vic and then back at me. "You believe in the justice, yes?"

"I do."

"That is weakness of you." He shook his head and collected his pistol, shoving it into his belt. "Neither the life or nature care for this construct of justice—it does not exist, and you are disadvantaged by your belief in this. In the world of nature man is the worst of all in his trust in this justice or that world is right. World is not right and never will be, and to believe this is blasphemy to natural order of things."

"Maybe I think we should rise above the natural order of things; it's called being civilized."

He poured two more shots of the vodka and attempted to hand one to me, but I shook my head, and he turned, holding it out to Vic.

She took it, still training the 9mm on him.

He glanced back at me. "This one, she understand, yes?"

Swigging down the drink, she tossed him the shot glass, which he fumbled to catch as she jammed the Glock in his crotch. "Look, Yuri, if I had my way, I'd just aerate your man parts and get the information out of you." She nodded toward me. "But he's a good guy and pretty much always does the right thing." She leaned in close, her nose about a foot from his. "Your mistake is confusing good with weak, and if you come back at either of us with that attitude, I'm going to do worse than shoot you in the man parts, you got me?"

The smile, again. "There is the worse than shooting man parts?"

"We have a saying here in the Wild West . . ." She eased back in her chair, drawing the gun away with her. "Fuck around and find out."

He chuckled and took his own shot, then rested the two glasses on the table before holding his hands up and standing as he made a great show of carefully pulling a card from his breast pocket and handing it to me. "Pay no attention to printed information; current contact is wrote on back." Turning, he edged away from Vic, still holding up his hands. "Fuck around and the find out—I like this."

"Dasvidaniya, Ivan."

"Poka poka, pupsik."

We watched him slide along the railing and then cross toward the stairwell before pausing and staring at the carpet. "When they are of calling you, Sheriff, and they will—call me. I am not believer in justice but am believer very, very much in revenge."

He continued down the steps, and I listened to the echo of his boots as they crossed the marble floor below and Vic looked at me. "So, are you the only sheriff in Wyoming with casual interactions with ex-KGB?"

"Spetsnaz of the Glavnoye Razvedyvatelnoye Upravlenie, please."

"Gesundheit." She yawned and stood, straightening her robe and dropping the 9mm into one of the front pockets. "C'mon, I'm tired and want to go to bed."

I put my arm around her shoulders and steered her toward the elevator where we waited for it to arrive. "So, what do you think?"

"I think he's twisty as a corkscrew."

"But other than that?"

The doors slid open, and we stepped inside where she pushed me against the wall and tucked herself under my arm. "Walt, he fucks people over and kills them for a living."

"Who else have I got on the inside of this mess?"

"You're actually considering teaming up with that asshole?"

We stayed like that for a long time, or until we got to the top floor. "I've got to find her."

"I understand."

Walking out, she trailed a hand back to me as we made our way to a door with a plaque that read PRESIDENTIAL SUITE. "Glad you went all out."

She slipped a card in the lock, pulling it out as it clicked and then pushed open the door as I followed her in. There was a short hallway leading to a large suite that overlooked the railyards to the south and the streams of traffic on the elevated highway.

There was a champagne bucket by the sofa with a bottle of Taittinger that was opened, a half-full glass and an empty one sitting on the coffee table. "You started without me?"

She picked up her glass and kicked off the hotel slippers, curling her legs beneath her. "You really think the Regis family has her?"

"What other explanation is there? She disappeared without a trace."

"So, you're not going to leave this to the authorities?"

I sat on the sofa and looked at her. "They're a very powerful family with a lot of connections."

"How about you call your pal at DOJ?"

"Mike McGroder?"

"Him."

"He retired."

"You don't know anybody else?"

"That maniac Cliff Cly, but I trust him about as much as I trust a fifty-year-old crate of sweating dynamite."

"So, what you're saying is that other than Boris Badenov, we're on our own?"

"Pretty much." I plucked the bottle from the ice bucket and freshened her drink and then poured myself one. "Saizarbitoria said there's a DOJ investigator, Blake Foster, in Iowa where they think her plane went missing."

"Have you spoken with him?"

"Not yet, I've been kind of wrapped up with this Blair McGowan thing."

"But you found her."

"Well, she found me and told me to buzz off."

She studied me. "Same thing. Hell, even better in that you've been booted off the case so it's not your problem anymore."

"Something's going on out there in the Red Desert with this cult, and I've got a feeling it's going to end in something bad."

She dislodged a foot and nudged me with it. "Need I remind you that that isn't your jurisdiction?"

"Yep, the problem is that if Grossnickle and his guys go out there, they're just going to close up shop and move somewhere else, dragging all those people with them."

"What people?"

"About forty of them, mostly elderly; followers I guess you'd call them. Some of them with some form of leprosy."

"Did you just say 'leprosy'?" She shook her head. "So, what are you, Moses? Going to part the waves and lead them out of desert?"

"Something like that, I guess."

She sipped her champagne. "You know this is how you're going to get yourself killed, right? Something stupid like this?"

"I hope not."

"I'm serious. It's when you least suspect it, Walt."

I started on my own champagne but then stopped. "What, exactly, are we celebrating?"

Shaking her head, she took both our glasses and sat them on the coffee table, climbing in my lap and giving me a smoldering and languid, lingering kiss while mumbling between our lips. "It's Friday."

We sat in our usual booth at the Luxury Diner on the Old Lincoln Highway under the watchful eye of the old Wyoming Motel sign that insisted it was still 1954, Vic eating her Athena omelet and me picking at my biscuits and gravy.

"You're not hungry?"

I shrugged. "Just wondering if I should even bother with heading back to Rock Springs."

She chewed, studying me. "Do I get a vote?"

"No."

"Does Dog?"

"No."

"Walt, let it go." She went back to eating, stuffing a piece of her omelet in her mouth and studying me. "I don't particularly care what the postal inspector has to say—you found her, and she doesn't want to be found. Case closed."

"I just . . ."

"The law . . ." She stopped chewing and looked at me thoughtfully. "You remember the law, that thing you swore to uphold?"

"Somewhat."

"Well, the law is very clear on the subject, so you need to let it go."

Something suddenly blocked out the light from the single window at the end of the counter and a booming baritone spoke from the darkness. "Let what go?"

We both looked up to find the Cheyenne Nation seating himself next to Vic, forcing her to move over. "Hey, I'm sitting here."

We watched as he raised a finger and the waitress almost left skid marks getting to him as he grinned his papercut smile up at her. "I am sorry, but could I bother you for a cup of coffee?"

The middle-aged blonde responded very differently from the way she had greeted us. "Cream and sugar?"

The Bear smiled back. "No, I am sweet enough."

As the waitress giggled and retreated, Vic gestured toward her food. "Please? I'm trying to eat here."

I sipped my coffee as he stole a piece of bacon from my plate. "How was your night with the player to be named later?"

He chewed and thought about it. "She holds promise, but I am sending her down to the minors."

My undersheriff glanced at him. "Needs seasoning?"

"Something like that."

"How old is she?"

He shot her a look. "Is this an official inquiry?"

"Just trying to save you seventeen to twenty."

"She is a registered voter."

The waitress brought his coffee, setting it before him with a yet unseen flourish with cream and an embarrassing assortment of sugars. "I know you said you didn't need them, but I thought you might change your mind."

The VistaVision smile again. "It has been known to happen."

The waitress swept away, leaving us with our dirty plates and half-filled mugs. "In answer to your question, I found the missing woman and she would just as soon remain missing."

He sipped his coffee. "I love those cases that solve themselves, do you not?" He studied me for a moment and then turned to Vic. "He does not?"

"He does not."

He turned back to me. "Why does he not?"

"Too much other crap going on with the case."

"Perhaps, but Michael Thurman only contracted you to ascertain that she was alive and well."

"He did."

"Then the case is closed, no matter how much you would like for it to remain open."

I nodded, looking at my plate but saying nothing.

The Bear glanced at my fiancée. "He has trouble letting go."

"That's the understatement of the century." She rolled her eyes. "Besides, don't you have enough to worry about with Mister Chekhov?"

The Bear turned to me with a more than quizzical look.

"Maxim Sidorov paid me a visit last night offering his services as an undercover operative in getting Ruth One Heart back from the global clutches of the Regis family."

"Does he have any proof of this?"

"He declined to elaborate."

"But she has not been found?"

"No."

"Hire him."

I stared at him. "Are you kidding?"

"No, whether you trust him or not is irrelevant. He is the first contact you have had from anyone who might know where she is and whether he is in the employ of the Regis family or an honest free agent, he is a contact, and the only one we have."

Vic interrupted. "How long has it been?"

I took a breath and slowly let it out. "Three weeks."

"And you've had no contact with her at all?"

"No."

She sat back in the booth as she and Henry exchanged a look. "I told you, call that investigator, what's his name?"

"Blake Foster."

"Call him and then go hire Der Komisar if you want to."

I stood, pulling on my hat. "Do you ever run out of those things?"

She smiled, all innocence. "What things?"

Shaking my head, I walked toward the cash register and confronted the waitress, who looked at me as if she'd never seen me before. Throwing a thumb, I gestured toward where my friends stood and started toward us. "The corner booth."

"Oh." Her eyes sharpened and the smile returned as she whispered. "Your friend, is he single?"

I thought about it. "He is the most singular person I've ever met."

I paid the bill in cash and left her to think about that before pushing open the door and stepping into the blinding sunlight of the parking lot and toward the Travelall, leaning against it as I searched through my pockets, trying to locate the slip of paper with the DOJ investigator's number on it.

"Nice ride."

I looked up to find Vic handing the Cheyenne Nation a stick of gum before offering me one from the pack. "Thanks."

He chewed and slid his eyes over the sheet metal as she leaned against the tailgate next to me, continuing in a walkaround. "Vintage, not your usual style."

"It belonged to the McGowan woman."

Vic chewed her own gum. "She gonna want it back, now that she's alive?"

I continued rooting through my pockets. "If so, she's going to have to pay me for it."

"What are you doing?"

"Looking for the Blake Foster guy's number."

She reached over and slipped her hand inside my jacket, her nimble fingers sliding in and pulling the slip of paper from my shirt pocket. "You always stuff shit in your left-side breast pocket."

I took the tiny slip with the numbers scrawled across it and said to her, "Sometimes I think you know me too well."

"Fortunately for me, I like what I know." She pulled her keys from her pocket and watched as I continued searching. "What now?"

"My cell phone."

She barked a laugh. "Where that is, I have no idea." I finally found it in my coat pocket and pulled it out, opening it as she laughed again. "Is that an honest-to-God flip phone?"

"What, they don't make many of these anymore?"

"Not for the past decade or so, no."

I thumbed at the thing, but it didn't light up or show any other signs of life. "I think it's dead."

She took it from me. "Yeah, probably from about ten years ago. At least it doesn't have an extendable antenna . . ." She fidgeted with it a bit more and then handed it back to me. "It was turned off."

"Oh."

The Bear joined us. "Oh, what?"

"I think I turned it off."

She shook her head. "Where the hell did you get that?"

"A head shop in Rock Springs."

"When we get back, we can buy you a real phone instead of that Fisher Price piece of shit."

I studied the tiny screen and there seemed to be some new, electronic hieroglyphics. "Okay."

"Okay?" She leaned her head down to get my attention. "We all go home and this shit in the Red Desert is over?"

"Yep." I pointed toward the phone. "This little guy here, what does it mean?"

She peered at the device in my hands. "It's a text message. No wait—that's a voicemail." Taking the phone from me she hit a few buttons and then held it to her ear. "It's a 303 area code, so it's your extended family member and resident postal inspector, Michael Thurman."

She started to take the phone from her ear as I reached for it, but then returned it before looking at me and swallowing as she listened. "What?"

Her face took on a somber expression as she handed it back to me, closed. "Blair McGowan is dead."

8

"They found her body on the County Road 4-21."

"Where?"

"Near Red Lake, east of Alkali Basin in the East Sand Dunes."

I leaned against the grille of the International. "Who found her?"

"A truckload of those guys doing geological surveys for one of the oil companies. They were driving along on one of the trails and one of them saw something lying out there in the sand." The postal inspector folded his arms and looked at the surface of the asphalt parking lot of the Sweetwater County Sheriff's Department.

"Grossnickle on this?"

He nodded. "The coroner has the body, and he can be difficult."

"How did she die?"

"Dehydration and a snake bite."

I turned to look at him. "You're kidding."

"It's what I heard."

I pushed off, circling around and petting Dog's head through the window before starting toward the building. "I guess I'll go find out."

"It's not your fault . . ."

"Maybe not, but I could've pushed a little bit harder."

He called out after me. "What're you gonna do?"

Muttering over my shoulder, I wasn't even sure if he heard me. "Push a little harder."

As I climbed the steps, I thought about my encounter with the cult members out in the Red Desert. As I opened the glass door, I was confronted by the young woman who had arrested me in the trailer park. "Hello, Sheriff."

"Howdy, Deputy—the boss around?"

She nodded down one of the hallways. "He's in his office, discussing the McGowan autopsy."

"They did one?"

"They were pretty sure you'd want it done."

"They're right." I looked in the direction she'd indicated. "Which way?"

"End of the hall, the one with the door that says 'sheriff.'"

"Got it." Walking down the hall, I found the door and knocked. "Sheriff?"

A muffled but recognizable voice called back. "Kind of busy in here."

I opened the door and stepped inside. "About to get busier."

"Cheese it, it's the cops." John stood and gestured toward a middle-aged man with an extravagant handlebar mustache, slicked-back dark hair, and a self-important demeanor. "Walt, this is Luis Diaz, the new county coroner."

We shook hands as I sat in the open chair facing the man. "Dehydration?"

He pursed his lips in contemplation. "So it would appear. That and a rattlesnake bite."

"Rattlesnake?" I glanced at my fellow sheriff and then back to the coroner. "I don't have to point out to you that one thousand people were bitten by rattlesnakes in this country last year and only one of them died, roughly zero-point-one percent."

He nodded. "Yes, but she was also in pretty rough shape with exposure, dehydration . . ."

"A rattlesnake bite?"

"Yes, Mister Longmire, she must've gotten lost out there and then got bit." The coroner's eyes darted toward John and then back to me. "Did I fail to mention that she was allergic?"

Thinking I might've heard him wrong, I asked, "Allergic?"

"Cardiac arrest along with dehydration and exposure, actually, but it was an anaphylactic reaction to the snakebite."

Easing back in the chair, I took a long breath. "You're telling me she was allergic?"

"From all indications."

Glancing at Grossnickle, I looked back to the coroner. "Was she bitten before the dehydration and exposure or after?"

"Excuse me?"

I grabbed the arms of his chair and pulled him toward me in no uncertain terms. "I repeat, was she bitten before the dehydration and exposure or after?"

"Well, we assume afterward." He glanced at the sheriff again and then reluctantly back at me. "The animals had done a number on her; the birds had gone after her eyes and there really wasn't much left of her face . . ."

With a yank, I pulled him in closer. "Was there visceral congestion, hemorrhages, or epicardial hemorrhages present?"

"Well, we didn't see any reason to—"

"And were they pre- or postmortem?"

"Well . . . I can't say I care for your tone."

I yanked his chair very close so that our faces were no more than six inches apart. "The hell with my tone. You check it with a coagulation screen, FBE and film, a creatine kinase test, and serial blood tests."

"I'm not going to subject that poor woman's body to—"

"Redness, swelling, bruising, bleeding, or blistering around the bite?"

"I don't—"

"Had she vomited or soiled herself?"

"I—"

"Did you do a protein analysis to discover the exact kind of rattlesnake venom?

"I—"

"The puncture wounds, were they far apart or close? Because if that was the cause of death, I'm thinking it was midget faded rattlesnake venom."

He shot a glance at John and then back to me. "Excuse me, a what?"

The Sweetwater County sheriff raised his eyebrows. "The rattlesnake with the most potent venom, and a resident in only our portion of the state." He picked up a folder from the desk and held it out to the coroner in an attempt to save him. "Looks like you've got a little more work to do."

I stood, towering over the man. "Do your job."

He tried to stand, but I was firmly in the way. "I need to get to my clinic on the north side of town."

I waited for a moment more before walking over to the window behind Grossnickle's desk, staring out at the open high-plains desert that looked a lot more southwest than my part of the state.

I listened as the coroner pushed one of the chairs out of the way and stood, taking the folder and starting toward the door, but when he got there, he turned and looked back at us, starting to say something.

I raised a finger to him. "Whatever it is you're about to say, you better make it count."

Thinking better of it, he opened the door and quietly closed it behind him.

John swiveled his chair and looked up at me, shaking his head. "Hey, nice to have you back, Walt."

I pointed at the door. "That's bullshit."

"Yeah, well, I don't think you made any friends there."

I looked at him. "What are you going to do?"

"You're sure Blair was with those people?"

I looked back to the window where I could see the coroner jumping in his Cadillac with California plates wheeling away. "Yep."

"I guess we'll go round them up and see if anybody knows anything."

"You want help?"

"With the mood you're in, probably not." He stood and joined me at the window. "More importantly, what are you going to do?"

"Go talk to some people."

"Just talk, right? No brandishing."

"Yep, just talk, I promise. No brandishing."

I knocked on the door of the singlewide three times and was preparing to leave when Flossy opened it a crack, the security chain still attached. "Ms. Frasier, can I speak with you?"

She grinned a ready smile. "Why, certainly—anything for my knight in blue denim."

Unhooking the chain, she gestured for me to enter and moved toward the kitchen where we'd sat before, but then paused and pulled a newspaper over something on the surface of the table and then moved it to the counter, out of our way.

I sat in the chair I'd occupied before. "Had any more troubles with your trash cans?"

She laughed, adjusting some kind of kerchief she had wrapped around her brassy hair that seemed to be determined to escape at every turn. "No, I hardly see him much. I think he might've switched to the night shift."

"I'm afraid that I have some bad news."

"Is it about Blair?"

"I'm afraid so."

"She's dead."

"Yes, ma'am. How did you know?"

She sat back in her own chair, straightening her robe and pulling a cigarette from the pack at her elbow, tapping it on the table to settle the tobacco. "Someone like Blair doesn't just disappear like that, so I figured that something must've happened." She lit her lighter and puffed on her cigarette, opening a window, and blowing the smoke outside, sort of. "So, what happened?"

"I'm not at liberty to say, but they found her out in the Red Desert. They say it was exposure and dehydration and a snakebite, but I'm doubting that."

"Do you mind if I ask why?"

"Because of what her friend Tess told me about the heavenly potholes."

She shook her head as if to clear it. "The what?"

"Ephemeral pools, sand-covered ice. If there was a drop of water out there in the entire Red Desert, she knew where it was."

"What do you think happened to her?"

I sat there for a moment considering what I was going to do and then just got on with it. "Ms. Frasier, I'm afraid I haven't been completely honest with you."

"In what way?"

"Ms. Frasier, I'm the sheriff of Absaroka County."

She studied me. "And where is that?"

"Here, in Wyoming."

"Is that so?"

She didn't seem particularly surprised. "Well, yes, ma'am."

Reaching behind her, she pulled out a large photo album from under the newspaper she had moved and sat it on the table between us. I stared at the wooden cover of the thing and then back at her, whereupon she gestured toward it with the cigarette and sat back in her chair. "You want something to drink?"

I stared at the weather-beaten retro album. "Am I going to need it?"

She stood and went to the avocado-colored refrigerator and retrieved two Rainier tallboys and sat them in front of us before sitting and gesturing toward the album with another extended drag. "Go ahead, I want to see the look on your face."

Opening the beer, I took a swig and flipped open the page, revealing a newspaper article about a railroad case concerning a murdered sheriff that I'd worked on as a deputy under Lucian Connally. Flipping to the next page, I could see it was an interview I'd given at the beginning of my career, and then another and another and another . . . Flipping through the pages, I could tell it was a chronological scrapbook of my entire law-enforcement career.

Raising my eyes, I looked at her. "You have got to be kidding . . ."

"Big fan."

I stared back at the open book of my life. "How did you . . . ?"

"A woman I roomed with in Reno was from your county and still got the newspaper. I started reading them and I guess I developed something of a crush on you over the years."

"You knew who I was when I knocked on your door the first time?"

"Of course I did."

I sat back in the chair, shaking my head. "You know, I don't think I'll ever go undercover again in my life." I looked back up at her. "I truly believe I am the world's worst at it."

She waved my words away. "Stop feeling sorry for yourself and tell me about your theories on Blair."

"I think the Order of the Red Gate had something to do with all this."

She took a long drag, tilting her head back to stream the smoke toward the open window. "Oh, she was too smart to get mixed up with that bunch."

"So everybody tells me, but I found her out there with them."

She leveled her eyes on me. "Goodness, no."

"And then she came and visited me, telling me to stop looking for her, that she was fine and didn't want to be pursued any longer."

She reached forward and stubbed out the cigarette in the vintage ashtray. "She said that?"

"She did."

"Did she mention why it was that she was out there with those wackos?"

"No, she didn't."

Picking up her can, she took a strong quaff and sat it back down. "There has to be a reason."

"She did that loony, quasi-documentary TV show about meeting aliens . . ."

"*Mysteries from Beyond*. She did that for some guy she knew out there."

"Excuse me?"

"The actor, he was an actor out there in Hollywood. He was also an executive producer on that show and got her to say all that crap and pretend it was true."

I sat there, going through my mental Rolodex. "Do you remember his name?"

"I remember it was something strange . . ."

A card stuck in my cerebral wheel and I blurted out the name. "Zeno Carruthers?"

"No, that wasn't it . . ."

"Was it Ritt Ravitch?"

She snapped a finger, pointing it at me. "You know, I think that was it."

I stood. "I'm afraid I've got to go."

"Where?"

"I have to go check something." Moving toward the door, I looked back at her. "Thank you for your help, Ms. Frasier."

She followed me out onto the small porch, calling after me as I climbed in the Travelall. "Let me know what's going on, please?!"

Dog followed me as I clamored up the steps to my room on the top floor of the Park Hotel, but when we got about halfway down the hall, I noticed the door to my room was hanging open.

I grabbed Dog's collar as I carefully slid the .45 from my holster and stood there for a moment, listening. I thought I heard something—but surely it couldn't have been what I thought it was. Just to be safe, I held the beast back as I slid along the side of the wall, nudging the door open even farther and swinging it wide to find the biker, Benny, asleep on my bed and snoring like a beached walrus.

I released Dog and watched as he approached the man, leaning against the doorjamb as the monster sniffed at one of Benny's stocking feet that hung off the edge. "Is he alive?"

Dog sat and looked at me without comment.

"Right." I pushed off the wall, moving toward the bed, and gave his shoulder a shake. "Benny?"

He snorted but remained unconscious.

I shook him again. "Benny."

His head lolled to one side this time, and then his eyelids fluttered as he looked up at me and smiled. "Man, I thought you were never coming back."

I glanced around at the empty beer cans and full ashtrays. "Looks like you made yourself at home."

He sat up and blinked, looking around. "I didn't figure you'd mind, man. It was a closer commute to work, and I didn't want to miss you."

Holstering the Colt, I sat on the only available chair. "Something up?"

"Yeah, Zeno wants to see you."

"Carruthers?"

"Yeah."

"Interesting, in that I'd like a word with him." I looked at the man, trying to figure how much was my responsibility to tell him. "Benny, did anything happen while I was gone?"

He picked up one of the beers and shook the can to determine if there was something in the bottom and took a swig, wiping his mouth with the back of his hand. "You're not going to believe this, but that woman who used to work with Blair gave this to me." He threw a thumb toward the window. "Right down there on the corner, crazy chick was just standin' down there, waitin' for me in a doorway—like to scare the shit out of me."

"What'd she say?"

He reached into the breast pocket of his shirt and pulled out a folded sheet of paper that looked as if it had been ripped from a spiral-ring notebook and handed it to me. "Nothing, but she gave me this with your name on it."

I took it. "What's it say?"

He pointed. "It says for your eyes only."

"And you didn't read it?"

"No."

I stared at him. "Really?"

"Well, I looked at it."

Sighing, I unfolded it and looked at what appeared to be a relatively well-drawn map.

"It's a map."

"Yep, I got that." I held it up and tried to get a scale on what I was looking at, following the dotted line to an X. "And this is where I'm supposed to find them?"

"I guess."

"No instructions?"

"No, she just handed me the thing and walked away." He thought about it. "Wait, she also said that if you want to see Blair again to not mention this to anybody."

Talking to Benny, I decided, was like conversing with a chicken. "When did she deliver this map?"

"Last night."

"You're sure of that?"

"Yeah, I got off work and rode over and she stepped out of the doorway and scared the shit out of me."

Folding the map, I sat back in the chair and studied him. "Benny, was there anything else, something big that might've happened in the last day or two?"

He looked at me blankly. "Nothing I can think of."

I shook my head. "I'm sorry to have to tell you this, Benny, but Blair is dead."

He froze. "What?"

"Blair McGowan is dead. She died of exposure and a supposed snake bite out there in the Red Desert."

He looked down at the worn carpet on the floor. "That doesn't make sense."

"No, it doesn't." I tucked the homemade map in my coat pocket and stared at him. "You're sure that's what she said and when she said it?"

"Yeah."

"The only answer is that they don't know Blair's dead, and if that's the case then why are they trying to get me out there?"

"Maybe it's a trap."

I let out an extremely dramatic sigh in hopes that he'd pick up on it. "Yep, I thought of that, but if I know she's already dead then why would I go?"

"Maybe they think you're dumb."

The statement was made in earnest, and I stared at him for a long while, not even getting close to making a dent. "I think you can go now, Benny."

"Really? I thought we'd head out there together."

"No, you've done enough, and I think I'd rather take care of this on my own."

"Well, okay . . ." He reached out to pet Dog, who growled at him. Benny withdrew his hand. "You'll let me know about Blair, right?"

I stood, hoping it might hurry him along. "You bet."

He pulled on his boots and then gathered the few items he had scattered around the room, lingering at the door. "When are you going out there?"

"Probably tonight."

"In the dark?"

Tossing the beer cans and emptying the ashtrays in the one trash receptacle, I nodded. "Night's like that, yep."

"I think you should wait till tomorrow morning."

"I'll take it under consideration." I watched as he finally left, feeling sorry for him in a way. I sat on the bed and looked at Dog, who joined me. "What am I going to do with you? I can't have you out there running around in the Red Desert, you're likely to get shot."

He nudged my elbow and rested his big head on my knee.

"That's not going to work. It's one thing if I get shot but another if you do. No one will ever speak to me again."

Standing, I loaded my things into my Filson bag and gathered up everything else, including two canteens, my shooting bag with my old binoculars, and even ammo for the Sharps. Dog waited until I got to the door, watching me with unwavering interest.

I patted my leg. "C'mon."

Tromping down the stairs, I found Mike Thurman leaning against the grille of the International with a large manila envelope under his arm. "What are you doing here at this time of night?"

He reached down and petted Dog as the beast sat on my foot. "I tried to call you, but it kept going to voicemail; you must have your phone turned off."

Remembering the thing, I pulled it out from inside my coat and flipped it open, looking at the dark screen.

"When's the last time you charged that?"

"You have to charge them?"

He shook his head and looked into the interior of the Travelall. "Have you still got the box? It probably came with a charger."

"I never got a box."

He reached for it and I handed it to him. "Where did you buy this thing, on a street corner in 1998?"

"Pretty much." I pointed toward the envelope. "What's that?"

As he looked at the phone, he handed me the folder. "Diaz, the county coroner, was stuffing this under your windshield wiper when I pulled up. I get the feeling he didn't want to meet up, so I took it and told him I'd give it to you."

Opening the tab, I peeked in to see the report and photographs inside. "It's Blair McGowan's new and improved autopsy." I tipped my hat back and glanced at him. "Do you want to look at it?"

"No, I do not. Ever." He handed me back my phone. "Go back to the street corner and buy a charger, is all I can tell you."

I closed the phone, stuffed it in my pocket, and then slipped the folder under my arm. "Some interesting developments have happened."

"Such as?"

"The Order of the Red Gate sent me a map through Tess Anderson, and requested a parley or else I'll supposedly never see Blair alive again."

"Not particularly keeping up with current events, are they?"

"No."

"Well, you're not going to do it, are you?"

I stared at him.

"That would be extraordinarily stupid."

"Benny Schweppe offered to go with me."

"That would be beyond extraordinarily stupid."

"Yep, I thought so too. Look, if they don't know about Blair's death, then perhaps they didn't have anything to do with it, and if they did, then I'm wanting to have a little chat with them anyway."

"Alone?"

"Well, that leads me to my next question. Do you know where I can find a dog sitter?"

"Walt, don't do this. Go over and give the map to Grossnickle and let him charge out there with all the troops."

"As far as I know there's nothing connecting Blair's death to the group, so they'd just walk."

"And you think an agent provocateur with a handgun and a vintage International has a better chance?"

"Maybe, but I can't risk Dog getting hurt." Nudging the beast off my foot, I circled around him and opened the door, pulling a retractable leash from the seat and handing it to him. "Here, Cady'll kill me if I get him hurt."

"And what about you?"

"Then you catch the blame."

"Thanks, just what I need is the attorney general of the State of Wyoming out for my scalp." He walked over and clipped the leash onto Dog's collar. "By the way, how did that reception go?"

I climbed in the Travelall and hit the starter as Dog strained against the leash, Mike using both hands to hold him back. "I'll tell you about it sometime."

Dog barked and once again lunged to get away from Mike, but the postal inspector held tight as I drove away, feeling like a heel.

I figured Flaming Gorge Vape was just the kind of place to stay open late for the convenience of the nocturnal patrons and was relieved to see the lights on and the same raven-haired human-pincushion kid behind the counter.

He looked up from some kind of gaming magazine. "Hey. You're, like . . . back."

"I need a charger for my phone."

"Oh, yeah. Which one was it?"

I took the thing out and sat it on the counter. "The JugBug."

"Right."

I waited as he rustled through the boxes under the counter. "So, you looked me up?"

He turned, resting what looked to be the what-not tray on the glass counter. "Huh?"

I gestured toward the device. "You put my name on the caller ID of this phone?"

"You have to have some kind of cellular ID." He shrugged but looked concerned. "You mad, bro?"

I nodded. "You're good with computers?"

"Yeah."

I tapped the screen on the counter to my right. "Do me a favor and look up Ritt Ravitch on this thing?"

He stared at me for a moment more and then, figuring he owed me a favor, slid his stool over and began pounding the keyboard and finally asked, "The actor?"

"Yep, let me see?"

He turned the screen and there were myriad photographs obviously from the actor's career, most of them black-and-white. I leaned against the counter and pointed to the center of the bottom row. "Can you bring up that one?" He clicked and it appeared along with the credit information that was too small to read. "What's it say?"

The kid leaned forward. "It's a production still from a TV show in the '90s called *Mysteries from Beyond*. I guess he was on the show." He studied it a bit more. "No, wait . . . He was the host . . . or something."

I indicated another shot where Ritt was wearing a lab coat and a stethoscope. "That one?"

He clicked on it and looked back at me. "Another TV show, something called *ER Doctor*."

I pointed at another. "And that one?"

He clicked it. "Another TV show, *Saddletramp*."

I pointed again at one of the actor wearing a robe, something like the one he'd been wearing when I'd met him. "That one?"

He clicked. "Some kind of religious documentary. I guess there was an entire series of them."

Sighing, I nodded. "Thanks."

He stared at me for a moment. "You still want the charger?"

"Yep, do you have one I can plug into the cigarette lighter in my car?"

"Your what?"

I spotted a round plug that would serve the purpose, holding it and the phone up. "Can you get from this to this?"

He studied the two devices and started rummaging through the tray, pulling out three more cables and connecting them before attaching them to the other two and handing the conglomeration to me.

Holding the unwieldy device, I said to him, "What do I owe you?"

"You know, I've done some sketchy shit in my time, bro, but I'm not going to charge you for that—I just hope it works."

"Thanks," I said before I walked outside and discovered a very large German shepherd–Saint Bernard mix sitting in front of the International. Dog wagged his tail, looking up at me as the glass door of Flaming Gorge Vape slowly closed behind me. "I take it we don't have to pay the ransom?"

He said nothing but followed as I walked around and opened the back door, allowing him to jump in.

I climbed into the front seat of the Travelall and plugged the electronic octopi into the dash. There was no light, so I couldn't tell if it was working so far. But when I plugged it into the phone, I heard a beep and could see a small lightning bolt hieroglyphic on the screen. I sat back and, knowing it might take a little while for the thing to come to life, plucked the autopsy file from the seat beside me and began studying it with Dog leaning over to join me. "Can you see all right?"

He said nothing once again and I took that as an affirmative. I started with the preliminary and then worked my way to the back, seeing where the coroner had retroactively applied the tests I'd requested.

Evidently it didn't take long for the phone to recover a degree of power because, as it sat on the dash, it rang. I flipped it open. "It's okay, he's with me."

"I swear to God, I let him out of my sight for an instant and he was gone. He must've turned the doorknob with his mouth."

Mike sounded pretty upset. "Yep, he can do that."

"And he blew through the screen door."

"He does that too."

"Jeez, does he know his sums?"

I glanced back at the beast, who wouldn't make eye contact with me. "I don't know, I've never tested him."

"You want me to come and get him?"

"What good would it do, he'd just escape again."

"Sorry, Walt."

"No big deal, I'll see you tomorrow."

There was a pause. "You're sure about this?"

"No, but seeing as how they've reached out to me, I don't have much of a choice."

"You do. Call in the troops."

I sighed. "I'll see you tomorrow, Mike." I closed the phone and sat it back on the dash, allowing it to continue gathering its energies.

I began reading the file again. "I think the postal inspector is worried about us."

Dog made no comment.

There were a number of additional photographs and, true to the coroner's word, her face had been destroyed by marauding birds and who knows what else, probably coyotes, which usually concentrate on the liver, heart, lungs, and viscera but sometimes took advantage of wounds inflicted by other scavengers.

There weren't too many other earthshaking insights, but it concluded that the snakebite had been inflicted after her death, indicating that she had indeed died of dehydration and exposure.

The only thing the coroner hadn't noticed on the second pass that I could plainly see from the photographs were the marks around her left ankle that indicated bruising and a few abrasions and cuts. It's likely that if you weren't in the business of human incarceration, you'd ever identify the effects of a manacle cuff to an ankle, but there they were.

The woman had been chained up until exposure and dehydration had killed her.

Studying the photos some more, I spoke over my shoulder. "I don't suppose you're going to tell me how you found me, huh?"

Dog sat looking at me first and then back at the file, his breath on my neck. "Hey, did you happen to notice that the woman in these photos has all her toes?"

He said nothing.

I closed the folder, turned the key in the ignition, and backed out, pulling the Travelall in gear and spinning the oversize wheel, heading out into the darkness of the Red Desert.

"Of course you did."

9

There's dark, and then there's in-the-middle-of-nowhere-Wyoming dark, and that's what we were driving through, but at least it wasn't raining.

The feeble headlights of the International failed to pierce the absolute black of the Red Desert and, not for the first time, I was having second thoughts about coming out here at night. My chances of finding the group in the day were bad enough, but attempting to figure out where they were at night was nigh on impossible—except for the map.

I'd unfolded the piece of paper and stuck it on the dash with a piece of stale gum I'd found in the glove box that I'm pretty sure was from when the Travelall had been assembled. My flashlight was tucked between the upholstery and aimed at the thing, but the pencil marks sometimes eluded me in that I'd already doubled back at least twice.

As near as I could tell, I was somewhere in the vicinity of the Jack Morrow Hills off BLM-4102 or possibly Freighter Gap Road, but I'd crossed Jack Morrow Creek three times and it was possible I was on the outskirts of Boise, Idaho, or Lyon, France.

Dog barked for the second time, and I was pretty sure he needed to hop out and lift a leg.

"Okay, okay." Easing the International to a stop, I pulled over and climbed out.

The air was sharp, the pungent smell of the recently anointed sage and juniper cleared your senses whether you wanted them to or not. Opening the back door, I watched as Dog trailed out into the grass near the edge of the road and disappeared.

Whoever made the map, whether it had been Freebee or one of the others, made sure it led in the opposite direction of where the body of the unknown woman had been found over in the Alkali Basin.

Why try to pass the woman off as Blair? She was, after all, wearing McGowan's clothing but, with Blair having been employed by the federal government her fingerprints and dental records, not to mention possibly her DNA, would be readily available.

What would they gain, other than a little time, by having a substitute body found?

Were they really that stupid?

And who was this woman, and how was she tied to the group?

And why send me the note and map?

On top of all that, what was the story with Zeno Carruthers and Ritt Ravitch? Obviously, the man had been an actor at one time, but he appeared to have lost the ability to drop the role of the week and was destined as a cult leader for the long run. Was it just another scam the group had worked up that was headed for a bad end?

Dog trotted back into the headlights and I opened the rear door, allowing him to climb in before closing it and noticing a set of headlights panning over the Steamboat Rim.

I pulled my coat back, unsnapped the safety strap on my Colt, and waited to see which way the vehicle was headed, but it was hard to tell from the angle of the road.

Watching the headlights, I finally figured out they were on the road I'd been on.

I reached through the open window and switched off the lights but allowed the motor to run at a soft idle. It was possible I'd need the Travelall to get moving quick, but for now I was at ease that whoever it was, it wasn't a Blue Bird bus like the one I'd seen at the camp.

Pulling the .45, I leaned against the door as Dog stuck his head out beside me.

"Don't get out of the car, you hear me?"

He didn't answer but sat and looked out at the approaching headlights along with me.

It was moving too fast, and the headlights were those brighter, more modern versions along with the illumination of a spotlight on the pillar of the driver's side that announced the follower.

The Toyota pulled to a stop, the passenger-side window rolling down as Rick Scout Traveler leaned forward and smiled up at me. "Don't shoot, white man. Nobody in here but us Indians."

I grinned at him as I resettled my Colt and attached the safety snap. "What're you doing out here, Ranger Rick?"

"Do you have any idea how tired I am of that joke?" He shook his head. "I saw some headlights and figured it must be some crazy tourist out here, lost—and what do you know, it is."

"Any sign of the Red Gate gang?"

"You still looking for them?"

I gestured back toward the Travelall. "They sent me a map."

"You're kidding."

"Nope."

He turned off the Toyota and climbed out. "Can I see it?"

I reached in, pulling the map from the dash. "Do you have a flashlight? I've got one if you don't, but the dome light on this International is about one candle power."

He pulled a nifty miniature flashlight from his pocket, shining it on the paper as we stood there between our vehicles. "Who drew this?"

"Somebody from the group, I'd imagine."

"It's actually pretty good, but I don't know some of these roads they've got you going on." He pointed at a portion. "This follows the deer migration corridor, but I'm not aware of any road in that area, so they either know something I don't, or . . ."

"Or?"

"It's a trap to get you somewhere you can't get out."

His finger traced farther. "It follows the rim but then heads into Indian Gap toward Essex Mountain."

"How far is that from the Boar's Tusk?"

"As the crow flies, maybe ten miles."

"Rough country?"

"Killpecker Dune Field?" He chuckled. "Like the Gobi or Sahara Desert or maybe the Atacama . . ."

"Never heard of that last one."

"The Atacama? It's in Chile; less than an inch of rainfall a year, it's the driest nonpolar place on the planet. Some parts are so inhospitable there are absolutely no signs of life—plant, insect, or animal." He looked thoughtful. "I really want to go there someday."

"You know, you Forest Circus guys are a strange breed." I stared at him for a moment and then looked back to our left where the rocky rim gave way to a vast expanse that, in the darkness, looked like an ocean of Bible-black ink stretching to the horizon. "Well, I guess out there is where I'm headed."

"I better go with you."

"No. I'm sure they want me alone and I'm not certain what kind of welcome I'm likely to receive."

"I am."

"All the more reason for you to stay out of this." I tossed the map back into the truck and turned to him. "Thanks for the help."

"I'm not sure it was much." He started back toward the Toyota before stopping. "Hey, I heard Blair was found dead over near Alkali Basin?"

"Yep, I heard that too."

He stood there looking at me, questioningly.

"Did you know she only had eight toes?"

"Blair? Sure, she lost those two on that miracle run up to Bairoil that one time—everybody knows that."

I nodded goodbye and climbed in the Travelall. "Evidently, not everybody."

With my head bouncing off the headliner, forcing my hat down over my eyes, I was coming to the conclusion that the nameless road I was on truly deserved the non-title. Dog was doing his best to stay standing, but even he was having a hard time staying afoot as he slammed against the interior, grumbling.

"I told you to stay in town." Sawing the wheel, I tried to keep the vintage SUV pointed along the rocky road, aware of the stone wall on one side and the sheer drop-off of darkness on the other. "So, do you suppose they just figured they'd kill us with the drive?"

He grumbled some more, and I eased to a stop where the road was now at least one and a half vehicles wide. Switching off the motor, I climbed out and opened the door for Dog because we'd been fighting the trail for the better part of an hour and nature was calling again.

I watched as he leapt out but avoided the edge, which looked as if it dropped off a couple hundred feet. "Be careful."

Standing there, I thought I once again might've seen something off to my left, possibly headlights.

I pulled out my old M19 binoculars from the front seat and traced the road leading along the drop-off but couldn't see anything. It was funny, because it looked like a single light.

I gave up and trained the powerful lenses along the basin, looking for any signs of life. I'd just about given up when I thought I saw traces of a few flickering lights—possibly campfires. It was too far to tell for sure, but it was the only thing that indicated anything living.

I waited as Dog lifted his leg and then gestured for him to hop back in the Travelall, closing the door behind him before following suit, starting the International up, and continuing our journey into the *Wages of Fear.* "Ever read the book by Georges Arnaud?"

He stared at the side of my head as I focused on the road.

"No? How about the film from 1953?"

He continued to stare at me.

"The story is about these guys who have to haul nitro over the mountains in Guatemala or some such place to blow out an oil well fire."

Dodging a boulder that had sloughed off onto the road, I felt the tires fight to continue going straight and just hoped the things wouldn't blow and send us off into the chasm. There was a crunch of something in the undercarriage and the exhaust started making more noise. "Two of them almost make it in the movie and the book, but one accidentally runs over the other, leaving Mario as the only survivor, but he dies on the trip back."

I was relieved when the road straightened and leveled out a bit, but it remained narrow as we approached a cornice that led into a canyon to our right and a spot I committed to memory if I found myself in a full-blown retreat. "When the author, Arnaud, was twenty-four years old, his father, aunt, and a servant were murdered in the family castle. He was the only survivor and was arrested, charged, and put in prison. It was during World War Two, so they pretty much forgot about him for nineteen months, but a jury finally acquitted him in 1943."

I turned the corner and could see an area where the little-used road below followed what could've been a wash. "I think the prison time might've influenced his worldview."

Making the turn inside the canyon, we drove across what looked to be an old logging road, even though there was no logging to be done as far as the eye could see, and headed south toward the lights I'd seen from above. "I'm hoping the way we came in isn't the only way out of here."

I now understood what Rick Scout Traveler had been talking about, where the small amount of scrub and sage gave way to a genuine desert, the dunes of which undulated in all directions. "I'm thinking we made a wrong turn."

Unsure of whether the International would simply bury itself in the sand with the tires it had, I coasted to a stop and got out again, gazing around at the world's biggest sandbox, and shook my head. Taking the map from the dash and looking at it, I tried to figure out where we were, exactly.

I opened the rear door and watched as Dog leapt out and looked at the surroundings as if we'd landed on the moon. "I don't suppose I could get you to stay with the truck, could I?"

Sniffing at the edge of the dunes, he turned to look at me.

"I didn't think so." Circling around, I opened the tailgate of the Travelall and pulled out two stainless-steel bowls, filling one with water from one of my canteens.

"Listen to me, okay?" Dog jumped up and took a perfunctory lap at one of them and looked at me, eye-to-eye. Grabbing his great ears, I stared into his face. "No, really listen. Okay?"

He got that look in his eyes that he acquired when I was sure he not only knew what I was saying, but why.

"If something happens—and I mean anything—if I say 'GIT,' you get the hell out of wherever we are and you come back here, you got me?"

He stared at me, not wagging his tail, and that's how I knew he was probably getting it.

"Even if someone is threatening me, if I say 'GIT,' you git. You got me?"

He didn't answer, but I thought he got it. Just to make sure, I pulled out the bag of dog food that I'd tucked in one of the side pockets and emptied the contents into another bowl as insurance.

I patted the tailgate. "You come here. Got it?"

He sat on the tailgate and looked at me.

"That's right. This is home; you come here if anything happens."

Taking the rucksack from inside, I pulled out the other blanket-sided canteen, then slung it and the one I'd used to fill Dog's bowl over my shoulder and the binoculars around my neck before straightening my hat and starting off toward the dunes to see if I could get a better view of our surroundings. As I'd expected, the monster leapt off the tailgate and followed me. "Just so you know, when that sun comes up it's going to get a lot hotter around here."

He ignored me and scaled the nearest dune, obviously having the same thought about visibility as I did. It was tough going in the sand and I was having trouble keeping up with him as his big muscles bunched and his four legs easily outdistanced my two. Finally catching up with him near the top, I took a breather and then summitted.

The skies were cloudy with intermittent moonlight, and the folded dunes lapped against one another like waves, it was as if Dog and I were on the edge of some great sea. The silvery light highlighted the sand, causing it to sparkle and shimmer and was enhanced by the movement of the clouds dodging the moon so that the wave effect was even grander.

A larger momentary opening in the clouds afforded a greater amount of moonlight for an instant, but it was all for naught in that, other than the four-hundred-foot monolithic volcanic plug, there was nothing to see when facing south.

"What do you think, head for the Boar's Tusk? Can't be any more than a couple miles, huh?" I looked down at Dog. "That's what they call 'famous last words.'"

I took a look back just so I'd have some point of reference if I needed to get back to the Travelall, and there was the canyon behind me and a small crease in the rim that should be visible even in the depths of the dune field.

I set off in a straight line for the Tusk as Dog shot ahead, angling a little to the right so as to not take the next dune head-on. I allowed him, but continued in a straight line to keep the angling from putting on more miles. The walk was tough but the air was cool, and I could've sworn I smelled the faintest hint of woodsmoke somewhere off in the distance.

Trudging on, I was glad I was wearing my boots, which kept the sand from pouring into my socks.

I figured it'd take two hours if I was going to make it all the way to the Tusk, but was hoping that I wouldn't have to go that far. Setting a pace, I figured I'd just keep moving for as long as I could before taking a real rest. I was pretty sure I had a good thirty minutes in the tank, but then again, maybe I was flattering myself.

If you've ever run on a beach, you quickly get the idea that running along on the hardened wet stuff next to the surf is the only way to go. There was no surf, though, so I felt myself slogging through like a posthole digger as I renegotiated my timetable, thinking I'd be lucky if I made it ten minutes before resting.

Even when I paused for only a second, I found myself paying for the same real estate twice by either sinking or sliding backward in the shifting surface. I kept forging ahead simply because it had to become the method of choice no matter how tired I got.

Dog started following in my boot prints, his tongue lolling to the side as the sand began taking its toll on him too.

After a while, any kind of movement became a battle with my breath as my boots fought for some kind of traction. Sometimes it worked, but other times it didn't as the pockets pulled me off-balance like quicksand.

Absentmindedly, I wondered if they made sandshoes, an alternative to snowshoes for the dune impaired.

Figuring I'd done a good twenty minutes, I stopped at the top of the tallest dune I'd encountered so far and stood there for a moment, swiping off my hat and running a sleeve over my face. I looked back from where I'd come and could still see the cleft in the rim that would guide me back to the Travelall. In the other direction, the Boar's Tusk didn't look one damn bit closer.

I placed my hands on my knees and leaned over, the binoculars hanging straight down along with the two canteens bouncing against my hip.

Dog appeared and licked the side of my face. "Try and preserve your moisture."

I took a deep breath and rose back up, realizing I smelled the campfire again, possibly off to my left. I lifted the vintage binoculars to my eyes and panned them over in that direction, thinking I might've seen a faint glow between two dunes, but it could've also been the moonlight playing tricks.

Starting off again, I'd gotten halfway down the dune when I turned back to where I could see Dog standing at the precipice, looking all the world like a movie still from a Rin Tin Tin film. His head was cocked to the side and his tail arched over his back and he was completely still in olfactory concentration.

"What is it?"

He sniffed and then huffed with his mouth open, tasting whatever it was.

"What?"

He looked down at me and then did something he rarely did: whine.

"What?"

Without another sound, he loped off the crown of the dune and took off to the right at an acute angle.

"Wait . . . what the hell are you . . . ?" I thought about shouting but figured I might alert the Red Gate folks and did the only thing I could, which was start off after the beast, wherever he was going.

Breathless, I half-loped, half-trudged after the monster, thinking about how I was going to thump his noggin when I caught up with him. What was he thinking, running off like this? As if I wasn't already getting enough exercise.

I'd made it over about the fifth dune when I heard something ahead, a growling, yipping noise that I knew wasn't Dog. Redoubling my efforts, I stumbled at the top of the next slope and fell to my knees before looking up to see a strange sight. There, cradled in the saddle of one of the spaces between two dunes was what looked to be a child, wrapped in a blanket, absolutely silent.

There was no blood, but the child didn't move.

Dog was only a few feet away, facing off three coyotes that were attempting to flank him to get to the child. One of them was limping where Dog must've tagged him in the leg, and one of the others drew off to the left as the monster turned toward him.

I guess they figured that there were three of them, but he was three times their size.

The one to the right moved toward me as I struggled to my feet, unsheathing my Colt and pointing it at him. I'm not sure, but he must've been shot at before and knew the .45 was something he wanted nothing to do with.

Pulling up short, he raised his head to get a better look at me and then glanced at the child as I took a step in his direction.

The wounded one in the middle didn't move, focused on the unmoving baby, but the nearest one darted back behind the wounded one as the one on the far left made a run at the swaddled baby. He was fast, but Dog cut him off and took his throat in his gaping jaws.

Head over dewclaws, the two of them tumbled down the dune, kicking up sand as Dog took advantage of his weight and size, pinning the coyote to the ground by the throat where he could've easily killed him, but instead just held him there as he continued to kick.

The wounded one, spotting his chance, shot toward the child as I used up my last shreds of energy to post-hole my way in that direction. He grabbed the tail of the blue covering and started dragging the child down the slope as I landed only a couple of yards away, slipping and falling to my side, pinning my gun arm.

I watched as the wounded coyote released the blanket but then made to leap on the child. He almost made it before the furry steamroller hit him like two tons of shit in a one-ton bag, slamming him into the sand.

I stumbled forward and onto my feet as the other two coyotes took to the dunes while Dog continued to hold the wounded one to the ground. "Dog!"

Dog released the coyote with one last warning shake, just so he'd know how close he'd been to breathing his last, and backed away with his head low, ready to hit him again. The coyote lay there for a moment before swallowing and then rising carefully, without making eye contact with Dog, and slowly limping away.

Four steps and I was to the child. I holstered the Colt and lowered myself, picking up the bundle but not feeling any movement. I prepared myself for the worst as I drew the blanket back to find a set of glittering hazel eyes looking at me and blinking in rapid succession.

"Howdy."

The baby's eyes were the only thing that moved, and she remained silent.

Dog started back toward us but then stopped when he saw the coyotes regroup on one of the adjacent dunes.

I called him. "I don't think they're going to come back, no matter how much you want them to." I turned and made a loud hissing noise at the trio. *"Tsssssssssssst!"*

With one quick look, they disappeared.

I turned my attention back to the baby and considered the surroundings, I suppose in hopes that there'd be some explanation as to why the child was out here, alone.

Nothing.

It was possible that whoever was with the child could've been attacked by the three coyotes, but I doubted they could take down a grown adult that would've been carrying the baby. It didn't make sense. I could see the prints of only the four-legged animals.

I opened the child's blanket a bit more, trying to get some kind of clue as to how the baby had gotten here. On further examination with my top-notch detective skills, I confirmed that she was a girl.

Wrapping her back up against the cool night air, I touched her chin with my forefinger, and she smiled. "Well, you're the best behaved abandoned desert baby I've ever met."

I slipped one of the canteens from my shoulder and unscrewed the top, dribbling some water on my fingers and placing the tips at her mouth, watching as she swallowed. I repeated the technique a few times and then screwed the top back on and slung the strap over my shoulder.

Looking around again, I still thought I could smell the campfire, but the scent seemed to come from back where I'd been—the southeast. It was time to make a decision: I could either go looking for the source of the smoke or head back to the Travelall, but that would take an hour at least and I'd be facing that drive back up the mountain goat path where I'd come from.

Clicking my tongue, I called the hound over and headed in the direction of the smoke, carrying the baby cradled in my left arm and cooing at her. My pace was slower, but I seemed to be making good time, probably because I was distracted by talking to the baby. "So, where did you come from, little one?"

Dog trailed along beside me, looking up at her.

"Hopefully you weren't raised by coyotes, and we just broke up the family unit."

She said nothing but appeared to be enjoying our one-sided talk.

"I wasn't led here by a star, and I didn't see any three wisemen, so I guess you're up for grabs."

She remained silent, and I was getting worried that there might've been something wrong with her, but she gurgled a bit and continued smiling.

"Somebody out here is losing their mind not knowing where you are." I thought about raising the pistol and throwing out a few shots, the location of the child's parents superseding my dealings with the Order of the Red Gate. I'd even gone so far as to have my hand resting on the security strap of my holster, but I wasn't quite ready to make that move just yet.

Maybe the campfire smell would reveal a few answers, but what was I going to do if I met with Curruthers, Ravitch, and the rest of the Red Gate gang and still had the child?

I glanced down at the baby. "You, no matter how cute you are, you're going to turn out to be a problem."

I kept slogging along until the dunes appeared to level out a bit, revealing a more flattened basin where the sand gave way, or were so big that you couldn't tell one from the other.

Dog was keeping pace and would, every once in a while, move out ahead only to circle back until we caught up.

"You're doing twice the distance we are."

The smell from the campfire was growing stronger, and I paused for a moment thinking about what I wanted to do. It wasn't like I could leave a baby out here in the dunes, but who had in the first place? There should've been people looking for her—vehicles, lights, shouting, maybe even helicopters . . . But instead, there was nothing.

I hadn't seen any children in the Red Gate group when I'd caught up with them before, but that didn't mean there weren't any, and why would they have left a child out in the wilderness? It just didn't make any sense.

Beyond the sand there was some grandfather sage and dry grass that broke up the topography, and I could see one of those Forest Service signs beside a pullout at the end of a dead-end road.

I circled around and could see a sign that warned of hazards in the area, which portions of the dunes where you could use vehicles, as well as the locations of stock ponds that were placed strategically for livestock and wildlife. I couldn't for the life of me imagine what animals would voluntarily enter this sand anvil of hell—but then I remembered the coyotes. It also said there was a two-track road leading to Steamboat Mountain to the east, but that it was closed from May to July for big-game birthing areas.

I looked back down at the baby. "Is that what you are, a big-game birth?"

She gurgled some more and then curled in against my chest, closing her eyes.

"I know how you feel, kiddo."

There were poles sticking out of the ground ahead, defining an area where you could park, but there was nothing in the area but a Forest Service outhouse, a few picnic tables, and firepits.

I pulled the map from my pocket and thumbed it open, wondering why in the world someone would've sent me on the route they had, rather than navigate me here on the designated roads?

I stuffed the map back in my pocket and pulled the JugBug out, flipping it open and then holding it up so I could see the illuminated screen. I peered at the little hieroglyphics but couldn't tell if anything might indicate that there was service. Just to be sure, I hit the green button and held the phone to my ear where it did, unsurprisingly, nothing.

Sighing, I flipped the thing closed and pocketed it.

I skirted the parking area, continuing westward where the smell of smoke appeared to be coming from, the looming figure of the Boar's Tusk hanging over us like a giant hand driving up from the sand as if attempting to exit a lonely and sandy grave.

Dog moved out a little ahead but then stopped to look at me. "What?"

He turned back and took a few more steps, stopping once more.

I caught up with him, halting at a ridge overlooking a cul-de-sac that you'd never see if you hadn't stumbled onto it the same way I and Dog had.

There, at the far end of the small valley was the multicolored Blue Bird bus, a number of wall tents, and a few feeble fires burning where a scattered group of people lay wrapped in blankets and sleeping bags, apparently asleep.

"Well, that's about how my luck has been running." I glanced at Dog and then at the baby in my arms. "It isn't like I can leave you up here."

With a shrug, I started down the hill, thinking about what my next move might be.

There was a group over to the left, which was the farthest campfire out from the main cluster, and I figured I'd start there and work my way inward. The fires seemed to be scattered at intervals of about fifty yards. I wasn't sure why they were arranged in that manner, but it allowed me to approach without alerting the others.

About twenty yards away, I noticed that the group around this fire was a lot smaller than the others, kind of an outlier of the whole.

I stopped and studied the sleeping bodies, four in all.

One of them moved, and I thought I'd better start with that one or I'd just be dealing with all of them when the action started.

I sat the baby down and gestured for Dog to sit beside her, which he did. Moving in a little closer, I could see it was an older man with a shaved head, readjusting himself.

I'd just about reached him when he threw the blanket back, lowered the hood of his robe, and reached over, tossing a few pieces of firewood onto the flames with a flurry of sparks.

I froze behind him but he didn't move; he just sat there propped up on one arm as he studied the fire. I could see he had some sort of terrible chemical burn–like wounds on his forearms. I checked on the twosome I'd deposited about twenty yards behind me, only to turn back to find the man staring at me as if he wasn't sure whether I was really there.

Raising a hand to my face, I placed a forefinger over my lips and made a quiet shushing sound. He didn't move, so I took the last few steps toward him before kneeling down and whispering. "Howdy."

He looked terrified and his mouth moved a bit, but no words came out.

"There's no need to worry. I'm not going to hurt you."

Finally finding his voice, he spat a few words out. "I am Richard Zevin, the Keeper of the Light of the Second Quadrant. Who . . . who are you?"

Ignoring his question, I posited one of my own. "Glad to meet you Keeper of the Light, where's Zeno Carruthers?"

He gestured behind him. "They're in the bus, the Triad of Greatness always sleep in the bus."

"Triad of Greatness, huh?" I could see no lights in the vehicle and figured that was for the better. "What about Blair McGowan?"

"Who?"

"The postal worker."

He looked confused. "We have no postal workers here."

I shook my head at him, getting exact. "Part of the group, brunette with a silver stripe in her fifties, missing two toes on her left foot?"

He physically pulled back from me. "That woman, she's . . . She was taken."

"Taken where?"

"Next Level, she was taken above."

I stared at him, trying not to roll my eyes. "By Higgo One and the clam people?"

"The what?" His face took on an earnest look. "Are you of the Order, brother?"

"Um, sure." I looked around. "Hey, I don't suppose you'd like to lie back down and go to sleep?"

"Certainly, but I must tend the fire."

"Okay, Richard. You do that but keep it quiet, okay?" I stood and he looked past me to where Dog sat with the baby. "Is that a wolf?"

"No."

"There is prophecy of wolves."

"Yep, well, he's not a wolf."

He kept staring past me in a kind of a rapturous fit. "Is that the child?"

I quickly kneeled back down. "*The* child?"

"There is prophecy of the child returned."

I thought about it. "This child?"

"The Child of Prophecy."

"Yep, I got that." I gestured behind me. "You know about this child?"

He started to stand, and his voice grew louder. "The Child of Prophecy returned."

I placed a hand on his shoulder, settling him as a few of the others in the immediate area began moving. "Look, no offense, but if you say 'prophecy' one more time, I'm going to belt you—and keep your voice way down."

He continued to try and rise, almost shouting now. "The prophecy foretold; the child has returned from the wilderness!"

Clamping a hand over his mouth, I slammed him back on the ground and held him there, checking the area. Some of the others were moving but no one had sat up . . . yet. Leaning in close, I whispered in his face. "You need to shut up and not make a sound, do you hear me?"

His eyes widened and he said nothing.

"All right, I'm going to take my hand away, but when I do, I don't want you to say a word. I want you to just roll over and tend the fire, keep the light, or whatever it is you're doing. You got me?"

He slowly nodded his head, and I gradually took my hand away, pointing a finger at him just to emphasize my statement. When I completely released him, he did as I said and rolled back, watching the fire and not moving.

I stood and retreated to where Dog was with the baby, carefully lifting the child and winding my way between the fires toward the bus. Dog silently walked alongside me, but after a moment he stopped and turned.

I whispered to him. "What are you doing? Come on."

He didn't move and I stopped too, turning to find Richard Zevin standing in front of his fire, his thin body wrapped in a robe, the desert wind rustling the fabric like pages, his hand extended with a boney finger pointing directly at me.

I looked around, but no one else had stirred.

Starting back toward him, I watched as his mouth suddenly hung open and he screamed at the bottom, middle, and top of his lungs, the single word screeching like a bird of prey. "Prophecy!"

10

It was an eruption with the remaining individuals, about forty in all, jumping up in different states of alacrity, some simply rolling over while others leapt to their feet grabbing branches, shovels, rakes, and other implements.

With the half dozen fires only a quarter lit, the place rapidly turned to bedlam as people faced off with one another and with nothing in the darkness.

I figured the only place to go where there might be cover was the underside of the bus, which was still a good sixty yards away, but in the confusion was probably the only option I had of getting the child, myself, and Dog out of the way before they collectively figured out what was happening.

Running in that direction, I watched as lanterns were being lit inside the bus, and I just hoped I'd make it before any real obstruction presented itself. It was then that one did in the form of an octogenarian with what looked to be a shepherd's staff. Placing himself directly in my way, he began shouting gibberish as I decided to make use of my old offensive lineman days and pushed out a hand in chuck-and-duck form with the baby tucked away in the crook of my arm like an NCAA football.

I steamrolled over the old guy and watched as he bounced off somebody else and fell backward into the fire, where he leapt up, his gauzy robe having caught on fire as he ran toward the others, who were now getting to their feet and running away from him like, well . . . he was on fire.

The bus was looming out of the crowd now, and I aimed for the sweet spot between the wheel wells, finally ducking down as Dog made it before me.

The folding doors of the bus were opening as I slid underneath it, holding the child and turning on my hand and two knees, Dog joining me but at least able to stand underneath the undercarriage.

A set of muck boots stepped down first, quickly followed by two sets of cowboy boots, and I figured the Triad of Greatness had finally woken up and arrived.

Carruthers addressed the crowd, hushing them as they drew near, a few slowed down by helping the man that had partially caught fire. "Calm, my brethren! Calm . . . Can someone tell me what has happened?"

Recognizing the voice of the zealot I'd talked with by the fire, I listened as he began screeching in the same singsong voice. "Brothers and sisters, the Child of Prophecy has returned, the child has been returned to us!"

"Brother Zevin, what is it you speak of?"

His voice came closer. "The Child of Prophecy returned from the wilderness."

Carruthers sounded a bit doubtful but still asked. "How did this miracle happen, brother?"

"The child was returned by man and beast, a large man along with a pack of wolves came from the wilderness and made themselves known to me, it is the sign of prophecy, my brethren."

"If that be the case, then where are they, introduce them to us so that we all might exalt in our transition to the Next Level."

There was a wholly pregnant silence.

"I do not see the child or its deliverers anywhere among you, so where might they be?"

Zevin's voice wavered a bit in the next statement. "Why, I'm not sure . . . I know that the man came to our point of light as if signaled to be there and simply appeared from the air."

"And what did he look like?"

There was more silence.

"He, he looked like a . . . cowboy. At least he was wearing a cowboy hat."

There was more silence, even though I thought some of the others might speak up and corroborate what the man was saying, but evidently the darkness and confusion had been on my side.

"You mentioned a pack of wolves, brother. And where are they?"

"I . . . I . . ."

"And of importance above all, where is the child?"

There was so much silence even I felt sorry for the old guy.

Carruthers continued. "Brothers and sisters, I'm afraid that brother Zevin has had a vision in his slumbers, and it will remain to be seen if this is a revelation of things to come."

I watched as his muck boot feet took a few strides out toward the group before stopping amid them. "I, for one, hope this is a foreshadowing of things that are meant to pass. No one wishes this more than me, but I think we should return to our slumbers and rest in preparation for the trials to come in the morning. The time of transference is upon us, and we must meet it clear-eyed and with the conviction our salvation demands."

I watched as his rubber boots backed away from the group and toward the bus, almost to the point that, if I wanted, I could reach out and grab his ankles.

"Return to your slumbers, my brethren, and dream dreams of prophecy so that you might share them with all of us."

I watched as the group disbanded, shuffling off into the night and to their communal fires as I pulled the child up, giving her a quick once-over just to make sure she was still conscious. The bright eyes were there looking back at me, and I had to admit I was a little amazed. "You are the quietest child I've ever met."

She gurgled a bit in response, but that was all.

Above, I could hear Carruthers, Freebee, and Lowell as they began talking in low voices among themselves in a very different tone than the one Carruthers had used with his followers.

Freebee was the first to speak. "The fuck, boss?" Carruthers remained silent as Freebee continued grumbling. "How in the hell did he find us? Do you think it was her?"

Carruthers finally spoke. "Someone is going to have to go check and see if the child is still there."

"Out there in the dark?" Freebee barked a laugh. "That kid is gone, we heard coyotes yipping all over the place."

Carruthers wasn't swayed. "Someone needs to check, and I'll speak with Blair."

"You don't think the body fooled them?"

The boss sighed. "If it is him out there, it didn't fool him."

"Why the hell not?"

"I don't know, but if it is him out there, we may have to up our game. Besides who else travels with a wolf?"

"Zevin said 'a pack of wolves.'"

"Zevin, as we know, has a tendency to fabricate." He lowered his voice. "They're becoming too active, so we're going to have to make sure we dose them in the morning."

Freebee stood, and I listened as his steps approached the front of the bus. "So you think this could all be bullshit?"

"We won't know until we find the child and I speak with Blair."

Freebee's voice called from the folding door as it opened. "I'll go, but I'm not going alone."

Lowell's tromping boots answered.

I watched as they trooped down the steps, heading in the direction of the dunes to the north. The way I figured it, they would reach the area where the baby had been left in less than an hour, but would they notice the tracks and follow them back to my vehicle or return to report to Carruthers?

Either way, I only had so much time.

I couldn't leave the baby under the bus—besides negligence, it was possible she'd be found again, and who knows what they'd do with her this time? But what was I going to do if I had to confront these idiots with a baby in my arms? It wasn't a situation to be envied, but it was pretty much all I had.

Five minutes or so later, I could hear Carruthers doing something in the bus, but I wasn't sure what. A few more minutes after that and I heard him get up from his seat and walk toward the front of the bus, even though it seemed as if he was taking his time. He walked down the steps of the bus and immediately took a left, going around the front and off between some juniper trees and a break in the dune field.

Moving out from under the bus on the other side, I stood, happy to straighten out my back. Dog followed as we waited a moment and then headed in the direction Carruthers had disappeared.

It was easy to follow his sandal prints in the moonlight as our unlikely trio continued after him, and it wasn't much of a surprise that he didn't go far. I wasn't sure where we would find Blair McGowan, but chained to a tree wouldn't have been my bet.

It was a Rocky Mountain juniper on the edge of the dunes, the sand having poured off and around the thing. The tree itself was a good twenty feet tall with a twisted and singular trunk that allowed for the chain wrapped around its base. The other end ran to what looked to be a manacle bound to Blair McGowan's ankle.

She sat at the foot of the tree, back in her robe and muck boots, a short distance away from the trunk. The prints around her gave a pretty good indication of what the limits of her mobility were. I also noticed that Carruthers was careful to not get anywhere near where she might be able to get ahold of him.

I pulled up at the nearest dune, peering through a couple of the stunted relatives of the juniper, then motioning for Dog to come sit with the child and me as we watched the odd homecoming take place.

Carruthers knelt just out of reach. "Blair?"

She didn't move.

"Blair, I need to talk to you."

I was amazed how well his voice carried in the dry air of the desert night. After a moment, her head rose, and I was stunned at her condition. Her hair was wild and there were dark circles under her eyes, her complexion sallow and her lips dried and chapped, her shaking hands folded in her robe. "I . . ." Her voice cracked. "I'm going to kill you."

"No, you're not." He breathed a laugh. "You're not going to do any such thing."

She croaked out the next words. "I swear to God I'm going to kill you."

Ignoring her, he continued. "We need to talk."

"I'm done talking with you."

Realizing this might take longer than he'd first surmised, he leaned over and sat. "He's here, or at least we think he is."

She cleared her throat and then sat there, trying as she could to not engage with him but finally giving up and asking. "Who?"

"Your friend, the sheriff."

For the first time, she smiled. "You're here because you're scared."

"Excuse me?"

"It's all going to fall apart; it's all going to fall apart and you're going to prison—that is, if he doesn't beat me to it and kill you himself."

He drew a handful of sand in his fist. "Funny, he doesn't strike me as a killer."

"You're not the first dead man to think that."

"Why would he kill me, Blair?"

She laughed this time, and it was harsh. "Don't forget, I know where all the bodies are buried."

He nodded his head, staring at his hand as he opened his fingers, allowing the sand to pour out. "Not all of them."

"Where's Penelope?"

His head rose and he looked at her. "I knew we'd get to that."

"Where is she?"

"We're checking on her."

"We?"

"Freebee and Lowell."

"You're letting those maniacs care for her?"

I looked down at the child in my arm, whispering. "I think they're talking about you, and you have a name, Penelope." She smiled and gurgled again as I threw my focus back at the two near the tree.

Carruthers stood. "To get what we want in life, we sometimes have to make sacrifices."

"Not sacrifices like this, and not unless you're a complete and utter psychopath."

He began pacing at the outer extremity of her chain length. "I know we have differences concerning my methods."

"How much more money do you think you can choke out of those poor, drugged people?"

He looked at her. "As much as I need."

She stood, holding part of the robe in her hand, and I noticed she was also wearing handcuffs. "There's never enough, I know that about you. I've seen you in action and I know there is no limit to what you'll do or who you'll sacrifice to do it."

"That's not true."

She rattled the cuffs, the chain swaying back to the trunk as she walked toward him. "Then why am I chained to a tree?"

"You've become unreliable in the last few months."

She reached the end of her tether and then stood there about a yard away, looking at him. "You mean 'unusable,' don't you? 'Cause that's pretty much the way you work; if someone is no longer of use then they don't really exist for you, do they?"

He stood there looking at her, saying nothing.

"I thought there were limits; I thought there were things even *you* wouldn't do, but now I see there really isn't anything you won't do, is there?" She shook her head. "My God, what kind of creature are you?"

He was about to say something in return when she produced a fist-size rock from the folds of her robe and threw it from point-blank range at his head.

He turned but the thing caught him on the temple, and I watched as he stumbled backward, falling to the ground. Even in that state he knew he was in trouble and began crawling away, holding his head where blood dripped between his fingers.

Leaping forward, she reached the length of her chain, which yanked her ankle back, but she was still able to get ahold of one of his feet and drag him toward her. His rubber boot pulled off in her hands as he moaned and feebly kicked at her, but she now had a grip on his robe and was desperately attempting to drag him to within her reach.

Realizing what was happening, he fought harder, even going so far as to use both hands in an attempt to get free.

The blood was pouring from the side of his head, and I was amazed that he was still able to put out that much effort.

He kicked harder, but she had a good grip on the robe now and was making headway in dragging him into her reach—and she might've made it too, except for his hand finding the rock where it fell. Sitting up, he grabbed the thing and began striking at her hand as she attempted to get her other hand on him.

Hers was a powerful effort, but he continued to pound at her, and she finally had to give up, falling in a heap, where she lay there screaming.

He touched his bleeding head again and kicked at her one last time. He even thought about throwing the rock at her but then wisely reconsidered. Dragging himself farther away, he sat there breathing heavily and mopping his head with part of his robe, the amount of blood making him look like a stuck pig.

Her screaming had subsided to a moaning, choking sound as she gave up all hope.

"Look at this mess! How am I going to explain this?"

Ignoring him, she lay there with her hair covering her face, the noises now gradually dying down as her strength faded.

After a while, he pulled his legs under him and attempted to stand but didn't have very much luck. He sat with one arm out for support, breathing heavily. Bringing his hand up, he stared at the rock. "I guess we should've checked the area a little more closely. I'm assuming you don't have anything else, or you would've used it on me?"

She raised her head, her face still covered by her hair as she screamed at him again, and threw the muck boot, which bounced off his shoulder and made him flinch.

He took a deep breath and stopped dabbing his wound long enough to slip the boot back on as he tried to stand. It was wobbly, but he made it this time, standing there breathing heavily as he placed a hand on his knee, holding his head. "I'd forgotten how strong you are."

Screaming at him again, she grabbed two handfuls of dirt and flung them at him.

He finally straightened and took a step before shaking his head and looking back at her. "I hate for it to end like this, but with the irreconcilable issues between us, I suppose there isn't any other way."

She screamed again, but the sound faded into words, screeching from her dry throat. "I'm going to kill you—I swear to God I'm going to kill you, old man."

He turned fully to face her, wiping more blood from his head as he laughed. "And what god is that, my dear?" He took a step toward her and then stopped, realizing he was getting a bit too close. "In all our time together, I would've hoped that you would've realized by now that there is no God."

She cleared her throat, spitting and pulling the hair away so that he could see her face. "We'll see how you feel about that when I get my fingers around your throat."

He glanced around. "Alas, within the context of your current situation, I don't see that happening."

They stayed like that, neither of them moving, until finally he turned and began walking away, continuing to dab at his bloody head.

Watching him go, she finally collapsed on the ground and lay still.

Dog, of course, got there first and her response was predictable.

She screamed again and quickly scooched away, raising her arms in defense of the wild animal attack I'm sure she thought was imminent. Instead, Dog looked at me and then back to her again, sitting with tail in full wag.

I shifted the child in my arms and swung one of the canteens around, spinning off the top and holding it to Blair's lips.

Forgetting everything else, she weakly supported the thing as she gulped.

"Easy. Go easy or you'll just throw it all back up." Swooning, she fell back as I lowered the canteen and propped her up with my free arm. "Take it easy and just breathe."

She lay there for a moment and then her eyes flickered open and focused on me. "You."

"Yep, me."

Her hand fumbled up. "More water."

"Sure." Releasing her, I helped to bring the canteen strap over my head and handed it to her. "Easy with that. It's all we've got till we get back to your truck; that is, if the coyotes don't drink it all."

Swallowing, she gazed around, focusing on Dog, who sat beside me. "Your dog."

"Yep." I gestured toward the bundle in my arm. "And I believe you know this little one here?"

Her eyes widened and then she took the baby from me, cradling who I assumed was Penelope in her arms and began wildly sobbing again.

Glancing around, I wanted to make sure Carruthers hadn't circled back, or that anybody else hadn't shown up after all the commotion. "Funny the things you stumble onto out here in the desert, huh?"

She croaked. "You found her."

"I did. She wasn't in a basket of reeds in a river. Is that standard treatment of infants in the Order of the Red Gate, to leave them abandoned in the dunes?"

"She was being sacrificed."

I reached into my pocket and I pulled out my keys to quickly unlock her cuffs, looking at her raw wrists where the things had chafed and bitten into her. I tried a key and finagled it in the manacle hole, finally hearing a click as it fell open from her bleeding ankle. "All right, but we better get moving before they come back."

She shook her head. "He's not coming back; they left me here to die."

Gathering her shoulders, I began lifting her onto her feet. "You can tell me all about it, but we better get moving."

She took a few steps with me, but I could tell she was having trouble supporting her own weight after all the exertion. "Are you going to be able to make it?"

"Where are we going?"

"Back to your truck; the route that was on your map."

"I hoped Tess would get it to you."

Peering back past the biblical-looking lone tree, I shook my head. "We could take the main road, but we don't have a vehicle, and they'd eventually catch up with us."

She stood next to me. "They won't catch up with us going this way?"

"I don't think so. They suspect I'm here and that I might've taken Penelope, but they don't know for sure and if they don't come back to check on you, they aren't going to have any idea where I'm going or where I came from."

She looked down at our tracks in the sand. "What about the prints?"

"They don't strike me as the most perceptive trackers of all time. Besides, once they figure out what's going on they'll have to play catch-up." I looked down at the baby in her arms, watching as she wet her fingers and held them to the child's lips. "Say, does Penelope, here, ever make a noise?"

She hugged the child closer. "Chronic absence seizure."

"And what's that?"

"She was traumatized at an early age, which caused these seizures.

Typically they're longer and more infrequent, but hers are shorter and happen more often; it's like she starts to make a sound but then everything shuts down." She handed me back the canteen. "The doctors say she'll likely grow out of it and be fine."

"How do you know so much about it?"

"She's my granddaughter."

"Excuse me?"

"It's a long story . . ."

I caught her arm as she slipped on the slope of sand, finally taking Penelope from her. "Well, it appears that we have plenty of time."

She clung to my arm as we topped the dune, looking out at the vastness of the nighttime Red Desert landscape. "Carruthers wanted my help with the whole Red Gate scam and when I refused, he sent that maniac Freebee out to kidnap Penelope."

"In Sacramento."

"Yeah, and even after I agreed, he wouldn't give her back."

We trudged along as I kept an eye out to make sure we weren't going to bump into the Red Gate group, but the chances were slim as far south as we were. Looking up, I spotted the cleft in the towering rock ridge to the north, giving me a good angle of trajectory that would lead us to the Travelall. "So, who got here to Wyoming first?"

"Me. I was just trying to get away from all the crazy crap, but when Carruthers found out about the Red Desert and the Boar's Tusk, it just fit his cult scenario too well. So, he followed me here."

"Correct me if I'm wrong, but the scam is to get elderly people to give up their worldly goods and then follow him out into the wilderness where Higgo One and the clam people will beam them aboard and take them to the Higher Place, or whatever it is?"

"Next Level, but they dropped Higgo One and the clam people thing; now it's just celestial angels."

"Right." I watched as Dog easily climbed the next dune, looking at us from his vantage point of four legs. "The TV show thing you did . . ."

She shook her head, softly laughing. *"Mysteries from Beyond."*

"Didn't you kind of hatch this thing?"

"You have to understand what the television industry is like; you get a call from someone that says you can make five hundred bucks in an afternoon by coming in and recording some shit. It's like these reality shows . . . I mean do you really believe this crap is happening spontaneously with three cameras and an entire crew watching? Or the guy that's out in the wilderness fighting for his life in the Amazon basin? Who's filming it? There isn't much reality in reality TV."

"Got it."

"So, Carruthers asked me to do that show and they gave me some talking points to just make a bunch of shit up, which I did, and then these Red Gate people took it and ran with it." She stopped to take a breath. "You'd be amazed how many people believe something just because it got on TV."

I took another scan of the horizon, thinking I heard something but once again not seeing anything. "Maybe not."

"Anyway, Carruthers started using that show on DVD and the internet as a recruiting tool."

"This is after his time in prison or before?"

"Both, he just refined it after he got out, really focusing on the retirees."

"And he followed you all the way to Wyoming?"

"Yes."

I gently jostled the baby. "How did he know about Penelope here?"

"He learns everything he can about you and then uses it to get what he wants. He was an actor, you know."

"What's that mean?"

"He has these personas that he uses. I mean, he can be anything he needs to be to get what he wants, and he's absolutely ruthless."

I gestured with the child again. "Why did he leave Penelope out there in the desert for the coyotes?"

"Prophecy."

"That, again . . ."

She looked at me sideways as we tromped on. "What?"

"I stumbled onto their camp after I found Penelope and had a conversation with one of the true believers and he kept talking about the Child of Prophecy."

She nodded. "Yeah, he trained them good. The Child of Prophecy was in the original horseshit and when he had Penelope, the followers just assumed that this was the child." She slipped again and I caught her arm. "The Child of Prophecy is supposed to be this transitional embodiment of the elemental change that the church members are supposed to undergo. The Child of Prophecy is supposed to be the final signal that the Order of the Red Gate is ready to be transferred to the Next Level."

"He just stuck her out there for the animals?"

"Pretty much."

"That's why you drew the map the way you did, to bring me in where the baby had been left?"

She stopped again. "It was a calculated guess, but I knew that was going to be his endgame. So, I left the note under one of the green rocks in hopes that Tess would get it to you."

"Well, she got it to Benny who got it to me."

"IQ-wise, it's almost like giving it to someone without a brain."

"I have a hard time arguing that point."

"So, what's your plan?"

I laughed and continued on, knowing we only had a certain amount of time until sunup.

"You have a plan, right?"

"In a way . . . I figure we've removed all the innocents from the group and my job now is to get you two to safety and then call in Sheriff Grossnickle and let him and the cavalry do the cleanup."

She looked at the sand, shifting with the wind underneath our feet.

"What?"

"They're not bad people."

"Who?"

"The followers, they're just gullible and looking for something meaningful in their lives."

"They won't be hurt, but what Carruthers and the other two are doing is worse—it's criminal."

She sighed. "It's more than that."

"Meaning?"

"He's gotten kind of desperate in the last few weeks."

I stopped. "Yep?"

"He's got some medical complications, and I know he's been talking to some doctors in Salt Lake City." She looked away, continuing the battle with the wind in keeping her hair from her face. "Whenever the members run out of money, they basically just take them out in the desert and kill them." Her eyes met mine. "They just tell the others that they achieved Next Level and have gone on."

"How many?"

"I don't know . . . dozens?"

Standing at the top of another dune, I listened and looked around. "If they get hemmed in, surely they wouldn't kill the rest."

She didn't answer.

"Would he?"

"I believe he would, yes."

Thinking I heard something again, I glanced at Dog, who stood on the next dune, looking off to our right and the area where I'd heard a noise. "Well, that doesn't change the first part of the mission, which is getting you and Penelope out of here."

"Then what?"

"I'm not quite sure." Continuing, I measured the distance to the cleft and felt reasonably sure that we'd make it back to the vehicle in less than an hour. "But it may have to be something drastic in nature."

I took a swig from the canteen and then shook it to get an idea of how much water was left, concluding that it wasn't much. Lowering the thing, I looked over Blair's head to where Dog was watching to the northeast, listening to the warbling, ghostlike sound.

"Coyotes?"

"Yep." I nodded toward the behemoth. "I'd like to take the credit, but he's the one that saved your granddaughter when the prairie poodles were getting ready to make a meal out of her." Stopping, I listened again.

She stared up at me and then in the direction of Dog's attention. "Something?"

"Yep, we've both been hearing noises in that direction, but maybe it's just the coyotes. Nonetheless, we better keep moving."

We crossed over a few more dunes and finally got to a spot where I could see the Travelall, parked only a little distance away from the two-track, exactly where I'd left it. The tailgate was still down and as near as I could tell nothing had been bothered. Stepping forward, I tripped over an old Marathon oil can, the five-gallon size from more than a half century ago, finally catching myself and giving it a kick before continuing toward the truck. "Well, that's a welcome sight."

She went so far as to smile as we made our way diagonally across the flat, harder ground. "I love that truck."

Dog leapt up on the tailgate, lapping up some of the water I had left as Blair sat, now holding the baby. "How was the road?"

"Scary as hell."

She actually laughed. "That's why nobody uses it; it's a goat path, really."

Refilling the canteen, I also took out the rucksack I'd thrown in the back, pulling out some beef jerky and some chips and handing them to her. "How do you feel?"

She tore open the bag and stuffed a handful of Fritos into her mouth, speaking through the food. "Better, now."

I scanned the horizon with my old Vietnam binoculars. "Good enough to drive?"

"Sure. I'm tired, but I'm okay."

Lowering the glasses, I sighed. "That's good, because they're coming."

She stood, glancing in the direction where I'd been looking. "You're kidding."

I brought the binoculars back up, but now couldn't see anything. "I wish I was, but there are two of them with flashlights. They just dropped off one of the dunes, but I'd estimate they'll be here in about twenty minutes." I lowered the glasses again. "You better get out of here."

I helped her load Penelope in the passenger seat, bolstered with a packing blanket. I then emptied the water back into the canteens and poured the dog food back in the bag, sealing it and piling the stuff on the seat.

With a deep sigh, I reached to the side and grabbed my shooting jacket and then carefully pulled a soft rifle case from the compartment in the back of the Travelall, unzipping the oiled canvas from the weapon and throwing the cover back into the truck.

"What's that?"

I handed it to her as I put on the jacket, then took it back and held the elongated, vintage piece up to where the moonlight gleamed off the surface and the owl feathers drifted in the slight desert breeze.

I still stood in awe of the Cheyenne Rifle of the Dead. "I call it 'emphasis.'"

"Looks old."

"It is."

"What are all the beads and feathers and shit?"

"Previous owners." Pulling the lever down near the beaded Dead Man's Pattern beadwork, I made sure the artillery was unloaded before reaching in and grabbing a fistful of ammunition from a range bag and dropping the bunch into my shirt pockets.

"What are you going to do with that?"

"They want to play, we'll play . . . Should buy me some time, and you."

I pushed a startled Dog back, shut the tailgate, and cranked the back window up. The beast stood there looking at me as I handed the keys to Blair. "Take the monster with you and get the hell out of here and don't look back. When you get topside on the ridge, circle back around on the BLM road to Chilton Road, there's a Forest Ranger there . . ."

She nodded. "Rick Scout Traveler."

I smiled. "I keep forgetting, you know this place like your two missing toes. Get to Ranger Rick and have him call in Grossnickle and the troops, pronto."

She climbed in and I closed the door. "When I start this thing, they're going to hear it and see the headlights."

I glanced back at the dunes. "Yep, they are."

"You got a plan for that?"

I saw the beams from the flashlights casting over the next dune. "There's always a plan for that—kind of Cain versus Abel."

"And which one are you?"

"We'll see." I stepped back and threw the strap of the rucksack onto my shoulder as she hit the starter and fired up the powerful V8. "Just one more quick question?"

She pulled the thing in gear and leaned out the window, looking at me. "Yeah?"

"Getting you to do that goofy TV show, following you to Wyoming to set up his crazy cult here in the Red Desert, kidnapping your granddaughter to sacrifice, and tying you to a tree—what's the connection between you and Carruthers?"

Her face took on a sad look. "He's my father."

I watched as she hit the gas and sped toward the incline, disappearing behind a cornice and the switchback, comfortably out of the range of the oncoming six-guns that were bound to be accompanying the jostling flashlights that moved steadily toward me from the dunes.

11

If I was to withdraw farther into the canyon, I'd be covered on both sides. I figured they wouldn't bother taking potshots at the retreating Travelall, which had already made the cornice and was slowly picking its way up the two-track goat path. I moved to the right in hopes of drawing them in that direction and watched as the flashlights bumped along about a quarter mile away.

There were a few higher spots in the canyon where I'd have a better vantage point, but who was I kidding? With the monstrosity I held in my hands I could shoot against a couple of wheel guns until the cows came home and then away to cow college.

I chose a copse of junipers near the base of the cliff where a shelf jutted out to a point and was partially covered. For the life of me, I couldn't imagine a better spot to lie down and wait.

I noticed that the shelf was much lower farther into the canyon. I walked the thick stratum of rock, moving in and out of sight behind the stunted trees where the vegetation had taken advantage of what little moisture there was in the arid plain as it brushed up against the wall.

I arrived at my chosen spot and knelt down, looking out at the flashing lights as they reached the smaller dunes.

They weren't following our track from the camp, and so they

must've come from the direction of where Dog had found the baby and then followed our tracks back to here.

I figured I'd give them the smallest possible target and assumed the most supportable prone position to begin assembling my defense, lining the rounds almost as long as my little finger along the edge but far enough away so as to not get in my way.

I loaded the Sharps .45-70 and then slipped off my jacket and folded it, laying the big rifle on the cloth and admiring the cold-blooded beast. I had shot the thing only a handful of times, but there are some weapons that become symbiotic, almost an extension of yourself.

Lonnie Little Bird and Henry said it was haunted, the Cheyenne Rifle of the Dead, but I didn't believe in ghosts—but the Bear said that didn't mean that the Old Cheyenne didn't believe in me.

Looking up at the massive constellations of the endless cosmos, I laughed. "I'd just as soon not kill anybody tonight, but if you could assist me in putting the fear of whichever gods happen to be around, I'd appreciate it."

I flipped the rear site to adjust it, but not too much in that there wasn't a great deal of atmospheric effect with which to contend. Just to be sure, I plucked a few needles off the nearest branch and held them up, dropping them and watching them fall straight down.

No crosswind, at least not here inside the mouth of the box canyon.

As near as I could figure there was a three- to five-mile-per-hour northwest-to-southeast breeze outside.

I gauged the distance at just over two hundred and fifty yards and smiled as I made the adjustment, wondering to myself what Americans would do for measurement if we didn't have football fields. I settled in and waited, raising my binoculars to my eyes and searching the area before the dunes.

It didn't take long to find them with the way they were waving their flashlights around. Freebee was in the lead as Lowell followed a bit behind with a bag slung over his shoulder, shining the beam of his light to the left and right.

I didn't want to shoot them if I didn't have to, even after the things that Blair had told me, preferring to bring them signed, sealed, and delivered to justice—but as the saying goes, there's no second place in a gunfight.

I tucked the stock against my shoulder and peered through the rear site, over the front, and zeroed in on the two shadowy figures just over two hundred yards away.

It was about then that I caught sight of the Marathon oil can that I'd tripped over, sitting upright about sixty yards in front of them, and figured it was time to issue a salutation.

Sighting in, I squinted into the darkness, pulling the hammer back on the big drop block.

There are a lot of theories on shooting, but the one I remember getting from my father was probably the most helpful: Wait until you feel it. The sense memory of the human mind and body is a remarkable thing and played a role in most of the more amazing actions I've accomplished in any physical sense in my life. I'd be hard-pressed to tell you how I did them. The argument could be made that it's just a case of hand-eye coordination or pure luck, but I like to think it's more than that. Any capable athlete would laugh in your face if you said it was only the two.

There's a moment—and if you're attuned to it, you can feel it when it arrives. There are ways to coerce it with breathing and the like, but in the end it's all timing and patience.

I pulled the set trigger and moved my forefinger to the next, feeling the smoothness of the machined metal of the Sharps Business Rifle.

There's a voice I hear in these moments, echoing down the hallowed halls of familial time.

Wait.

A familiar voice, low and steady.

Wait.

A voice that has never failed me.

Wait.

One of the voices that begat me.

Now.

Gently squeezing the trigger, I felt as the wooden stock kicked and watched the can fly into the air.

Thanks, Dad.

I drew the binoculars to my eyes and could see the two more clearly now. They didn't move as the can fell to the ground after having flown a good ten feet in the air, and I didn't blame them. With the distance, it was likely that the can had jumped before they heard the shot, which sounded like thunder echoing from the canyon.

"What was that?"

Freebee's voice carried pretty well in the dry desert air, but I wasn't tempted to reply.

"Did you see that?" He turned to look at his partner, who predictably said nothing.

I set the binoculars aside and dropped the breechblock with the lever, picking out the spent shell and then inserting another round, bringing the hammer back to prepare to fire.

They still weren't moving, which was fine by me in that all I was doing was trying to eat up time until the cavalry showed up.

"Was that a shot?"

I let them think about it for a while, but when Freebee started for the can, I figured I better reintroduce myself. What the hell else was I going to shoot, the sand?

Focusing, I took aim at the can again as he approached it, letting him get about six feet away before squeezing the second trigger and watching the can go tumbling toward him. Even with the roar of the rifle I was pretty sure that he yelped as he skittered away from the thing as if it were alive and wanting to attack him.

Pulling up the binoculars again, I focused on his angry face as he scanned his eyes across the cliff, looking for me high and low.

"Recompense to no man evil for evil . . ." When I didn't respond, he added. "I suppose you think this is funny, huh?"

I still didn't answer, learning a long time ago that not knowing was the worst.

He raised the pistol in the air. "I can throw a few shots your way, if you'd like."

It was possible he could hit me, but with the effective range of his pistol being less than a quarter of that of the Sharps's, it would have to be the shot of a lifetime with a trajectory of a rainbow, and I didn't think he had it in him.

"For the wrath of man worketh not the righteousness of God." He holstered the pistol and shouted. "Look, Sheriff . . . Yeah, we did a little research on you." He smiled, still looking around, finally walking over to the can and kicking it. "What do you say we just call her quits and go our separate ways?"

I quietly dropped the breechblock and pulled out the spent brass, inserting another round. I closed the lever and pulled the hammer back, but then laid it on its side on my jacket to pull up the binoculars so I could get a better look as he tried to make up his mind about what to do next.

He looked a little more nervous and then shouted. "Never take your own revenge, for it is written that vengeance is mine and I will repay, sayeth the Lord!"

Playing the binoculars about, I couldn't see his friend Lowell.

I swept the area at the bottom of the dunes, especially the spot where he'd been standing behind his friend, but couldn't see anything other than a set of footprints that looked like he might've backtracked into the dunes. Widening the area, I tried to see if he'd found some way to flank me, but I didn't even see prints indicating as to how he could've gotten any closer.

Maybe he had turned back.

Smart man.

Sitting up, I looked toward the interior of the box canyon and the road that curved to the right and continued upward, but there was no one there. Turning the other way, I could see where the ledge I was on continued to angle upward, but the drop-off was particularly sheer. I was sure a person could get up that way, but it would be dangerous and time-consuming, something I wouldn't want to face with the business end of a large caliber rifle pointing at me.

"For if ye forgive men their trespasses, the heavenly Father will also forgive you. But if ye forgive men not their trespasses, neither will your Father forgive you."

"How about I just shoot you to shut you up?" I'd figured what the hell, talking to him was only going to slow him down.

He froze, but then a thin smile crept across his face. "Well, howdy!"

"Where's your friend?"

"Oh, he's around." He still cast his eye about the area, the echo from the canyon making it hard to pin down exactly where I was. "Say, why don't you come on out here and we'll discuss this like reasonable people?"

"I'm kind of comfortable where I am, thanks."

He crossed his arms, shaking his head. "I don't think you're going to shoot me, Sheriff."

"You can think that, if you want."

He threw out his hands. "Now, why would you want to kill me?"

"Why wouldn't I?"

He nudged the can with the toe of his boot. "You're the one who took the baby, right?"

"Yep."

"Got her with you?"

"Maybe."

"I doubt it." He glanced to his right and upward. "Unless I'm mistaken, the taillights we saw were that old International with Sister Blair at the wheel." He paused, considering the situation. "Hey, just so you know, that's a family deal. I don't have anything to do with that."

"Who does?"

"Carruthers, that's his thing."

"Killing children?"

"Oh, he wasn't going to kill her, she's his great-granddaughter for goodness sake."

"You could've fooled me when I barely got there in time to keep the coyotes from tearing her to pieces."

His head dropped as he did his best to sound apologetic. "Yeah, that one might've gotten away from us . . ."

"The three of you went to bed."

"Look, I'm not defending his actions . . ."

"Then defend your own."

There was some noise from behind him as I watched Lowell Ommen return from the dunes with another man who I recognized as the one I'd awakened when I'd entered the compound, Keeper of the Light of the Second Quadrant, Richard Zevin.

Freebee turned back from watching their approach, the smile back on his face. "I don't think I'm going to have to."

Lowell pushed the elderly man in front of him until he stumbled and fell alongside the other gunman, visibly weeping. "Richard here is from up near Evanston, and you two have met, right?"

I didn't answer.

Placing his hands on his hips, he looked at the man and then back at me. "Richard here knows this desert like the back of his hand, and he's been really helpful in our time around these parts." He pulled the Colt Peacemaker from his holster, half-cocking the hammer and spinning the cylinder on the sleeve of his shirt before turning and aiming it at the back of the sobbing man's head. "And now I'm going to shoot him."

I studied him through the binoculars a good long time before countering. "You do, and I shoot you."

He cocked his head. "Really?"

"Yep."

He gestured with the pistol. "I shoot him, you shoot me, and then Lowell here takes a shot at you? That's a lot of shooting." He glanced down at the elderly man who continued to sob, silently. "What if somebody misses?"

"If I can hit a five-gallon oil can from this distance, I can most indubitably hit you."

"I suppose that's true, but I don't think I can miss Mister Zevin from this distance, either."

I waited a moment and then responded. "Then the question becomes whether or not Lowell there can hit me, which I doubt."

"Lowell's a pretty good shot with that big Smith and Wesson of his."

"Then maybe I should shoot you first."

"That won't help Mister Zevin."

"Maybe, maybe not."

"The thing is, Sheriff, we've got a nearly inexhaustible supply of victims to haul over here and shoot. Granted, we had Richard here to help us navigate so he's kind of handy, and one of us would have to go fetch anybody else and bring back . . ."

"Nonetheless, you shoot him, and I shoot you, and I'm betting I can also shoot Lowell there before he can get back into those dunes."

"So, Mister Zevin here will be dead, but so will Lowell and me?"

"That's the equation, as simple as it is."

"And you walk away?"

"Oh, I won't be walking away. My next step after dispatching the two of you will be to head over to your compound and round up Carruthers and wait for the cavalry to arrive."

He continued to smile. "And what cavalry would that be? The one Blair is supposed to fetch?"

"Among others, your world is about to become very small, Freebee."

"What if that cavalry you're waiting on isn't coming?"

"Meaning?"

"What if I told you we had somebody up there to intercept Blair? That'd be a whole new cup of tea, now wouldn't it?"

"I don't believe you."

"It doesn't matter if you do or not, nobody's coming." He nudged Zevin's head with the muzzle of the pistol. "*Now*, what's the equation?"

"Same as it was before, you shoot him, and I shoot you—no matter what else happens, you die."

That information seemed to shake him just a bit. "What if you just wound me?"

"This weapon I'm holding will drop a horse at five hundred yards. I'm pretty sure that wherever it hits you, the damage will be substantial enough that if you do survive, at best you'll be crawling—and I call that a slow-moving target."

"But Richard here will be dead and that'll be your fault."

"No, if you pull the trigger his blood will be on your hands, but you'll be putting into action a chain of events that will result in me fulfilling my sworn duty to serve and to protect, which will bring about the deaths of you and your friend."

"So, our blood will be on your hands?"

"By doing my duty, yep."

"Your duty?" He shook his head as if not quite believing what I was saying. "But Mister Zevin will still be just as dead, so what do you gain by shooting us?"

"You won't ever kill anybody again."

"Hypothetically, but that doesn't help us with this standoff, now does it." Raising the pistol, he lowered the hammer. "Hey, do you have that .45 of yours handy? How about we make a deal?"

"Such as?"

"Let's go at this mano a mano. We'll let Mister Zevin go and you just come down here and have a gunfight with one of us just like in the movies."

"Now why would I want to do that when I've pretty much got you right where I want you?"

"Why, Mister Zevin, here." He gestured toward the elderly man, who had now raised his head and was looking up at him. "He can either run off or head back over to the brethren, and then we can settle our differences."

"That would take a certain amount of trust on my part."

"Yes, it would, but either way Richard here lives."

It was about then that Zevin, sensing this might be his only chance, leapt up and ran toward me. Dropping the binoculars, I lifted the Sharps and tried to aim as Freebee pulled his pistol from the holster and began aiming it at the fleeing man.

Zevin had just cleared me a shot at Freebee when I pulled the trigger and watched in shock as he took that moment to suddenly raise his hands. I'm not sure if he was confirming to me that he wasn't attacking me, or if he did it in hopes that the two gunmen might not shoot him if he did, but the result was horrifying. The large round clipped the two fingers on the elderly man's hand, completely removing one as the round continued on, slapping into the side of Freebee's love handle and spinning him around like a dervish before he collapsed in the sand.

Jacking the lever, I plucked out the round and slid in another, pulling the block back up and thumbing the hammer back. Focusing on the second gunman, Lowell, I could still see Zevin struggling forward as he held his mangled hand to his chest, the blood soaking his white robe.

Lowell, as near as I could tell, hadn't moved, but upon seeing the elderly captive making a break for it, finally lifted the big Russian Model from his holster and took aim.

I fired.

Maybe it was because I'd clipped Zevin in the hand, or possibly because I'd overcompensated for the extra distance to the second man, but the round literally blew the hat off Lowell's head. It must've struck a little bit of his skull as his head snapped back, summersaulting him backward, with the Smith flying in the air.

Reloading as quickly as I could, I sited back in on Freebee to make sure he wasn't going to make any action, but he lay there unmoving, giving the impression that I might've hit him better than I thought I had.

Lowering the rifle just a bit, I watched as Zevin ran to the flatter, hard ground and stumbled forward, falling and then getting back up. Struggling to hold his wounded hand, I watched as he began to sway a bit, and knew I was going to have to go down and get him.

I set the Cheyenne Rifle of the Dead back on my jacket and patted it. "Not your fault, old girl."

I picked up the rucksack and canteen and hustled my way down the rock ledge to where it stopped behind some more of the junipers, hopping down as the elderly man came into sight and then tripped. Zevin fell forward, momentarily forgetting about his wound and sticking out his hand to catch his fall and then immediately regretting it.

He screamed and then dragged himself up, struggling to keep moving. But when he saw me, he got a sudden rush of adrenaline and stumbled forward at twice the speed he'd been moving.

Stepping forward, I pulled my .45 from the holster and kept a watch on Freebee, who continued to lie still out there on the hard ground.

Zevin stumbled into my arm as I caught him and turned in an attempt to find Lowell, but he must've been lying on the other side of a low dune because I couldn't make out any sign of him.

The old man was sobbing as I lifted him and when he raised the hand I could see why: His left ring finger was completely gone and the pinky held on by what appeared to be a single tendon, dangling over the back of his hand.

Pulling a bandanna from my pocket, I held his hand up and began wrapping the mess together as he screamed again. "Look, you've got to stop doing that or they're just going to home in on where we are."

"Oh God! Oh God!"

I gripped his wrist as he stood there shaking, doing my best to stop the bleeding. The bandanna was saturated in no time and I told him to hold it as I flipped open the rucksack, pulling out some ballistic swabs and a few rags. It was far from sanitary, but it was going to have to do.

He was looking a little pale as I sat him on the rocks, opened the canteen, and gave him a sip as he greedily tried to guzzle. "Richard. Hey, Richard! Listen to me. This is the only water we've got, so go easy on it, okay?"

He nodded and drank with a little more restraint this time.

"I've got to go out there and check on those two to see if they're dead or need some assistance."

He lowered the canteen, gasping as it bumped his other hand, growing silent and then blurting out. "The hell with those sons-abitches."

I stared at him.

"They . . . They were going to kill me."

"Yep, they were." Unholstering my .45, I checked the pipe and mag, sliding it back together and looking at him. "Nothing so zealous as a convert, huh, Mister Zevin? Did you know 'zealot' comes from the Hebrew, an ancient sect in Judaism. They believed that the only alternative to Roman persecution was violence"

Stuffing the canteen under his arm, he cradled the hand some more, rocking back and forth. "What . . . What in the hell are you talking about?"

I took a step toward Freebee's sprawled body, still supposedly lifeless or unconscious out there. "That loss of a finger sure knocked the religion out of you."

"They were going to kill me."

"Yep, I think I knew that a long time before you did." I half turned toward him. "How in the world did you get caught up with this bunch, Keeper of the Light of the Second Quadrant?"

Using the sleeve of his robe, he dabbed at his eyes. "It was my wife. She got the cancer and there wasn't anything anybody could do, so we got to listening to Carruthers on this blog that he does and pretty soon we were in deep. When he moved his operation here to the Red Desert, I promised I'd help him if he'd do the same for Elisabeth."

"That your wife?"

"Yep."

"What happened to her?"

"She moved on to the Higher Level." He lifted his head to look out at the dunes, glowing in the moonlight. "They don't believe in modern medicine, that bunch."

"Well, when we get out of here, I'd advise you to get those remaining fingers looked at by some modern practitioners."

I started off when he called after me. "Hey?"

Turning, I called back. "Yes, sir?"

"If you would, see if you can find my finger out there and bring it back to me—it's got my wedding ring on it, and I hate to think of it ending up as crow bait."

Nodding, I turned back and trudged on. "Will do."

I found the finger with the wedding band still on it, amazingly enough.

It was lying in the sand about thirty yards in front of the motionless body of Freebee.

Stooping, I picked up the gruesome object and studied it, amazed at what a lead slug the size of your little finger traveling a thousand feet per second could do—which, evidently, was cut through human flesh like a hot knife through butter. There was a commensurate amount of blood and gore where the splatter had exploded, but all in all the cut was pretty clean.

I'd once been told by Doc Bloomfield that you had to get the disconnected digit on ice, which we didn't have, and sewn back on in six hours, which we probably weren't going to make.

Oh well, it would make a nice keychain for the old guy.

Fresh out of bandannas, I wrapped the finger in the map Blair had made for me and then tucked it in my shirt pocket, where Vic said I carried everything.

Wait till she found this in the laundry.

I approached Freebee and circled to the left to get a better look at him. There was blood, but not as much as I would've expected, possibly soaking into the dry sand underneath him, but he was breathing.

I aimed the Colt at the back of his head and nudged him with the toe of my boot, but he still didn't move. I attempted to roll him over, but with his one leg splayed out to the side, he wasn't rolling. Moving around him, I knelt down and grabbed his side to roll him my way. Just as I'd expected, he'd been playing possum and quickly tried to bring the Peacemaker on me, but I was able to grab his wrist and force it against the ground, where it fired harmlessly off to the left.

Biting his lip, the young man looked up at me. "Didn't go for it, huh?"

"Not particularly."

He grunted, gripping with his other hand just above his hip bone where the blood saturated his clothes. "My side's really killing me."

"I bet it is." Straddling him, I placed a knee on his arm and then took his weapon, then after stuffing it in my belt, climbed off and knelt there beside him. "First time?"

"What?"

"First time you've ever been shot?"

His eyes widened as he looked at me with an incredulous smile. "Have you not then made distinctions among yourselves and become judges with evil thoughts?"

"A couple of times. So many times in fact, I've been shot in that exact same spot."

He grimaced, crunching into a fetal position. "Jesus, am I gonna die?"

I scanned the dunes, looking for Lowell. "Hard to say without looking at the wound but there's quite a collection of organs in that quadrant: the liver, gallbladder, duodenum, the upper portion of the pancreas, and the hepatic flexure of the colon—none of which respond particularly well to high-speed lead. Heck, even if they just get nicked . . ."

He stared at me, shaking his head. "Are you really a sheriff?"

"I get that a lot." I continued to scan the horizon and scratched my beard. "What'd you eat last?"

He blurted out a breath and then spoke again. "What?"

"What's the last thing you ate?"

"Who gives a shit?" He gasped, started to speak again, and then paused before trying once more and finally blurting the words out. "A breakfast burrito."

"That's not good."

"Aahhh . . ." He groaned a bit and then looked up at me. "Why?"

"Any kind of hole in your gastrointestinal tract like your intestines, colon, or bowels can leak food or digestive fluids into your abdomen causing peritonitis—inflammation—and can kill you as quick as if you were stuffed with rat poison." I shook my head. "And that doesn't even take into consideration the other organs I mentioned—"

"Jesus, so . . . I am gonna die?"

Still scanning the horizon, I didn't see anybody out there in the dunes by the moonlight, but that didn't mean that Ommen wasn't lurking. "Well, it's not doing you any good to be out here leaking into yourself and the sand, so we have to get you some medical attention." I stood and took a step toward the endless dunes. "I'll be back."

His voice took on a genuine panic now. "Where are you going?"

"I'm going to go check on your buddy Lowell."

"Did you shoot him too?"

"As a matter of fact, I think I did, but I think I hit him in the head."

"Jesus."

"Yep, let's see if he's as merciful with your buddy as he has been with you." Moving away, I kept my .45 out and ready, just in case. It was going to be a trek through the sand again, but like any good hunter, you followed your shots.

I was approaching the distance where I thought I should've seen him, but there was nothing. Continuing on, all I could think about was Vic's remark about how this would probably be the way I died, monkeying around with this kind of foolishness.

What was I going to do if I did find Lowell out here missing half his head or wounded like the other two men? The night was rapidly turning into a traveling trio of triage with me the only unimpaired . . . if I remained lucky.

I heard a noise to my right and turned to see a coyote off to the side of one dune, looking at me. It was possible that he was one of the ones Dog and I had chased off from Penelope, drawn in by the scent of fresh blood. Interesting that he wasn't skittish about the sound of firearms, but then people were probably shooting around here all the time.

He studied me for a moment and then dipped his head, turning and running off.

If I'd tagged Lowell there would've been blood galore, but even if I'd just grazed his head there would be blood somewhere. Turning in a circle, I looked back toward the cliffs, finding the cleft and then thinking maybe I was to the left of where I'd hit him.

It was the only answer.

I glanced back to where I'd seen the coyote and figured I'd take a look that way just in case Lowell was lying over the next dune providing room service for the local wildlife.

I trudged up the hill and finally saw a slight blood trail where a few drops had fallen, but I couldn't help but think it might've been the coyote, possibly the one Dog had steamrolled earlier in the night.

I knelt down to check the blood, feeling the tacky, dark substance between my fingers. It was fresh, whomever or whatever it was from. I then looked to my left and could see a much larger stain in the sand.

Back toward the cliffs I could see the cleft and the spot on the low ledge where I would've aimed from, so this could've been the spot where I'd gotten him. He'd lost a lot of blood but still had the strength to get up and walk away.

Tough kid.

Standing, I followed the blood trail where he'd continued to leak. I followed along as the blood seemed to disappear almost entirely, with only a drop or two here and there. Maybe he'd been able to bandage himself up.

The coyotes called from the northwest, that ghostly sound warbling through the night, probably complaining about all the tourist traffic in their desert.

I continued and found another dollop of blood, this one even fresher than the others.

It had to be a head wound with the amount of blood he was sporadically bleeding, with the blood vessels so close to the surface. I'd hit him in the head with a slug from one of the most powerful rifles on the face of the earth, but if I did, how the hell was he still out here wandering around?

Circling the large dune, I could feel the fatigue in my legs catching up with me and slowing my rate, the sand sinking every step.

More blood.

Taking a breath, I stooped, feeling the wet sand that had hardly set up at all.

Wherever he was out there, he wasn't far.

I'd just started to stand when there was a noise behind me, a sound exactly like the one that a big Russian Model 3 being cocked would make.

He was wounded, that much I knew, and it was possible that I could turn and breathe on him and he'd fall over, but until I saw what I was dealing with, discretion might be the better part of valor.

Turning slowly with my .45 raised, I was confronted with the silhouette of Lowell Ommen, backed by the full moon, the barrel of his pistol extended toward me from a distance of only a couple of feet.

"Howdy, Lowell."

He said nothing but took a surprisingly steady step in my direction, extending the .44 directly at my face before flicking the barrel a few times to indicate that I should drop my weapon.

I did as he said, letting it hang from my finger and then fall to the sand.

He took a step closer but wavered just a bit. I thought about making a move, but he steadied himself, carefully lowering and picking up my Colt and stuffing it in his belt before slowly standing straight again.

"Freebee's over the hill here. He's shot and he's going to need some attention."

Predictably, he said nothing.

He was a lot closer now and as I allowed my eyes to focus, I began making out the features of his blood-soaked face. He smiled, revealing the grotesque visage of bright white teeth set against wet crimson. He then casually lifted his hat as if to adjust it and a fresh coating of blood poured out from under it.

I could now see the deep crease in his forehead, open wide and exposing the viscera and the bone white of his uncovered skull.

12

"Do you have any idea how tempting it is to tell Lowell to just shoot you in the face, right here and now?"

"I've got an idea."

"Well, I would, but we need transportation—at least I do." He gasped again and then tried to stand, failing and then looking up at me. "When ye are in the service of your fellow beings, ye are only in the service of your God."

"Found religion again, did you?" I felt the nudge at my back from Lowell's Smith & Wesson and extended my hand, pulling Freebee up on his one leg and catching him as he started to fall. "What did you have in mind?"

He hugged onto my arm with both arms. "You're going to carry me back to the camp."

I stared at him. "You've got to be kidding."

"I'm not. This is your mess, so you get to help clean it up. Now turn around so I can climb on your back."

I shook my head in disbelief. "If, and I say if, any of those conditions I mentioned pertain to your prognosis, you'll be dead by the time we get back to the camp."

"What other choice have I got?"

Not willing to give away Zevin's position I pointed to our right toward another grouping of trees at the base of the cliffs. "We put you over there in the shade with some water and go get help."

He shook his head, snarling a smile. "I don't think Lowell and I want your kind of help."

I looked off to the east where the blood-red orb was just beginning to make itself known. "Two hours and that sun's going to heat this place up like a frying pan."

He cocked his head. "I didn't say it was going to be easy, certainly not for you."

"I'm not going to be in good shape, but you'll be dead by the time we get there." I threw a thumb over my shoulder. "And so will he."

"Well, it'll just be you and the dead guys, huh? Besides, if we die you can just run off, but I've got a sneaking suspicion that the last thing ole Lowell here will ever do is plant a bullet in your head as a return favor."

I swiveled just a bit, relieved to see Ommen had placed his hat down tight over his eyes. "Could you do me a favor and ask him not to adjust that hat of his again? I'd just as soon not have to see another ten gallons of blood pour down over his face. Besides, the last time he did it I think that wound winked at me."

"Turn around and shut up."

I did as he said, feeling him climb on my back, or at least try.

"Can you stoop down, you big son of a bitch?"

I did as he asked. "Boy, that religion of yours kind of comes and goes, huh?"

"We'll see how yours does in the next couple of hours." He rested his arms on my shoulders and climbed the rest of the way up as I took his legs in my hands in a fireman's carry.

Feeling the tension in his body, I listened as his breathing stopped and then began again. "Are you all right?"

He gasped out the words. "Yeah, yeah. Let's get going."

I turned and was faced with the bloody mess of Lowell, watching as he stepped aside and motioned for me to go ahead. I studied him for a moment more in hopes of seeing some lessoning in his physical abilities, but he stood still and appeared readily capable. "I'll take the lead, okay?"

Without waiting for an answer, I began trudging in the sand flats leading into the dunes, feeling the heat rising and wondering how far I'd get before I fell over.

Freebee's voice sounded against my neck. "Well, I suppose you want to know how me and Lowell got involved in all this?"

I couldn't help but breathe a laugh. "Not really."

"You're not curious?"

"Not particularly, I'm concentrating on not dropping you."

"That's okay, I don't know how long I'll be able to talk before I pass out." Repositioning himself nearer my ear, he started up again. "The first person I ever killed was a guy in a bar back in Burns, Oregon, where I'm from—stabbed him with a knife."

With the extra weight of him, I was really sinking in the sand, which forced me to lift my knees even higher just to clear my boots.

"I was eighteen."

The sun was now visible on the horizon to the east, and I could feel the ambient temperature rising as I trudged along, following their trail where they'd followed mine.

"I was washing dishes in the back of this shithole where I was working, and I came outside for a smoke. There was this guy and his girl sitting on the trunk of his car, and the asshole tells me to put out my cigarette, and I told him to just cool his shit and I'd be gone in a few minutes. I guess it was because of the girl, but he came over all big and bad . . . I don't know, I guess I'd just had enough, you know?" He was silent for a moment, his breath raspy and rancid. "You should've seen the look on his face when I stuck that butcher knife into him."

The first trickles of sweat slipped down from under my hat.

"Ran off into the Malheur National Wildlife Refuge, and I knew that place like my gun hand. Took 'em three months to finally get me." He coughed. "I guess it was a mistake."

"Sheriff Grossnickle said it took them one month to get you, but what was the mistake?" I shifted him a little and could feel him tightening his grip on my shoulders. "Knifing the guy?"

"Naw, I should've gone north into the National Forest or the Ochoco."

"Right."

"The eyewitnesses kind of dried up when one of 'em got hit in the head with a tire iron, and then an old buddy of mine who also worked at the bar, Jimmy O'Conner, who happened to be there that night, remembered that the asshole had had a gun in the parking lot—so I walked."

Taking a deep breath, I powered up the next dune, only to be faced with another.

"My man Jimmy, we decided to head out and celebrate near Crater Lake, you know where that is?"

Huffing a breath, I answered in a hoarse voice. "I do."

"And then it turns out Jimmy's an asshole too. He says if I don't pay him some money, he's gonna recant his testimony and get me thrown back in prison." There was a long pause. "I tell you the water in Crater Lake is cold, and it's deep too." He laughed, softly. "You know, I think one of the big things in life is to find what you're good at, and then the rest is just work. You know, refining your technique."

"Then there was a fourteen-year-old girl, as I recall?"

"You been reading up on me, Sheriff?"

"A little."

"Well, you see that's something else I'm good at . . . She could've passed for sixteen, by the way, and I was only nineteen at the time."

"Well, I don't think the Romeo and Juliet provision entertains the appearance of the three-year gap between a girl of nonconsensual age. I still believe that's statutory rape according to Oregon law."

"It was Portland, and Portland is different from the rest of the state."

"I don't think so."

"You know, and that's the unfortunate attitude her daddy took." He was silent for a moment. "He changed his mind when he came out from work, and somebody had left a knife stuck in the driver's seat of his car."

The heat was starting to wear on me, and I could feel the extra weight in my legs as I began trailing the toes of my boots in the sand. Pausing for a moment, I waited to see if Lowell was keeping up, finally feeling a muzzle in my ribs as he reached around Freebee to prod me.

"He's tough, isn't he?"

I started off again, speaking over my shoulder. "If he's that tough, let him carry you."

"Naw, we'll just keep using you. You know, saving our energy."

Reaching the top of the next dune, I looked ahead where the sun was creeping toward us, rising in the east like an egg yolk of lava.

"But at that point I decided that the great Pacific Northwest just wasn't big enough for a man like me . . ."

"Sounds like that's the same conclusion Oregon law enforcement took."

"Maybe so. Anyway, I'd always wanted to be an actor and decided to try my hand at an audition down in Los Angeles. I did a hell of a tryout, but they went with this other guy, but then he got hit by a car and they went with me."

"You're kind of a dangerous guy to be around."

"Seems like it, doesn't it?"

"Is that where you met Carruthers?"

"*Saddletramp* was the name of the show. Did you ever see it?"

"I'm afraid not."

"Piece of shit. I kept tryin' to tell the producers what they were getting wrong, but they didn't want to hear it."

"Imagine that."

He readjusted himself. "His name was Ritt Ravitch at that time. He was a support player in the show and took me under his wing, but then they fired me, and things got rough. I had to pull a job off up in Bakersfield and they said I robbed a guy, which meant—"

"Felony-only offense."

"You know, I do believe you are a sheriff."

I paused at the top of the next dune. "I don't suppose either of you brought any water?"

Freebee gigged me like a horse. "Sixteen months, do you believe that? Sixteen months they gave me up in Delano, where I found God."

I could feel my tongue thickening. "He moves in mysterious ways."

He chuckled. "By that time, they'd canceled *Saddletramp* and ole Zeno was on to something else . . ."

I mumbled the words, aware that my mouth was becoming exceedingly dry. "I believe the Securities and Exchange Commission refers to it as affinity fraud or a Ponzi scheme."

"These rich folks out there in California are getting old and looking for some way to buy their way into heaven, so along comes Zeno. He'd changed his name by that time, and he starts offering them these stocks and bonds."

"Unregistered security offerings."

"There was risk involved, but pretty soon he was making real money, I mean raking it in. Millions through this church of his, the Holy Trinity Empire. First, he'd offer 'em salvation for their soul and then financial salvation to go along with it. Then Zeno got stupid and started spending the money like it was going out of style—cars, trips, private jets . . . Now, you can't do that shit and get away with it for long without drawing attention to yourself, and pretty soon the State of California sent him up to North Kern where I was having a brief sabbatical, and I met up with him."

"So, this whole Red Gate thing is just the same thing he was doing before but designed to keep a lower profile."

"Yeah, I mean the downside is that you've got to take care of these motherfuckers at least until you can get rid of 'em."

"Blair mentioned that."

He chuckled to himself. "You have to cull the herd every once in a while."

"That how you continued to develop your technique?"

He was quiet for a bit. "How many folks did you say you'd killed, Sheriff?"

"I didn't."

"Oh yeah, that's right. You think you've killed as many as me and Lowell, here?"

I slipped in the sand and almost fell. Catching myself, I slowly stood and half turned to see Lowell trudging behind me, wavering a bit. Swallowing what spit I had, I strained to get the words out. "I . . . I hope not."

"Yeah, you ought to hope about a lot of things." He readjusted himself and I could feel his blood saturating the back of my jeans. "Hell, I bet we've killed some twenty or thirty of these sorry ole bastards and buried 'em out in different deserts."

"And Blair has a map?"

"So she says. Got it from one of the old fuckers who used to follow us when we'd take 'em out. She wouldn't tell us who it was but I'm betting it's that poor ole Richard Zevin . . ." There was a pause. "He's dead, right?"

Not wanting to give them any reason to go back after the old man, I told a partial truth. "He was bleeding out when I last saw him."

He chuckled again. "Well, you gotta have a mission in life."

Pausing again at the top of the next dune, I looked ahead but couldn't see anything that looked like our journey would be coming to any kind of end. Freebee kicked at me again, but it was weaker this time. Turning, I could see Ommen struggling to get up the dune where I now stood, trying hard to not fall over.

I thought about when it was that I wanted to make my move, and then I wondered if I'd waited too long and was going to fall over when the time came. The best tactic would be to stumble and fall back on top of Lowell, blocking him with Freebee and buying myself enough time to get my .45 back.

I glanced behind me again and was relieved to see that Lowell was now fully staggering up the dune, his gun hand hanging to the side as he struggled to keep up.

It was now or never, but timing was everything.

I stooped over and pretended to stretch my back, waiting for the exact moment when I would launch myself backward and on top of him. I figured with the weight of both me and Freebee, we'd smash Lowell into the sand long enough for me to roll to the right, because he was right-handed, pin his arm, and get my 1911.

It all sounded good in theory, but my energies were fading fast.

Hearing him draw closer, I stiffened to fall backward and suddenly heard a voice in my ear. "You know . . ." Nudging the muzzle of his Peacemaker into the left side of my head, he continued in a breathless and rasping voice. "Now would be the time when a smart guy would think of trying something clever." I listened as he rolled the hammer back. "And that would be pretty stupid."

Lowell was approaching and I thought about what I was preparing to do, and what the odds of success were.

One thing was for sure, they weren't going to get better.

Suddenly lurching back with all the strength I had, I felt the muzzle of his Colt slide forward just enough to miss my head as the thing went off. The pain in my left ear was excruciating as I slammed backward, literally landing on Lowell as Freebee and I landed on top of him. His gun fired too, and I'd assumed it would go off to the left, but instead it went off to the right as the three of us tumbled backward down the dune.

My right ear joined my left in feeling like my head had been submersed in a bucket of water as I scrambled off Freebee, who lay beneath me like an empty weather balloon, evidently knocked out.

Unable to hear anything, I began flipping him over but couldn't see any of the weapons, finally glancing over to the right where both our guns lay about ten feet away.

I pushed up and staggered to a standing position, but from my peripheral vision could see Lowell lying on the ground aiming his pistol at me between the holes in his boots.

Neither of us said anything as I slowly turned toward him.

His hat had come off and I could now see where the .45-70 had creased his head, the bald pate pulled apart and the copious amounts of blood having congealed into a massive, sopping scab.

The gun wavered in his hand, the streak of blood pouring into his dominant eye as I stared at him speaking, my voice muffled and distant. "You're not going to make it without my help—I'm tired, but I'm intact."

We stayed like that for a moment, him unable to talk and me barely able to hear.

I looked at Freebee. "He might make it, but my guess is he's poisoning himself from the inside out. If we don't get him some help, he's going to die. Hell, he might die anyway with the limited medical facilities you've got back at the compound. But you, my friend, aren't going to make it." Licking my dry lips with a tongue that felt like a roll of tar paper, I listened to the echoing in my ears, wondering if I'd ever hear again. "You've lost and are losing too much blood, and I'm not sure if that big Sharps that creased your cranium hasn't concussed you or caused all kinds of cerebral hematoma that's swelling your skull fit to pop like an overinflated balloon."

I took a step toward him rather than going for the guns, watching as he raised the barrel of the vintage weapon, centering it on my chest.

"You shoot me and we're all dead." My voice sounded like someone else speaking; someone I didn't know and could barely hear. "Holster that thing and I'll go get those two other weapons, then I'll holster his to him and take mine and we're all armed, fair and square. Then I'll haul both of you out of this blistering hell, deal?"

The pistol still wavered, but I watched as it slowly dropped to his inverted lap and his head fell back.

Standing there, I thought about just walking away and leaving the two of them and heading back to where I'd left the old man with one canteen half full of water.

But a deal is a deal.

I trudged over to the two pistols, stuffed mine back into my holster, and then walked back to Freebee, careful to not let Lowell see me thumbing the .45 rounds from the six-shooter and depositing them in the ever-trusty left breast pocket along with Richard Zevin's ring finger. Lowering myself down, I shoved the vintage weapon in Freebee's elaborate holster.

Watching him breathe, I checked his pulse at the throat, satisfied he was still alive, and then reached down and pulled him up by his shirtfront, half turning and sidling him on my hip and onto my back. I took his arms and pulled them over my shoulders, grabbing the cuffs I'd taken off Blair and then attached them to his wrists so he was essentially strapped to me. Then, lifting his legs, I walked back to Lowell, stretching my jaw in an attempt to get the ringing out of my ears.

"Get up." His head lifted a bit but then fell back. "I can't carry both of you, so you're going to have to walk, holding on to his belt."

His head came up again, but then fell back once more.

Exhausted, I nudged his boot with the toe of my own. "C'mon, we've got to get going or all of us are dead."

I watched as he rolled into a fetal position to get his knees under him. He then struggled up and took a quick breather before holstering his gun and snagging his hat from the sand.

He stooped there considering the hat.

My disembodied voice sounded from my head. "It's not sanitary, but I doubt that matters much right now."

He tugged the thing on and then stood, looking all the world like a walking corpse.

Turning, I offered him Freebee's gun belt. "Grab a hand onto his belt and don't let go. If you do let go, I'm not likely to notice and you'll die out here alone, you got me?"

He said nothing, but I could feel him pulling at the man on my back and figured it was time to get moving.

I began climbing that first dune I'd already climbed twice but could feel the weight of both men bearing down on me. I tried to swallow and clear my throat but couldn't work up the spit and just settled into a slow march to the south and slightly west.

What the hell was I thinking, carrying the weight of three men across a desert? Granted, I was twice their size, but I was also twice their age and more than a little dog tired.

Speaking of, I wondered where Dog was, and if he was safe.

I did my best to find a pace, a tempo that would allow me to surrender to the dull thrumming in my head, concentrating on placing one boot in front of the other. I wanted to laugh, but all I could afford was a smile, thinking about being in this position before at about eleven thousand feet in a spring blizzard in the Bighorn Mountains.

I could've done with a little of that cold and snow.

In that instance I'd desperately wanted to keep those two individuals alive but couldn't say the same about the two connected to me now. What was I going to do if Lowell let go and fell—go back and get him? And then what? I was barely capable of hauling Freebee.

I wondered if the Old Cheyenne would come to my rescue again but doubted it. They weren't invested in these two and would just as likely prefer to see their animal-gnawed, bleached bones littering the Red Desert.

But what about me?

Certainly the Crow Shaman could carry all three of us.

"Virgil . . ." Choking the word out with a chuckle that still sounded like my head was wrapped in cotton, I coughed and added, "Are you out there?"

There wasn't a response, not that I was really expecting one.

I felt Lowell's hand slipping, but then felt him grab Freebee's gun belt and the drag of his weight as I pulled on like a shattered tank wavering to one side of a dune with one track unreeled.

My head started to drop, but I couldn't allow it, knowing that without a point of reference on the horizon I was likely to be out here wandering in circles until I finally dropped face first in the sand—and then it would be over.

The salt-encrusted sweat of my clothes chafed against me like 500 grit sandpaper, alternating between damp and dry as a bone, and I was pretty sure I was hardening up out here in the desert. Maybe that was the way they'd find me, standing out here like a statue with two corpses attached to me.

How did it go?

My voice rang in my head like a broken bell, echoing and meaningless like the words. "Look upon my works, ye mighty, and despair." I could feel my lips moving but could no longer hear the words that recited from my lips.

I met a traveler from an antique land
Who said: two vast and trunkless legs of stone
Stand in the desert . . . Near them on the sand,
Half sunk, a shattered visage lies, whose frown,
And wrinkled lip and sneer of cold command,
Tell that its sculptor well those passions read,
Which yet survive, stamped on these lifeless things,
The hand that mocked them and the heart that fed;
And on the pedestal these words appear:
My name is Ozymandias, King of Kings:
Look upon my Works, ye Mighty, and despair!
Nothing beside remains. Round the decay
Of that colossal wreck, boundless and bare
The lone and level sands stretch far away.

"Very good, Walter."

Squeezing my eyes together, I glanced around but could see nothing but the endless dunes of the monochromatic desert, humping up to defeat me.

"What is the form?"

Clearing my throat again, I mumbled the words. "Iambic pentameter, which speeds the narrative with a sense of foreboding."

The voice of Betty Dobbs, my high school English teacher, was strong and clear. "'Ozymandias' is one of Shelley's shortest poems, but it has three speakers. Who are they?"

"The narrator, or the poet himself, the person he meets traveling on the road, and then the king, Ozymandias."

"Historically, who was Ozymandias?"

"It was the Greek name for Rameses II of Egypt. Shelley wrote the piece in 1817 not long after the British Museum acquired part of a statue of the pharaoh, and it's possible that was the inspiration for the poem."

"What do you think it's about?"

My hearing was still sketchy, but I could hear her clearly. "It's about the vanity and fleeting quality of human power in the face of the inevitable passing of time, a theme that was very popular during the Romantic period, mostly in response to the overindulgence of the French Revolution."

"Did you like it, Walter?"

"Very much, Mrs. Dobbs."

"Why?"

"The subversive simplicity of the language and clever, two-sided construction. I guess I enjoyed the sly irony."

"What irony?"

"The hubris of a king, thinking that his legacy would last forever and instead it's a wreckage in a vast desert, alone and forgotten."

"Something like the hubris of trying to carry three men from a desert?"

I stopped and felt Lowell walk into the back of me.

He didn't say anything and neither did I as I stood there panting and looking around. Squinting, I watched the waves of heat roll up from the sand and blinked, trying to remember where my sunglasses were as I started off again.

"'Photokeratitis' is what they call it." This was a different voice, but another one I knew. "A painful eye inflammation caused by UV rays burning the cells covering the clear cornea, reducing its transparency and resulting in a loss of visual acuteness."

"Snow blindness."

"Do you see any snow around here, Walter?"

I smiled and could feel my lips cracking as I remembered my sixth-grade science teacher. "No, Mister Miller."

"Any reflective surface can have the same effect, such as water or sand. You have light-colored eyes, Walter, which makes you more prone to snow blindness. Do you know why?"

I coughed, trying to spit but then gave up and just sputtered out the words. "Less melanin pigment to absorb UV radiation and protect the photoreceptor cells."

"Very good."

I stumbled in the sand, seemingly losing the ability to lift my boots. "So, I'm going blind?"

"Only temporarily, so long as you get out of this desert."

"Good, I don't think I could face being both deaf and blind."

"Dehydration is what you should be concerned with." He paused audibly, making the sound that all the kids teased him about. "Aaaaaaaa . . . The dead do hear and see, though."

"Are you sure about that, Mister Miller?"

"I'm dead, aren't I? I was approaching retirement when I was teaching you in the sixth grade, and that was quite some time ago."

I stumbled again, falling to the side enough so that I had to place a hand against the steeper dune to my right to steady myself. I wasn't sure if I could feel Lowell back there, but when I started off again, I felt the familiar tug. ". . . A dozen days."

"Excuse me?"

"The average human in the desert can last about a dozen days without water.

"In perfect conditions, such as shade, and temperatures no higher than seventy degrees, but as the temperature rises closer to a hundred and with no shade your time is cut to two and a half days."

Gazing about with my impressionist pupils, I was having trouble differentiating the sand from the sky. "Not much shade around here."

"And you're exerting yourself to an incredible degree."

"How long have I got?"

"Hours, at best."

"Then what?"

"Aaaaaaaaaaa . . . You join me, and we can test out theories about blindness and deafness."

I smiled, the cracking of my lips seeping blood, tasting the salty liquid with my swelling tongue.

"What are you smiling about, Walter?"

"Nothing."

"My aaaaaaaaaaa . . . verbal tic?"

"The kids used to make fun of you about it."

"But you never did."

I struggled to get the words out, unsure if they were even discernible. "No, sir."

"Why?"

It was a down slope, and I lengthened my stride just a bit in hopes of making time. "I was brought up to be better than that."

"And that's why you're sacrificing yourself, carrying these murderers from certain death?"

I started to pause again but figured I couldn't really risk continually stopping. "They're human beings."

The voice changed again, but this one I didn't recognize. "They're going to kill you."

"They'll certainly try."

"Hubris, again. If they live and kill others, won't their blood be on your hands?"

"Too many factors to take into consideration. If they survive . . . if they survive, what if they change?"

"What if they don't? Wouldn't it be better to let them die in this hellish burning wasteland?"

"I'm not a judge or a jury."

"But you have been in the past?"

"Only when given no choice."

"I guess what I'm telling you is that you have no choice now. If you keep at this, you're going to die."

"Then I die."

"You're willing to risk your life for criminals such as these?"

"It doesn't matter who they are, they need saving."

I tripped, allowing the toe of one of my boots to get caught in the sand, sending me head over teakettle, toppling over and down a dune where the three of us rolled to a powdery stop.

13

"You're alive."

"Howcayowtill?"

"There's a bottle of water there by your right hand, careful you don't knock it over. You're going to want it. Your mouth and tongue are so dehydrated, no one could understand what you were saying once they got you to talk."

"Miblind?"

"Excuse me?"

"Ami blind?"

"Hard to tell, but we put a damp cloth over your eyes and that's why you can't see anything at the moment." I listened as he adjusted himself. "You came staggering into camp with Freebee in a fireman's carry, your right hand latched around Lowell's wrist, dragging him on his back. To be honest, you were a frightful sight with your face and mouth horribly dried up. I wasn't there but they say you couldn't see, couldn't hear, and couldn't speak—that you lurched your way through camp and would've likely kept going if they hadn't forcibly stopped you. Even then they said you put up a terrific fight and broke the nose of one of the brethren."

Pulling the cloth from my face, I gently tried to pry open an eyelash, but the grit and emulsion from my eye must've joined together to make a powerful glue, and I finally gave up. Reaching very gently to my right, I felt the base of a plastic bottle and closed my aching fingers around it. "Koolaideu?"

"Excuse me?"

"Koolaid?"

"Oh, no, we're not into that kind of thing; much more advanced these days." He laughed. "They say you were talking in a way that as near as they could tell you were arguing with yourself, evidently taking both parts."

Raising up on one elbow, I lifted the bottle and took a shallow sip.

"That's right, a little at a time. From what I'm to understand they gave you too much at first and you threw it all back up, so let's go easy, shall we? Water is something of a limited commodity here in the desert."

Lowering the bottle, I felt something hard at my shoulder and scrunched back, resting against whatever it was. "Dithey makit?"

"I'm sorry?"

"Did they makit?"

"Freebee and Lowell, yes. A little worse for wear but they're alive."

I took another swig of the water, relieved that the ringing was gone from my ears.

"Why in the world would you do it? I mean, I'm assuming you're the one who shot them."

"That'swhat I was arguing with myself about wheney found me."

"What did you shoot them with, a howitzer?"

"Sharps buffalorifle."

"Well, I think Lowell will have a permanent crease in his skull, but he's coming around, and we did the best we could with Freebee. It would appear that there's no cataclysmic damage to any of his internal organs, but something is wrong inside him and we're going to have to get him looked at, which introduces a number of perils to the group." He paused. "Do you know, you're the first thing he asked about?"

Pouring a little water on the damp cloth, I gently rubbed the one recalcitrant eye, and then the next.

"We took the opportunity to take off your boots and place you in the shade, letting you rest through the afternoon."

"What time issit now?"

"Approaching midnight, I would say."

"I was out all day?"

"I'd say you're lucky to be alive."

Easing open the one eye, I could see my bare feet stretched out in front of me in the sand, and a steel manacle attached to my left ankle. "No one came?"

"I'm afraid not, an agent of ours intercepted Blair and Penelope and brought them back here."

"What about my dog?"

"There was no mention of a dog."

Raising one eyelid, I could make out Carruthers seated about twelve feet out, sitting cross-legged in the sand, his white robe and flowing hair seemingly iridescent in the moonlight as he puffed on one of his trademark Cohiba Robustos.

"What are we to do with you?"

"Exuseme?"

"After such an astounding act of heroism, we can't simply kill you; it would cause unrest within the brethren."

I took another mouthful of water and then tempted the fates with a minor grin, feeling my lips splitting again. "Let mego?"

"No, I don't think we can do that." He sighed, deeply. "We'll be heading out of here in a day, the environs around these parts are becoming rather unwelcoming, but you can come with us."

I didn't say anything.

"I thought not."

It took pretty much all I had to get the next statement out. "How-many of them are you going to kill before youleave?"

"Excuse me?"

"The brethren, how manyave you killed?"

He paused, holding the cigar, suspended in midair. "Why none. Who told you such a thing?"

I took another sip. "Your daughter, for one."

"Well, it's a complicated relationship between the two of us."

"Shesaid that too."

He looked off in the direction of the compound, continuing to smoke. "They're all my children, why would I kill them? What would I gain? No, we simply separate them from the group and then ship them home on a bus."

"Broke."

He shrugged. "Salvation costs money."

"What aba . . . about your great-granddaughter?"

"Unfortunately, within our prophecy there had to be a sacrifice, but then you came along and saved her, which was fortunate since Freebee and Lowell lost her."

"Lost her?"

"Yes, we were going to go back and get her, but then they couldn't find her. No one was more concerned than me."

"Concerned enough tha . . . that the three of you turned in and went to bed?"

He spread his hands. "Well, I mean there was really only so much we could do in the dark."

I shook my ankle, rattling the iron links. "And your daughter?"

"As I said, it's complicated between Blair and me."

"My relationship between my daughter and me is complicated too, but not enough so that I chain her to a tree."

"Perhaps she's not as complicated as Blair."

"Hmm." I grunted.

He sat there, looking at his lap. "I haven't been a good father."

"Blair said that too."

He nodded, his head still hanging down, the cigar clutched in the corner of his mouth. "I really shouldn't have had children; I should've concentrated on my career, or what there was of it."

"You were the narrator for *Mysteries from Beyond*, where Blair first talked about her experiences with the clam people."

He smirked. "You saw that?"

"A friend loaned me a copy."

"VHS?"

"No, it had been updated to a DVD."

He thought about it, straightening his robe and tightening the sash. "Not my best work, but by that time I was doing mostly voice-overs."

"And you blame Blair for that?"

"No, no . . . It's a pitiless business. Once you get to a certain age in Hollywood, you're suddenly playing the father, the uncle, or the next-door neighbor."

"Parenting can be kind of pitiless too."

"I'm finding that out." The smile faded. "Be that as it may, we're going to have to do something with you." At the sound of footsteps, he turned and looked off toward the camp. "Well, here comes an associate of yours."

My eyes still weren't focusing all that well, but I could make the outline of the skinny figure with a ponytail that approached from behind Carruthers.

"Hey, Sheriff."

I stared at him.

"It's me—Benny."

"I'd like to say I'm surprised, Benny, but I'm not." I watched as he sat next to Carruthers. "You were in this all along?"

"No, but when Tess gave me the map that Blair made, it was just too much of an opportunity to pass up."

"They paid you?"

"Yeah."

"You better watch your step, Benny. You're liable to get in over your head." I took another drink of water. "Are you the one that intercepted Blair, the baby, and my dog?"

"Your dog ran off."

I stared at him. "What?"

"When I stopped them, she opened the door, and the dog came at me, so I went for my gun, but by the time I got it out of my saddlebag, he was gone."

I glanced around the dunes, half expecting to see the monster. "You better hope nothing happens to him, Benny."

"Really? What're you gonna do, chain me to a tree?"

I raised the bottle of water in a toast. "I'll do much worse than that."

Carruthers interjected. "I'd imagine you're hungry?"

"I could eat."

The older man tapped the ash from his cigar and then placed a hand on the biker's shoulder. "Benny, go get somebody to bring the sheriff here some stew, would you?"

Begrudgingly, Benny stood and gave me one last look before raising his finger and pointing it at me before pulling the imaginary trigger and raising the make-believe barrel and blowing the smoke away.

We both watched him go. "You know, I might be persuaded to leave Benny in the desert."

"Those of limited intellectual capacities have their uses too."

"Somehow, I knew that would be your opinion."

He slowly stood and I could tell he was in pain. "Sheriff, I'm willing to make you a deal."

"Not the first time I've heard that."

Ignoring my remark, he continued. "As I said, we're going to be leaving here very soon, and I don't want to have to do something cold-blooded if I don't have to."

"And what are you proposing?"

He took another puff of the Cohiba, the ember end glowing. "Letting you live."

"So much for all that benevolence for the returning hero?"

"My proposition is this: We leave you with enough water and food to survive long enough for us to get away."

"And where is away?"

"I think it might be best for you to not know that."

"Higgo One and the clam people, huh?"

"The more outrageous the lie, the more people are apt to believe it."

I took another sip of the water and looked at the vast panoply of stars and the thick part of the Milky Way galaxy that stretched from horizon to horizon, what the Cheyenne referred to as the Hanging Road. "Take a look at those stars, would you? It's like a fresh bedspread being pulled over the heavens every night."

"I'm assuming there's a reason we're discussing the sky?"

"It's like a brand-new start each night."

He studied his cigar. "And your point is?"

"Carruthers, or whatever you're calling yourself these days, you've got an opportunity here to set things straight. Whether you're aware of it or not, those two psychopaths you've got on the payroll are not taking your people out and putting them on a bus, if that's what they're telling you. Now, I got the same story from both your daughter and them."

"Why would they tell you?"

"They were pretty sure they were going to kill me, but then fate took a turn."

"If that's the case, once again, why did you save them?"

"And, once again, I'm not a judge and jury. I know what they were going to do to Richard Zevin, the Keeper of the Light of the Second Quadrant, which is why I blew holes in them."

"And where is poor Richard?"

"Parked out there on a rock ledge with a water supply and food. He's missing a finger or two, but I think he's going to make it."

"What if I don't believe you?"

Carefully reaching into my shirt pocket, I pulled out the grisly keepsake, unwrapped it, and tossed it at Carruthers's feet, where he stared at it. "Do you believe me now?"

His eyes slowly rose to mine. "You cut off his finger?"

"Shot it off, actually, but that was only because he was running toward me and raised his hands unexpectedly."

"So you shot him?"

Setting the bottle down, I reached over and gathered my boots and socks, stuffed in the leather shafts. "No, I was trying to keep your guys from shooting him."

"And why would they do that?"

"Good grief—because they figured if they had a hostage, I wouldn't shoot them."

"But you did."

"Only as a last resort." I pulled my socks out and looked at him, shaking my head. "Look, Carruthers, you seem like a smart guy, so if those two have been taking these people out and shooting them in the back of the head and burying them in the desert, then the legal terms 'murder in the second degree,' 'manslaughter,' and 'negligent homicide' suddenly loom large in your immediate future."

He continued to smoke, staring at the finger but made no motion to pick it up. "What happens to me doesn't matter."

"Look, I know you're facing some medical issues but that doesn't mean those two get to play *God's Little Acre* out here in the Red Desert."

"What do you know about my medical condition?"

Putting my socks on, I watched him as he continued to study the disembodied finger. "Not much, and at the risk of being callous, I don't really care. You see, you're not my problem if you don't know what's going on, but you could be part of the solution. Now, just from the small time I've spent with your two followers, I can say without a doubt that they've been doing this stuff. So why don't you go get your daughter and have her show us the map."

His eyes came back to mine. "What map?"

"The map that shows where all your dead followers are buried."

The eyes widened. "There's a map, for God's sake?"

"That's what your daughter says."

"Look, I took advantage of people financially, but I never killed anyone. I find it hard to believe . . ."

"I'm inclined to believe you, but unless you help me now, that may not play in the court of law."

He leaned forward, struggling to get up and then stood there, looking off toward the camp and smoking. "I need time to think."

"Yep, well, there isn't a lot of that right now. Those two have had the props knocked out from under them, and if we're going to do something about this situation then we're going to have to do it quick."

"I . . . I need time to think. I picked both of them up out of the gutter . . ."

"That's all fine and well, but in all honesty, you might've done better to leave them there."

He started off toward the camp and took the last puff of the stogie and then flung it into the sand without looking back at me. "I'm sorry, I need to think."

"Carruthers? Hey, we haven't got a lot of time here."

Ignoring me, he continued as I sat back against the tree watching him go. "Well, hell . . ."

I took my boots and thumbed open the leather flap inside and started to take out the handcuff key I kept there. I'd just started fiddling with the manacle when I saw another shadow working its way down the path toward me. Putting the key away until I could figure out who it was, I lifted the water bottle and took another drink, thinking about how bad I wanted a Rainier.

She didn't stop at the perimeter of the chain length but continued on toward me where she sat in the sand in the same place she'd been imprisoned before. She held the bowl of steaming stew out toward me, a slice of sourdough bread clinging to the rim along with a large spoon. "Fancy meeting you here."

She got herself settled and looked out at the disembodied digit lying in the sand, the wedding ring glimmering in the moonlight. "Is that what I think it is?"

I took the bowl. "It is."

She studied my hands. "Whose?"

I ate a spoonful, starting slowly. "Richard Zevin."

"Richard Zevin?"

"Yep, do you know him?"

"He's the one who made the map of the bodies out in the desert."

"You've got to be kidding."

"No, he got suspicious, and when they started taking people away, he'd follow them."

"So, he actually witnessed them killing these people?"

"I suppose so."

I gestured toward the grayish-looking finger, lying in the sand. "Can you just hand it to me, I'm thinking he might want it back." I shrugged. "The ring, at least."

She stared at it. "I'm not touching that thing."

Sighing, I sat the bowl down and then reached over, slipping the key back out of the small pocket in my boot and then inserting it into the manacle, tripping the catch and dropping it to the ground before slowly lumbering up and taking the three steps to where the finger lay. I scooped it up and poked it into my shirt pocket, finally returning and sitting where I'd been and going at the stew again.

"That can't be sanitary."

"You have no idea how far I am past personal hygiene."

She then stared at the manacle lying in the sand. "I forgot you had that key."

I paused eating long enough to respond. "It's come in handy over the years. How's Penelope?"

"Sleeping."

"Good, and my dog the last time you saw him?"

"Headed back down the road looking for you."

I took another mouthful of the stew and savored every drop. "Not good."

"Why?"

"He'll show up here looking for me sooner or later." Unable to help myself, I ate another spoonful. "I'm surprised it's taken him this long. I'd imagine he found Richard and remembered what I said about staying there."

"It sounds like a lot happened out there in the desert."

"It got exciting there for a minute."

She watched me eat and then looked back toward the cliffs to the north. "Do you think something has happened to your dog?"

"More likely he's done something to somebody else."

She shook her head at me. "He's just a dog."

"You haven't seen him in action." I finished the stew and began eating the bread, swabbing it in the bowl and finding something that looked foreign. Thinking it might've been part of the finger, I flicked it out with a nail. "Okay, so I had an interesting conversation with your father."

"Trust me, they're all interesting."

"He says he didn't know about Freebee and Lowell taking members out in the desert and shooting them."

She stared at me. "And you believe him?"

"I'm kind of an expert on reading people and I think he was genuinely shocked and more than a little spooked when I told him about the map."

"Wait . . ." Her eyes came back to me. "You told him about the map?"

I sat the bowl in the sand between us. "I assumed it was something he knew about."

"No, he didn't. No wonder he looked spooked and shocked."

"Uh-oh."

"Um, yeah."

"So, who has this map?"

"Richard says it's hidden where they'll never find it."

I chuckled to myself, mostly. "You know, this is turning out to be the most inconvenient case of my career."

"And you're laughing about that?"

"No, something my undersheriff said about this being how I was going to get killed, this foolishness."

"Foolishness?"

Ignoring her question, I asked. "Can you get Penelope?"

She now grew serious. "I can."

"What about my sidearm?"

"Possibly."

"Where's your truck?"

"Parked near the bus but I might be able to get a key."

I picked up the bowl and started to hand it back to her when I saw somebody else come down the trail from the compound and quickly placed the loose manacle back over my ankle, unattached. "Jeez, this place is like Grand Central Terminal . . ." I lowered my voice. "Look, give it a shot but don't endanger yourself."

Benny appeared at the periphery of the chain length. "Blair, baby, you dad wants to speak with you."

"I bet he does." Picking up the empty bowl and spoon, she walked past him without looking at him as he watched her go. "And don't you ever call me 'baby' again."

He faced me. "You know, I may have to tap that one more time."

I shook my head and took the last sip of my water. "Benny, how about you just go away?"

"Hey, big man, you don't make the rules anymore—didn't anybody tell you?"

"Did you get your money yet, Benny?"

"No, but they're good for it."

I stood up, careful not to disturb the manacle and watched as he checked the sand, making sure he was just out of reach. "Are they, now?"

"Look, man, I know you think I'm an idiot, but I was just playing you along, see?"

"Sure you were."

"If I wanted, I could just shoot you now, so you better be cool."

I took a step toward him, trailing the chain after my ankle. "Shoot me with what?"

He pulled back his vest, revealing the Colt six-shooter as he raised his eyebrows to show me he meant business. "This, man."

"Is that Freebee's Colt?"

"Yeah, but he doesn't need it in his condition."

I took another step toward him and watched as he stepped back, supposedly out of arms reach. "Neither do you."

He pulled the elongated revolver out and pointed it at me. "I can shoot you, man."

"No, I don't think you can." I took another, final step toward him, now supposedly at the end of my tether.

He drew the single-action hammer back, leveling it at my face. "I'm warning you . . ."

"Benny, have you checked to see if that thing is loaded?"

He studied me with one eye from over the sights. "What?"

"Seeing as I dumped all the .45 rounds out of that particular gun more than twelve hours ago, unless you reloaded it, you're pointing an empty pistol at me right now."

He kicked the thing to the side in his hand, peering at the back of the cylinder, looking for brass.

As I stepped forward, he pulled the trigger and the firing pin fell on the empty chamber, making a loud snapping sound as his arm drew back from the imaginary recoil.

We stood there looking at each other as he quickly took another step back and pulled the hammer again, once more squeezing the trigger, whereupon it did not fire again, and he stared at the thing in utter disbelief. He finally looked up at me, half screaming. "Doesn't matter, you're still chained to a tree, man."

I took another step, the manacle falling free as I grabbed the pistol from him, flipping the thing forward, then taking Richard Zevin's finger and handing it to him. "Here, hold this for a minute."

He took the thing, staring at it as I retrieved the rounds from my shirt pocket and began loading the big Colt.

He cleared his throat, his voice pleading as he looked up from the finger at me. "Please don't chain me to the tree . . ."

The International wasn't parked very far from the bus, but there were people everywhere and I couldn't see Blair, assuming she, her father, and the two henchmen were inside the multicolored Blue Bird conveyance.

The thought was confirmed in that, even in the darkness, I could see and smell the smoke coming from the small stack in the rear. The loading deck of the Travelall was extended and there were blankets and a pillow, informing the fact that they were probably going to have to use the International to haul Freebee and Lowell into the hospital in Rock Springs and try and explain the gunshot wounds to the local authorities.

I could steal the Travelall, but I'd have to get Blair and the baby in there, and that meant leaving the rest of the crowd at the hands of the psychopaths for as long as it took me to make it back into town and get Grossnickle and the cavalry out here before the muscle started using the old folks as target practice.

As near as I could figure, I didn't have too many options: Go in there and kill all three of them, or at the very least the two really crazy ones, and then chain Carruthers to the tree with Benny, which was worse enough torture for anybody.

The rear of the bus was backed into an area with the same stunted juniper trees from earlier and some wooden crates that could provide cover. I ducked under the branches and got to the rear of the bus, then sat with my back against it, listening.

"That's what he said."

Blair's voice responded. "I don't know anything about that, besides, it was just something he said . . . Where would I get something like that?"

"Do you know what that could do to us?"

"I don't care, I just want my granddaughter and me out—that's all I've ever wanted."

Carruthers's voice was different than it had been when I'd been speaking with him earlier, and it was possible he was a better actor than I'd given him credit for. "Blair, I'm trying to give you more than that."

"Whatever you've got to give, I don't need."

Freebee's voice chimed in, weak but not as weak as I would've thought. "You keep talking like that and you're going to end up out there chained to the tree with your friend."

Carruthers interrupted. "What are we going to do with him?"

"I honestly don't want to kill the big bastard, but I don't know of any other way. He knows too much."

"So we kill him."

"I suppose so."

Blair's voice rose. "Just like all the others?"

There was a loud smack, and I could only assume that she had been rewarded for her decency as Curruthers's voice continued. "What are we going to do about you?"

Freebee's voice was dismissive. "I'm fine."

"No, you're not, and we have to get you to a hospital or a doctor or something, you and Lowell both." Carruthers's voice sounded a little desperate. "We'll take the two of you to the clinic on the north side of town where our friend has set up practice. He's the one I've seen, and he'll patch you up without notifying the authorities."

It was odd hearing him talk like this after just striking his own daughter, and I couldn't help but wonder what the connection was between him and the young gunman that would lead him to take as big of a chance as what he was contemplating.

"So do we kill the sheriff now or when we get back?"

Freebee's voice again. "When we get back, I'll get my gun from that idiot Benny, and I'll do him myself." He then added. "I owe him that much."

Generous of him.

"I'll drive us to the clinic, since I'm the only one that knows him."

"What about her?"

"We'll take the keys to the bus. I don't think she's foolish enough to try and walk out of here with the baby."

I listened as they moved around, obviously getting ready to head into town.

Sitting there with my back to the bus, I started wondering about what it was I could do next—either step out there and take my chances, shooting the three of them and saving Blair, or try to figure out something else? I wasn't in the best shape of my life after my little jaunt through the desert.

Slowly standing, I placed a hand on one of the crates and stood as the lid shifted, revealing what was inside—it was full of the light-colored robes that seemed to be the uniform of the day.

I stared at them, thinking.

There was more movement in the bus, and I listened as they made their way toward the front, even going so far as to move to the corner where I watched Carruthers help Freebee down the steps and deposit him in the passenger seat of the Travelall. Blair came out next with Lowell and put him in the back as Carruthers came around and shut the door, confronting her.

"Perhaps we should take Penelope with us, as insurance."

"No."

He smiled. "No?"

She stood her ground. "No. You don't know how to take care of her and I'm not risking you harming her again."

"What if I said that you don't get a vote?"

"Then you go ahead and take her, but if anything happens to her, I'll see you dead."

He laughed again, pulling out the keys to the International. "I suppose she'd be more trouble than she's worth."

My eyes followed him as he climbed in and started the Travelall, backing it up and then driving it out of the small area and scattering the forty-odd people who were still seated around the campfires.

Blair watched them and then reentered the bus to rejoin her granddaughter.

I pushed the open lid of the crate and pulled out one of the robes, the tag of which read XXL. I then stared at the Blue Bird Conventional model from the early sixties, trying to remember how many people the thing would likely hold.

Its top speed?

Downhill with the clutch engaged.

There are crazy ideas, and then there are really crazy ideas. The one I was thinking of was probably the latter more than the former, but how would I get all the crazy people on the bus? And once I got them on the bus, where would I take them?

Folding the robe over my arm, I crept alongside the elongated Blue Bird and slipped in the doorway, climbing halfway up to find Blair already on her way down the aisleway with the swaddled babe.

She froze as I folded my arms on the partition and rested my chin there with a smile. "Hey, have I ever told you about the time I hotwired a bus?"

14

"I was sixteen and had a driver's license, so it wasn't completely illegal."

Blair sat in the passenger's seat with Penelope still wrapped in her arms, her legs propped up on the transmission hump, allowing me to trail my legs down the aisle to get a look underneath the dash—the hooded robe under my head and a flashlight nestled in the crook of my neck and shoulder. "Will you please hurry up before they come back?"

"What's it going to take, an hour into town, a couple of hours there and then an hour back?" I'd already removed the ignition switch bezel and dropped the cylinder down to where I could get at the wires and attempt to disconnect them. "By then, we'll be long gone."

A few of the old folks had come up to the bus and were now standing in the stairwell, uncertain about what exactly was going on but were being reassured by Blair that everything was fine. One of the robed individuals was limping, an elderly woman with a Germanic accent. She asked, "Did . . . did you lose the keys?"

Blair reassured her. "We did, Mrs. Wasserstein, but we've got a mechanic here who thinks he can get it going."

"He doesn't look . . . He doesn't look like a mechanic."

"Well, we have to make do out here in the desert."

"He looks like the one that dragged the two men in from the desert."

Blair cleared her throat. "He is. Aren't we lucky?"

There were two tabs on either side of the ignition assembly, and I pushed them with my thumb to release them from the plug attached to the wires. I stared at the thing. It was different from what I'd been used to back in the salad days, and I was unsure as to how to get the wires loose and just as unsure as to how to attach them to start the aged Blue Bird.

"How's it going under there?"

I watched as Mrs. Wasserstein got bored and wandered off, which seemed like something they all did. The flashlight fell and I worked to get the beam repositioned. "Hey, can I ask you something?"

She laughed. "I don't think there are too many secrets between us anymore."

"Are those people on something? I mean, when I first ran into Richard Zevin out there by the campfire, he seemed pretty much like a zombie, but when I met him again with the shooters out in the desert, he seemed as though he'd come out of it."

"They're drugged." She adjusted Penelope in her arms. "Xylazine."

I ducked my head to look up at her, the flashlight falling again. "Horse tranquilizer?"

"Yeah, the cheap powdered stuff. They mix it in with the Tang they give them at breakfast. It's also what causes the lesions in the ones they have to inject."

"The sores, like the ones Zevin has?"

"Yeah, not only that but it depresses their breathing, heart rate, and blood pressure to dangerous levels and the results are those blackened, chemical burn–like flesh wounds . . ."

"Not leprosy?"

"No, but that way they think they're cursed and in need of redemption and it also keeps people away from them so there aren't so many questions."

"My God."

"Pretty horrific, huh?" She stared at my shocked and repulsed face. "So, how's it going under there?"

I reexamined the wires and tried to get my mind back on the job. "I don't suppose you have a paperclip or two?"

"No, but I've got a couple of hairpins."

"Those might do it."

I watched as she reached into her hair, pulling a few pins out and handing them to me and I was relieved they weren't the plastic-coated variety. "So, back in the day, why did you steal the bus?"

Aware that she was attempting to keep my mind off the plight of the true believers, I went along, retelling the story written in my mind as I worked with my hands. "We had this bus driver who was kind of an asshole and since I was the last drop-off on the route, I had to put up with his comments on race, religion, politics, and women the whole way. Another thing he did was stop periodically and get out to light up the most rank-smelling cigars in human history."

"Like my father."

"Kind of. And we'd have to sit there in that bus and wait for him to finish up before continuing on. Well, it was the last day of school, and I'd pretty much had enough of him."

"So what'd you do?"

Finding the live wire, I placed one end of the pin in a hole and then paused before inserting another. "Can you check that stick shift and make sure it's in neutral?"

I watched as she rattled the lever, making sure.

"Contact."

"Roger that." I watched the small spark as I inserted the other wire. "That's the ignition circuit, now I have to find the starter."

"So, what'd you do?"

"While he was out there on the Powder River with his stogie, I closed the door. At first, he didn't notice, and by that time I'd hot-wired the thing and fired it up." Inserting another wire, I tapped it on the live one and watched as the lights came on throughout the bus. "Crap."

"Then what?"

I switched the wire again and the horn tooted before I plucked it away. "Then I drove everybody home and left the bus at the last stop, my family's ranch road."

"Not smart."

"No, but it wasn't like everybody didn't already know who stole the bus."

"Well, they say that outlaws make the best cops . . ."

Preparing to insert the wire in the last hole, I once again adjusted the flashlight so I could see what I was doing. "I somehow doubt that."

"What happened?"

"That, along with a fight with a good friend of mine, got us both a week of community service."

"Bummer."

"Not really. We basically babysat Robert Taylor, who was the grand marshal for County Fair and Rodeo Week."

Mrs. Wasserstein, who had evidently wandered back over, interrupted. "*The* Robert Taylor?"

"Yep."

The elderly woman continued. "*Quo Vadis*, *Ivanhoe*, *Westward the Women*, and *Devil's Doorway*? *That* Robert Taylor?"

"In the flesh." Tapping the wire, I listened as the starter on the ancient conveyance turned the motor over with no results. Reaching over my shoulder, I pumped the accelerator with my hand. "Hey, Blair, is there a choke on the dash?"

"The little yellowed plastic one with a *C* on it?"

"That'd be it. Pull it out as far as it'll go."

She did as I'd instructed and I touched the wires, the starter kicking in again, but this time the big engine responded with a grumble and then finally a roar. As Blair pushed the choke partially in, I tapped the accelerator at my shoulder and listened as it loped into an uneven idle. "There we go."

"That's it?"

"For now." Shimmying out, I sat up and grabbed my hat from the dash. "Okay, so what do we do to get everybody on the bus?"

She stood, looking out to where the folks were milling about like livestock. "It's pretty easy, we sing."

I looked up at her. "We *what*?"

"We sing. No kidding, it works every time. We just start singing and they'll all just pick up their stuff and file onto the thing."

"What do you sing?"

"Doesn't matter; they usually sing hymns, but I've seen them use Buddy Holly."

Climbing up, I sat in the driver's seat, adjusting the choke the rest of the way as the motor smoothed out. "Well, get out there and sing 'em in."

She rocked the baby gently and looked at me.

"What?"

"It works better if more than one person sings."

"You've got to be kidding."

"Nope."

"I don't sing."

"What? Are you nuts? Everybody sings."

"Not me, I'm horrible. I can play the piano, but I can't sing. Honestly."

She glanced behind her at the wandering denizens. "What do you think this is, Carnegie Hall? They just need it to be loud enough for them to respond. It'll also help if you put that robe on . . ."

"Oh, good grief." I did as she requested and then followed her to the doorway of the bus where a few of the old people were milling about. Allowing her to stand on the steps, I stood to the side. "Okay, which one of your greatest hits do you want to do?"

"How about the state song of Wyoming?"

I finished tying off the sash of my borrowed robe. "Excuse me?"

"I had to sing it for the state postal meeting, it was Poppa Bear Mike's idea. I've actually got a pretty great voice—do you know the lyrics?"

I shook my head in disbelief. "I used to, back when I was hot-wiring buses."

"Well, I'll sing and you just join in when you can?"

"Sure."

Clearing her throat, I watched as she straightened and began singing. I've always been envious of people who can sing, but particularly envious of people who can really sing, and Blair was one of the chosen few. The voice that flowed forth from her was nothing short of astounding, and all I could do was stand there and watch as she began.

"In the far and mighty West,
Where the crimson sun seeks rest,
There's a growing splendid State that lies above,
On the breast of this great land;
Where the massive Rockies stand,
There's Wyoming young and strong, the State I love!"

Picking up on the tune, I jumped in on the chorus and as bad as my singing voice was, in comparison with hers it was a hundred times worse.

"Wyoming, Wyoming! Land of the sunlight clear!
Wyoming, Wyoming! Land that we hold so dear!
Wyoming, Wyoming! Precious art thou and thine!
Wyoming, Wyoming! Beloved State of mine!"

I watched as the brethren began packing up their meager items and shambling toward us like sheep. My belief that my singing voice was possibly the worst known to mankind was confirmed as Blair couldn't help but side-eye me as I struggled to remember the words.

"In the flowers wild and sweet,
Colors rare and perfumes meet;
There's the columbine so pure, the daisy too,
Wild the rose and red it springs,
White the button and its rings,
Thou art loyal for they're red and white and blue."

Taking a moment before we launched into the chorus again, I asked, "Do we have to keep going?"

"Just another chorus." She belted the song out and I did my best to keep up.

"Wyoming, Wyoming! Land of the sunlight clear!
Wyoming, Wyoming! Land that we hold so dear!
Wyoming, Wyoming! Precious art thou and thine!
Wyoming, Wyoming! Beloved State of mine!"

She stepped aside and allowed the followers to enter the bus in single file as she rocked the baby, and for the first time, I was surprised to hear Penelope crying. "I thought you said she didn't cry?"

"Evidently that voice of yours is enough to bring even her to tears."

Not allowing my feelings to be hurt, I watched as the majority filed on the bus and then helped the more enfeebled ones in getting up the stairs. With the last one, Mrs. Wasserstein, seated in the front row, I saw Blair and the howling baby seated behind me. "Okay, here we go."

I'd just turned back when I noticed something important. "Does the gas gauge on this thing work?"

I could barely hear her over the yowling baby. "I think so."

"Then it's out of gas."

"Oh God, no."

"Yep, as near as I can tell we've got about one sixty-fourth of a tank of gas."

She leaned over my shoulder, looking at the gauge. "That's not going to get us far."

"There's the fuel dump."

We both looked toward the accented voice from the first row where Mrs. Wasserstein sat. "Excuse me?"

"They have spots where they bury fuel for the bus, it uses so much of the stuff."

I glanced at Blair and then back at the woman. "Fuel dumps?"

She nodded, kneading the sash from her robe in her fingers. "There must be a half dozen of them."

"Who does he think he is, Erwin Rommel?"

Blair sighed. "I think he actually played him in a Scholastic film . . ."

I leaned across the aisle and placed a hand on Mrs. Wasserstein's. "And how do we find one of these fuel dumps?"

Her eyes brightened, and for the first time she revealed a mischievous grin, raising a crooked finger toward the windshield of the bus. "They're marked on the back of the sun visor."

I made the right turn toward the Boar's Tusk, just hoping there were enough fumes in the tank to get us to one of the numerous X's on the abbreviated sun-visor map. "You know, I'm really getting tired of these maps . . . By the way, do we have a physical one of where the bodies are buried?"

"I don't know who has it, but I know it exists."

"You've seen it, this map?"

"No, but I heard Richard talking about it, before they started giving him the injections; he referred to it as the 'map that blocks the sun.'"

"Right." I thought about the lone individual I'd left with food, water, shade, and a missing finger near the cliffs. "Maybe he was confusing it with the fuel-dump map."

Pulling up to a dogleg in the roadway, I peeled off to the side and noticed a rock outcropping. I turned off the engine to conserve what fuel there was and flipped down the sun visor, staring at the marks made in Sharpie on the cardboard surface. There was an *X* near a wavy line and some dots at the dogleg, and I could only imagine it was the spot I was now gazing upon. "Is there a shovel on board?"

Blair nodded. "There are hand tools in the back by the stove—pickaxes, rakes, and shovels."

I started toward the rear of the bus, looking into the gaunt faces of the people seated in the tiny bench seats like prisoners. Isn't that what they were? But they were more than that—they were fathers and mothers, brothers and sisters, husbands and wives, even somebody's children—and what had they done to deserve treatment like this?

They'd had faith.

They'd had faith and had entrusted it in the wrong people, kind of like Rommel.

Halfway down the aisle, I felt my boots stop and words coming out of my mouth. "It's okay." I took in the sight of their hollowed eyes and the sores on their bodies. "I know you've been through a lot, but it stops here and now, and you're all going to be okay."

"Are you here to save us?" I looked down to see an elderly man with his head against the glass, two black eyes and a bandage over his nose, not even looking at me.

"You bet your ass I am."

I watched the reflection of his face as he grinned a wan smile, some of the others even going so far as to chuckle.

I wasn't so sure they believed me.

I headed toward the back again, finding a number of shovels and picking the broadest and heaviest one. Tossing it onto my shoulder, I started toward the front as Blair joined me in getting off the bus.

Limping out to the spot, I rested the shovel in the sand, searching in the darkness, pretty sure I could see a disturbance in the surface, which could've been caused by the wind, but I hoped not.

"Are you all right?"

I turned back to look at her. "What?"

"Your leg, I was just asking if you were okay?"

"Yep, I just must've post-holed it a bit hauling those two psychos out of the desert." I placed the shovel in the sand and easily plunged the blade a full depth. "Well, somebody loosened the dirt and sand hereabouts, for whatever that's worth."

"I knew Erwin Rommel."

Blair and I both turned to see the old woman a little way off with a few of the others who were wandering about, obviously curious as to what we were doing.

"Mrs. Wasserstein, I think you and your friends should get back on the bus."

She paid no attention to me as I watched her gaze out at the mountains to the north. "Actually, I knew his older sister, who was an art teacher in Heidenheim. I was born in Danzig, where they had the officer cadet school, and he visited her once when I was receiving a lesson."

"He was one of the ones who tried to kill Hitler, you know."

It was another man, the one with the black eyes and bandaged nose who had been resting his head against the window.

Blair tried corralling them. "Mister Holt, it might be best if you were to get back on the bus?"

"No, I'd rather not." He glanced around at some of the others who weren't coming out of the walking coma so quick. "I owned a lumber company up near Medford, Oregon, and I'm not a stranger to a shovel."

My turn to smile. "Mister Holt, if you'd be so kind as to get yourself an implement, I'd be happy to have you join me." He walked back as a few others came off the bus, gathering about to see what was what as I began digging, the robe somewhat impairing my efforts.

The sand was loose and was easy digging in the cool of the night, but I was glad when Holt returned and joined me in the hole I'd made. After a few moments others joined, and before long we had a growing chain in moving sand as some scooped with their hands, pulling the stuff away from the hole.

Even amid the dire situation, I had to admit that it brought a smile to my face, watching the octogenarians come back to life and, after a while, I had to ask some of them to vacate the hole in that we were in danger of conking each other with the shovels. I was surprised at how, when no longer under the influence of the tranquilizers, their personalities were starting to exhibit themselves.

"I've got something here."

Another man, a burly individual a little over five feet in height who'd owned a trucking company in Riverside in a previous life, was poking at something in the sand.

I moved around the man and pulled the flashlight from my pocket, shining it at the area, but unable to see what he'd been talking about. "Excuse me, Mister Espinoza."

I dug around with the corner of the scoop shovel and felt it graze something. I then swept more sand away to reveal a withered, darkened, skeletal human foot encased in a plastic shoe.

"It's Mister Eggers. He's the only one that wore Crocs." Espinoza nodded his head as we did our best to slide a plastic tarp underneath the body.

To my surprise, none of the others moved away from the spectacle, continuing to hover near the hole as we continued in our grisly chore.

A tall woman in the group spoke up. "They told us that he'd gone on."

"Well, Mrs. Bellamy, in a way, he has." I stopped digging for a moment, tipping my hat back and wiping the sweat from my forehead. "When did Mister Eggers . . . um, move on?"

Holt, in the other end of the hole, sighed. "About a month ago, as I recollect."

Having now slipped the tarp under the body, we gently lifted it from the hole and slid it onto level ground at the crowd's feet. "That would make sense in the five stages of decomposition—fresh, or autolysis; bloat; active decay; advanced decay; and dry/skeletonized, such as with Mister Eggers here. Each stage has specific characteristics that are used to identify the chronology of the remains, and I'd say Mister Eggers here is about a month old, give or take."

Perhaps too much information in that they were all staring at me now.

"Who are you?"

I looked up at Mrs. Wasserstein. "I am Walt Longmire, Absaroka County Sheriff."

She glanced at the others and then back at me. "And where is that?"

"Excuse me?"

"What country is that in?"

"The United States, ma'am."

"Of America?"

"Yes, ma'am. The state of Wyoming."

"I wondered why it was you people were singing that song." She looked thoughtful for a moment. "You're not a very good singer, young man."

"No, but I'm a pretty good sheriff." I leaned against the side of the hole, thinking about what to do next as Blair, still holding Penelope, appeared within the crowd and knelt down to talk with me.

"What's the story?"

"With Eggers? Oh, he was shot all right and probably with this pistol of Freebee's that I've got tucked in my belt."

"Well, at least you found your map."

"Yep. 'Your Honor, I'd like to introduce as evidence, the sun visor of a '61 Blue Bird bus . . . ' All I know is that it's the desert and you need transport or you're dead, and we seem to be fresh out of gas."

"There's the fuel dumps."

Blair and I looked at Mrs. Wasserstein, who had knelt to join us. "Yep, ma'am, but as it turns out the map on the sun visor actually marks the . . . How can I say this, the undiscovered country from which no traveler returns."

"No, the other sun visor."

I stared at her. "Excuse me?"

"The other sun visor is the one with the fuel dumps marked on it.

If I pointed toward the wrong one, then I apologize. My mind has been very foggy but I'm getting better. I know that one of the sun visors has the fuel dumps marked on it, so it must be the other one."

I looked over at Blair, but she had disappeared.

"Mrs. Wasserstein, why were you asking me who I was and where we were? Do you mind if I ask where you folks thought you were?"

"We're not in the Holy Land?"

"No, ma'am."

"We always wear our hoods when traveling but we were told we were in the Judean Desert between Jerusalem and the Dead Sea."

I was starting to see why Carruthers had chosen the areas he had in which to hide his little group. "No, you're in the Red Desert in south-central Wyoming."

"Not the Holy Land?"

"Well, some folks think of it that way."

"It's here." Blair, still holding Penelope, knelt down again, holding the sun visor out to me. "There are six of them and one is back down the road and to the left, about a mile I'm guessing."

I took the thing and flipped on the flashlight to see that the dumps were distributed evenly throughout the area and determine which one was indeed the closest. "Well, let's hope that one has fuel in it."

We carefully loaded the body of Mister Eggers in the aisle at the back of the bus, and I had to admit I was glad he'd achieved the level of decay he had, happy to forgo the liquification or gaseous stages in the environs of the bus.

I sat in the driver's seat and took one last look at the sun-visor map, then touched the one hairclip to the other and listened as the V-8 obediently rumbled to life. Slipping her in gear, I glanced back toward the much more alert and anticipating faces on the bus as they raised their hoods and placed them over their heads. "Hang on!"

Spinning the wheel, I turned a U and headed back whence we'd come. I threw a look at the woman seated beside Blair. "Mrs. Wasserstein, I hope you don't mind me asking, but were you in other places before here?"

She nodded emphatically, her face framed in the hood. "Oh, yes. It's been quite a tour."

"And what were those places?"

"We were in the Desert of Sin, the Sur, Sinai, the Judean Desert, and the Negev."

I turned the corner at the cutoff to the Boar's Tusk and headed east, hoping the fuel would hold out. "Wow, you really covered some ground."

"Yes, but I'm beginning to think we might've been bamboozled."

"It's possible." I checked the gauge but was pretty sure that it was pegged at the bottom. I couldn't be certain, but I was hoping that the gauge was somehow broken.

I slowed to a stop farther than I really wanted to go up the road and checked the map with the flashlight, but couldn't see any cutoff to the right this time, where the *X* was. I switched off the ignition and opened the door, noticing a change in foliation of the branches that covered a large area.

Stepping off and onto the dusty sand-filled road, I reached out and grabbed one of the dead branches, pulling it away to reveal a hidden road that led into the juniper bushes that surrounded it.

Some of the others climbed off the bus and began assisting me in clearing the area, and after a few minutes we were good to go. Gathering the group onto the bus, I connected the wires with a touch and grinded the starter to no avail.

"You have got to be kidding." Pumping the gas, I hit the wires again and watched the gentle spark. Still nothing. "I don't believe this."

Blair, now holding Penelope again, leaned forward. "What is it?"

"I think we're out of gas."

Touching the wires I tried again, and with the same results.

"We are out of gas."

"What are we going to do?"

"I don't know."

"We push it."

We looked back to find Mister Holt standing in the aisle. "We've got almost forty people here, and we can at least push it off the road. Then we go get the gas from the dump and refill this thing."

I gestured toward the back of the bus. "Do you really think they're up to the job?"

He shouted at the group. "Brethren, we must lend a helping hand in moving the bus!"

To my amazement, the group began moving and filing out the door.

I turned the steering wheel and made sure the emergency brake was off and that the transmission was in neutral. Climbing out, I joined the group as they all laid hands on the Blue Bird as if it were a religious experience.

I had my doubts, but it was a lot of people, even if they were a little long in the tooth. "Okay, everybody ready?" Anchoring the left corner where I thought I'd do the most good, I put my back to the rear of the bus and dug in with my boots, which accomplished nothing.

Peering over to the other corner, I could see Holt anchoring that side. "On three?"

He nodded. "On three!"

"One, two, three . . ." I dug in and, to my amazement, the bus actually began moving. "Keep the pressure on, now that we've got momentum!"

The bus was moving at an extremely slow pace, but it was rolling toward an opening at the side of the road and maybe even gaining a little momentum. "Keep pushing!"

There was a slight berm to the right and the bus eased momentarily as both front wheels rolled over and then gained a little more momentum as the thing started heading toward the bushes to the right.

"Oh, hell . . ." Running around the others, I got to the door and leapt up as best I could, getting to the steering wheel and straightening it down the cutoff that appeared to have the slightest slope. "Thank heaven for small favors."

Holding her steady in the short road, I flipped on the lights and could see an opening where, hopefully, the *X* might have indicated the next fuel dump was. I hit the brakes and switched off the headlights—just what I needed was to find fuel and then have a dead battery.

I put the thing in park and ratcheted the emergency brake, hoping that we hadn't run over anybody in our efforts. Grabbing my shovel and climbing out, I could see the ragtag group in their robes coming down the cutoff where the Blue Bird had outflown them.

Blair was first, still holding the child. "Are we good?"

"I think so, there's an opening in front of the bus and I'm hoping they weren't stupid enough to actually bury the cans in the road."

I made good on my word and began digging, almost immediately striking something in the sand as the others gathered around, some with shovels. "There's something here."

Moving a little more to the side, I scooped the sand away, hoping to not see any more body parts. Instead, I could see the integrated handle of a metal jerry can. "Jeez, maybe it is Rommel's fuel dump, after all."

Prying the thing up a bit, I reached down and pulled it the rest of the way out of the ground and could tell from the weight of it that it was full of something. Turning the cap, I pulled out the spout to the delicious perfume of petrol. "We've got gas!"

There were small cheers and some applause as I screwed the cap back on in reverse, attaching the spout and handing it to Holt, who was the first in line. "Fill 'er up."

"Will do!"

He disappeared and Espinoza took his place, some of the others falling in line as I went back to digging and extricating another of the five-gallon metal cans, following the same procedure and handing it up to the former trucker. "Here you go."

He nodded and Mrs. Wasserstein limped over and took his place. "Ma'am, I'm afraid that these cans are much too heavy for you to lift."

She smiled, shaking her head at me as she readjusted her leg. "Young man, I don't think you know what I'm capable of if properly motivated."

I scraped away more sand and pulled another can out, taking a breather before unscrewing the spout. "And what exactly are you capable of if properly motivated, Mrs. Wasserstein?"

She folded her hands and studied me. "When my hometown Danzig was sieged by the Soviets chasing after the Nazis, my sister Reva and I joined the Polish resistance and dropped marvelously huge cobblestones down on the Nazis and killed eight of them. Then, once the Russians came in and started killing and raping everyone, we started dropping rocks on them."

"How many did you get?"

"You don't want to know, young man."

I nodded, unscrewing the tap and reversing the spout and threading it back in before handing it up to her. "You're probably right."

Others took their place as I dug up the rest and trundled off until Holt came back around for the last can. "This it?"

"I think so. There might be a few more in here, but I think that's plenty of fuel to get us to Rock Springs."

He took the can from me and then stuck out a hand to assist me in getting out of the hole. "Then what?"

"The Sweetwater County Sheriff's Office."

"Think they'll help us?"

"I know they will." Using the shovel as another source of leverage, I grunted my way up and stood there with him, looking at the faint glow in the sky to the east.

"It'll be daylight before long."

"Yep, but it should take less than an hour to get into town." I watched as he removed the bandage from his nose, revealing a great deal of swelling there along with more of the two black eyes. "Mister Holt, are you the one I punched in the nose?"

He nodded. "I believe so. As best I can remember, you were bound and determined to keep on walking after you got out of the dunes and I stepped in front of you to stop you."

"I'm sorry."

"Don't worry about it. It might've knocked some sense into me."

Patting him on the shoulder, I took the can from him and started toward the rear of the conveyance. "Do me a favor and get all these folks back on the bus. When I get this thing started, we're going to be heading out of here like a Blue Bird out of hell."

"Roger that."

I couldn't help but ask, so I called back to him. "Mister Holt, were you in the military?"

"Air force. Yourself?"

"Marines."

He cocked a grin. "They still give you guys crayons to write home with?"

Playing along, I replied as I continued to head toward the back of the bus with the gas can. "No, we kept eating them."

He laughed and began corralling the group and herding them toward the open door of the bus as Blair appeared with Penelope, moving toward me. "Think we're going to make it?"

Lifting the back of the can, I inserted the spout and began emptying the five or so gallons into the tank. "I think so, if this thing'll start. I'm worried about the amount of sludge in the bottom of this half-century-old tank, and how much dirt and lacquer has been pulled up in the lines and fuel filter." I finished filling the thing and lowered the can. "Have they ever run this thing out of gas before?"

"I have no idea." She glanced back at the group as they filed on, pulling up their hoods.

"Why do they do that?"

"What?"

"Mrs. Wasserstein mentioned it, that they raise their hoods every time they travel on the bus?"

"More of my father's bullshit, supposedly to keep them from looking upon the wickedness of the world, but it was actually just to keep them from knowing where they were."

"And they still do it?"

"Habit, I guess." She looked back at the group and smiled. "It's amazing though, isn't it?"

"What's that?"

Her gaze stayed on the brethren as they raised their hoods and climbed on the bus, chatting with one another, some of them even laughing. "A lot of them, they're turning back into people."

Thinking about tossing the can to the side, I instead fastened its cap and brought it with me in case we needed another gallon or three. I couldn't help but smile as I thought about what she'd said. "The desert is a place of encountering and transition, it's where God brought the Israelites into the wilderness, because He wanted to speak to them at Mount Sinai. The desert is where God spoke to Moses, met with Elijah and John the Baptist. Heck, it was the place where the devil tempted Jesus." Tightening the bus's gas cap, I listened, thinking I might've heard something but then turned back to her. "How's Penelope?"

She stuck a finger in and touched the child's nose, which to my surprise caused her to make a small noise. "Did she just say something?"

"She did. I'm thinking your singing broke the spell."

"Wouldn't be the first time."

Ushering her and the baby back toward the doorway, I heard the noise again. Taking a few steps, I studied the opening back at the road just in time to see a 1968 International Travelall streak by.

15

"Do you think they saw us?"

Lodging the jerry can in the front row, I sat and gave the old bus just a bit of choke, pumping the gas and then saying a detailed prayer to those desert angels that might still be ministering our way. "We're not sticking around to find out." I continued to pump the gas but heard nothing but the grinding of the starter. "Damn . . ."

I let up and allowed the thing to rest for about fifteen seconds, then hit it again. This time, it caught for just the briefest of moments. Turning it off, I waited only ten seconds this time and then hit it again, pumping the accelerator for all I was worth and hoping I wasn't flooding the thing with the newly found gas.

It roared, and so did I.

I let off the gas again and it stumbled, but I punched in the choke and threw off the emergency brake, then switched on the headlights and jammed it into reverse, barreling backward and shouting at the hooded group, "Everybody hang on!"

It was a short run to the road, especially in reverse. It was probably the lowest gear the old bus had, but at least we were moving.

We'd almost made it halfway back to the road when I saw the International again, swinging into the entrance as we reached top speed. The headlights blinded me as I peered out the side mirror, but I watched as Carruthers tried to get the Travelall to stop and make use of its own reverse gear.

The lights receded, in that they were faster than we were, but we had momentum, and by the time we made it to the road they were backing out at an angle, trying to get out of the way of the oncoming behemoth.

Not for an instant did I let off the gas, and the Travelall never made it out of the way, the rear end of the big bus slamming into the front driver's-side fender of the International and crunching it. There was a surprisingly small amount of impact, but the bus riders screamed and yelled and were tossed around a bit.

The speed had carried us out onto the main road, and I wasn't taking any chances, shifting the Blue Bird in gear and stomping on the gas, watching in the mirror as the sand and dust filled the roadway from the spinning dual-set wheels.

We'd gone a couple hundred yards when I hit third gear and yelled back at Holt. "See 'em?"

He looked out the side. "No, but let me get to the back!"

I concentrated on the direction ahead, sawing the wheel and taking up the entire road, hoping we didn't meet anyone coming the other way. I'd just about gotten ready to yell at Holt again when I got my answer, a gunshot from outside the back of the bus. "They're still there?!"

I watched through the oversize rearview mirror as the elderly man stumbled over the dead body and lurched down the aisle, grabbing the rails on the back of the seats and finally reaching me. "Worse than that! They're attached to the back of the bus!"

I leaned farther out the window and could now see the tail end of the International swaying with the bus every time I took a turn. "Oh, good grief!"

There was another shot, and I yelled at the folks in the bus, "You people in the back, you need to move up here toward the front right now!"

Waiting until they all got settled as best they could, I shifted into fourth and began making evasive moves with the tonnage of the bus in hopes of getting loose from the Travelall and then praying I'd done enough damage to the thing to keep it from following.

People were still screaming and yelling, but I concentrated on the road. In a sweeping turn, I watched as the damn International skidded to the side, still locked onto the back of the bus, refusing to let go. "How in the hell is that thing holding on?"

Holt was beside me. "I got one quick glance through that window at the bottom of the emergency exit before they started shooting, and the bumpers are locked together."

"It's only a question of time before they try and blow out our tires . . ."

We hit a swell and the bus lifted on its suspension, crashing down like a makeshift roller coaster. "That get us loose?"

He stood straight, looking out the back. "No, they're still there."

I continued to swing the bus right and left as we hit a series of washboards powerful enough to knock the fillings from your teeth. "Still there?"

"Still there!"

"Damn it!"

Spotting a berm ahead with a log backing it up, I shifted down into third and wondered if the suspension on the bus would be able to take it and turned that way. "Hang on!"

The berm gave us a little height before we hit the log, but the jarring effect felt as if we'd bent a wheel for sure. I just hoped the tire would hold as the rear wheels hopped up and over the thing and the

Travelall bounced higher than the bus and jolted loose, heading straight into the bushes as we sped on.

"Hallelujah!"

I watched the thing set back there like a sinking ship in a cloud of dust, then I shifted into fourth and hit a straightaway that must've been a mile long.

Espinoza called from the back of the bus. "Our bumper just fell off!"

"Let it, we'll get better gas mileage!" Easing off the gas a bit for fear of pushing the old girl any more than I already had, I turned around in my seat to see the majority of the folks still crowded toward the front of the bus. "Is everybody okay?"

Blair answered. "I'm afraid Mrs. Millet might've broken her leg and Mister Keysen hit his head!"

"Well, make them as comfortable as you can, we can't risk stopping!"

Driving on, I couldn't help but feel as if the bus was pulling to the right, just as it would if the right front tire was losing air. I thought about pulling over, but if by any chance they got the Travelall out of the bushes and back on the road, I wanted to be long gone.

"Can you see anything?"

"Nope, we're free as a bird!"

"I'm going to pull over and get a look at the front tire." I coasted to a stop and unfolded the doors, leaving the motor idling. "Everybody stay in their seats."

Climbing down, I pulled out the flashlight and shined the beam on the wheel, confirming my feared suspicion.

The lip on the wheel was indeed bent, and when I knelt down, I could hear a tiny whistling even over the motor as the tire lost pressure.

"Bad?" I looked up to find Blair standing in the doorway, adjusting Penelope in her arms.

"Bad enough."

"Can we change the tire?"

I stood and walked back to the doorway, my attention back down the empty road. "We could if we knew where the spare was, and if it has air in it, and we can find the jack, and it works, and there's a tire iron."

"That's a lot of *ands.*"

"It certainly is." I took another step down the road. "By the time we do all of that, they might be able to walk here."

"I checked inside but didn't see any spare, but maybe this will help?"

I turned to find Mister Espinoza standing on the step behind Blair, holding a device out to me that I could see even in the half-darkness. "Is that my phone?"

He handed it to me. "I don't know, but it was lying on the floor."

I took the JugBug and flipped it open, surprised to find that it had power—and no signal. "You know, I'm having more trouble getting out of this desert than Moses." Just on the outside chance, I punched in 9-1-1 and held the thing aloft just in case it got through, but then lowered it and looked at the message across the bottom that read CALL FAILED. Fighting the urge to throw the thing into the dunes, I pocketed it. "And people wonder why I don't carry one of these things."

"Can we make it to the main road?"

I looked up at Blair. "Possibly. It's also possible we could get service there or flag somebody down, but sooner more than later that tire is going to be flat and then we're stuck." I looked down the road but still couldn't see anything. "If they're walking, we could pull away as far as we could and get away from them, and if they're driving then we can find a hiding spot long enough to change the tire, if we can find the spare."

"You can take a tire off the back and put it on the front."

I turned to Espinoza. "What?"

"You'd probably have to bolt the flat tire on back there because you might have to have a wheel as a spacer to get all of it to bolt together. It's risky, but it might work better than nothing."

"How do we break them loose?" I studied the massive lug nuts threaded on the hubs. "I'd imagine these things are torqued on with an air wrench."

"I checked, there's a heavy-duty plastic body air torque gun, one of those Ken-Tool shock-bar lug nut wrenches, a torque limiter extension, and a full toolbox—I don't think it's ever been used."

"Okay, from all that I'm going to assume you know what you're talking about, but what do we power the thing with?"

He laughed. "This bus has two pneumatic air lines out, one for tow usage to release the air brakes and the other is a utility line with an auxiliary compressor. If everything is operable, we should be able to get those wheels off in a blink. There's only one problem."

"What's that?"

"We only have one jack, but if we can pull that inside wheel on the back onto a rock or something then we can suspend the outer wheel and unbolt it."

I looked down the road, again, fully expecting to see the three horsemen of the Apocalypse headed this way. "Well, the cutoff for 17 is up ahead and we could take it as a shortcut to get to Rock Springs rather than continuing on to the pavement—if they are driving, they'd never suspect that we took that route."

"Why?"

"It's a rough road and in a bus without all its wheels . . . I wouldn't try it if I didn't have to."

"Do we have to?"

"I'm afraid so." Sticking a boot out I tapped the rubber sidewall. "Besides, the longer we sit here the flatter this tire gets."

There was another pullout toward the end of the straightaway but I decided to push it a bit. Too much, as it turned out. The blast from the exploding tire, which sounded like incoming mortar fire, was enough to almost send me into the ditch.

I slowed to a stop and jumped out to look at the damage, knowing full well we'd be lucky if we could get her moved another hundred yards. "Okay, that's it."

Looking up and down the road, I thought I could see the turnoff to the petroglyphs. "Six million acres and I find the one spot where there's no place to hide."

Holt and Espinoza climbed out to look down the road. Holt was the first to speak, indicating a road and sign about a quarter of a mile away. "Is that the road you mentioned, 17?"

I moved around to the front of the bus and was relieved to see where they were pointing. "Yep, that must be it." Climbing back in, I waved for them to follow. "Come on!"

They piled in and I closed the door, easing the bus forward, glad we were on the loose sand and talcum powder dirt at least. The thing vibrated like one of those old exercise machines as I tried to keep it pointed straight, the cutoff getting closer as I looked into the side mirror hoping to not see the Travelall.

We'd finally gotten to the southbound road as I wheeled us to the left and made it with a great deal of effort, deciding if I wanted to take the cutoff toward the petroglyphs to the right or push my luck again and try and make it to the Cedar Canyon cutoff to the left. Both were dead ends, which meant if they got the International drivable and found us, I'd have to press my luck yet again and use the bus as a battering ram.

"I'm sorry, but I have to go pee."

I looked back at Mrs. Wasserstein, who sat next to Blair. "Excuse me?"

"I have to pee, young man."

"Mrs. Wasserstein, you do realize we're running for our lives here?"

"Yes, but the fact remains that I have to pee."

"Right." Turning my attention back to the road, I figured "what the hell" and took the right. Why not take the route that had vault toilets?

After creeping along about two miles, there was an open area where I could circle the bus around and it'd at least be pointing in the right direction for our glacially slow escape. The humped-up sandstone buttresses off in the distance were just catching the first rays of sun as it crept its way into the darkened sky, the stars grudgingly giving way to the new day—and I was thankful that I wasn't out in the middle of the desert dragging two bodies along with me.

"There were a couple of busted concrete blocks in the back, along with a few solid ones, so I think we can get that one tire off the ground." Espinoza was standing in the aisle, holding on to the railing behind the driver's seat. "I don't know how much weight they'll hold, though, so I'm thinking we're going to need to get the people off here."

I saw the Forest Service sign ahead and the sturdy-looking bathroom with two stacks, stopped the bus, and stood to address the hooded group. "Bathroom break!"

As they got off, I joined Espinoza, Holt, and another man in the back where we grabbed the blocks, jack, auxiliary hoses, and air gun and moved toward the front. "Where's the pneumatic connection to that line?"

Espinoza pointed toward the rear and handed me the end of the hose as I made my way back. "Right there, where that panel is above the wheel well, where I got most of this stuff."

"Got it."

I dropped my concrete block and turned the wing nuts that held the thing, flipping it open. Looking inside past a pretty prodigious pack-rat nest, I pulled out the hose with the brass coupling and connected the two. "Now what?"

He knelt by the front tire and examined it with the two other men. They placed the jack under it and then moved back toward me, all of them carrying blocks or portions of blocks. Espinoza glanced around and then gestured forward. "Hop in and pull her forward slowly when I tell you to, and then be sure to stop when I tell you to do that."

"Got it."

Climbing in the driver's seat, I looked off to the right where Blair had the group lined up for the bathrooms like it was Disneyland. I ground the thing into first, then waited for Espinoza to give me the word.

I watched the crowd as they dropped their hoods and continued to talk and laugh, and it struck me how glad I was that they'd gotten their lives back.

I took a breath and waited.

I got curious and put the thing in neutral, climbing down the steps and looking back where they were still arranging the blocks. "Be sure to not be under that thing when I pull it forward, okay!"

They waved and I stood there looking out at the massive rock that contained the White Mountain Petroglyphs, thinking about the grooves in the stone they say had been there for hundreds of years.

"Penny for 'em?"

I looked down and could see Blair, cradling Penelope, who had circled around to check on the progress at the rear of the bus before coming up to see about me. "I'm afraid you'd be overcharged."

"I'm willing."

I nodded my chin toward the monument, and encyclopedia of the Shoshone tribe. "The birthing rock, it's on the panel to the left, decorated with petroglyphs of different animals giving birth."

She rocked her granddaughter. "Interesting."

"But that's not all. There are finger marks in the stone, some of them worn almost a foot into the rock, numbers of them."

"Why?"

"Shoshone women with child, they would come here and place their hands on the rock as a blessing and during the pain of the birthing process pressed their fingers against the rock, wearing the stone away."

"Really?"

"If we had time, I'd tell you to go up there and have a look."

"Kind of a hallmark for the strength and persistence of women, huh?"

"Never doubted it." Espinoza whistled and I gave him the high sign, climbing back in, but not before warning Blair. "You might want to step away from this rolling disaster."

She did as I said and I put the bus in gear, taking off the emergency brake and pulling it forward just a bit. When I didn't hear anything, I pulled forward a bit more but stopped when they began shouting. I put the emergency brake back on and stepped down, watching as they used the pneumatic wrench to take off the outside rear wheel.

"What're you going to do when this is all done?"

"Go find my dog."

She looked around. "Still expecting him?"

"Kind of, but if he got down to where Zevin is, he probably smelled the blood and then stayed with him. I told him to remain in that area if anything happened—he's nothing if not loyal."

We watched as the men rolled the tire toward the front and then climbed under, positioning the jack and lifting the shredded tire and wheel. The wrench made quick work of the job, then they lowered the thing back down good as relatively new, rolling the embattled tire toward the back.

"Do we have to worry about that thing doing damage to the good rear wheel on that side?"

Espinoza glanced at me as they continued. "Yes, we do."

Blair studied me, and then raised a hand to cover a laugh.

"What?"

"I'm just thinking about Benny, chained to that tree."

"I left him a bowl of water, so he'll make it as long as we did."

"He better hope we get to the authorities eventually, huh?"

I gazed back up the road. "Yep, he better."

Holt yelled out. "I don't want to break anything up, but we're almost ready!"

"Duty calls." Shrugging at her, I resettled my hat and robe and climbed back on the bus, sitting in the driver's seat as I waited for the call.

I sat there and waited, and waited, finally wondering if I'd missed the yell over the idling motor.

After a few minutes, I got concerned and started to climb down the steps when I heard something I wasn't prepared for—a gunshot.

Scrambling from the seat, I pulled the Colt Peacemaker from my belt and leapt down the steps only to be confronted by Lowell pointing his own revolver in Blair's ear.

He looked a little better than the last time I'd seen him with bandages wrapped around his head and his cowboy hat perched on top like a bottle cap. Saying nothing, he held the muzzle there and eyed the gun in my hand, nodding that I should throw it away.

There really wasn't any choice, in that all he had to do was pull the trigger and she was gone.

Stepping down to the last step, I placed Freebee's revolver on the tread of the second and looked at him, where he motioned for me to step down, which I did. He pulled Blair, still holding the baby, back.

To the right I could see the others standing against the side of the bus with their hands laced behind their heads and the slumped body of Mister Espinoza crumpled against the wheel where Lowell had shot him in the back of the head.

I looked at the gunman, who smiled.

"I will see you dead."

He smiled some more.

"You ever shoot somebody facing you?"

The smile faded just a bit.

"Somebody armed?"

The smile was gone now.

"I didn't think so."

Without his permission, I moved toward the back of the bus and past the men standing there. I carefully avoided the pool of blood drying in the sand, gripped Espinoza's shoulder, and pulled him back to me where I could cradle his body and lift the dead man from the ground.

Carrying the man forward, I placed his body in the shade near the door and then looked back at where he'd been working, finally turning to the gunman, who held Blair by the hair a couple of arm lengths away. "I don't know where your compatriots are, but I'm assuming the International isn't running and we're going to need something to drive, which also means somebody's going to have to finish the work he started before you killed him."

He stared at me.

"We have to get the tire on this thing before it'll move."

Predictably, he still said nothing.

Deciding I finally had enough, I ignored him and moved back to the wheel well and began threading the lug nuts onto the hub. It was a calculated move, and I could just as easily have ended up crumpled in my own pool of blood, but I was past the point of dealing with the psychopath.

Picking each lug nut up, I bided my time, thinking about what it was I was going to do—and exactly how I was going to do it.

Finally getting all eight on there, I started for the air wrench but then saw that Espinoza had also gotten the lug wrench from the compartment inside just to set the nuts after using the pneumatic gun.

I reached down.

As he'd said, it was one of those Ken-Tool shock-wrench bars, as the old ranchers used to call them, a two-piece monster of iron that assembled to make a four way with three sockets and a pry-bar edge that I'd used on tractors enough times growing up.

My fingers had just closed around the thing when I felt the muzzle of the .44 against the back of my head. It's what I would've done in his place, and I could fault him for being crazy but not stupid—more important, though, it meant that the pistol was no longer against Blair's head.

Ignoring him again, I began slipping the middle of the one piece, sliding it through the hole in the other until it made an impressive iron-forged four-way wrench.

I placed the socket over the one lug nut and started to stand, swinging around with all the momentum I could muster and bringing the tire iron against his arm as the gun went off.

It fired harmlessly into the dirt as he scrambled backward, his arm now hanging to the side with a horrible compound fracture, exposed bones showing as he still, miraculously, held on to the revolver.

He mouthed a horrible, screeching scream, then clumsily switched the Smith & Wesson from the one hand to the other, still trying to get used to the amount of pain he was no doubt enduring.

His eyes were wide as he lifted his face and started to raise the revolver at me, but I'd already drawn back with the heavy tool and threw it at him as hard as I could, hoping to knock him off-balance enough so that I could get to him.

But it did far more than that.

Maybe those desert spirits were with us, or possibly the thumb of chance decided to rest on the scales in our favor, but the one-in-four chance of the pry bar end hitting him first was something like a million to one—but the sharp edge of the thing buried itself in the center of his chest.

The penetrating stab wound must've gone completely through the edge of his sternum, his heart—if he had one—and possibly into his spine.

His hat fell off and he stood there still fighting the impact of the thing, trying not to fall backward, and still holding the gun. His head raised just a bit and his mouth hung open, his blind eyes darting about in search of I know not what. He stumbled a half step toward me and then slowly began raising the pistol.

I was still two steps away as he continued to lift the sidearm, but the weight of the thing seemed to be too much for him as the bloodstain bloomed from the center of his chest in the bright white T-shirt under his flannel shirt like justice incarnate.

I took a step toward him as his eyes seemed to find me but then searched more as his aim drew up toward my own chest, his wrist unintendedly lolling to the side.

It was as if he couldn't see me.

But what *was* he seeing?

I hoped it was the face of every individual he'd ever killed and buried out there in the desert—all of them. Most important, I hoped it was the former trucking-firm owner Espinoza smiling back at the killer and letting him know that it was now, undeniably, his time.

The pistol went off, missing me by a good four feet and rattling into the side of the bus as the others behind me screamed and scattered.

I took the last step forward and brought my hand up, stripping the weapon from his dying grip.

It was strange looking into those eyes without eyelashes or eyebrows, making him seem incomplete and not quite human. He slumped forward, the socket end of the wrench bumping against my stomach as he lifted his head some more to look up into my eyes.

I guess a better man would've said something comforting, if anything at all, but I didn't. I simply looked into that questioning and confused face and dismissively shrugged to the side, letting his lifeless body fall to the dirt.

He landed square on the wrench with a thud and, if possible, drove the four-way farther through his body and tent-poling the back of his shirt as his arms and legs quivered a bit before growing still.

Studying him for a moment, I turned to see the assembled group of forty-some people now at the front of the bus, staring at me in varying degrees of horror.

I gazed back at them for a moment and then stuffed the pistol in the back of my jeans before retrieving the air gun and kneeling to torque the lug nuts onto the bus. I thought about letting it go after using the air gun, but it was what you did, finishing the job.

I sat the pneumatic tool down and then stepped to the dead man's body, flipping him over and then reaching down with both hands as I placed a boot at his throat and pulled the four-way wrench from his chest with a sickening, sucking sound.

With all of them watching, I moved back over and put one last twist on each of the eight lug nuts in a pattern that made sure they were even.

I then tossed the heavy blood-dripping tool toward the dead man, where it thudded onto his perforated and leaking chest.

"What?" I dusted off my sticky hands and stared at the blood-soaked ground for perhaps longer than I should have, aware the group was still watching me as the words spilled from my mouth. "You gotta snug 'em up."

I'd carried Espinoza's body onto the bus and wrapped it up in another tarp before returning outside where some of them, not understanding what had just happened, didn't want to get on the bus. I guess I couldn't blame them, as they probably felt like they were just trading one psychopath for another.

Blair cooed at Penelope and watched as some got on, and others attempted to talk to the ones who didn't want to. "They're confused."

"Understandable." I nodded toward the body. "But if that one found us, the other two can't be too far behind. We need to get moving."

She looked down the road leading to 17 south and the way to safety. "Where do you think they are?"

"Difficult to say. He was probably the one in the best shape and the other two could be trailing along and be here any minute, or maybe they stayed back and are trying to get that truck of yours going. Either way, we need to get out of here."

She looked at the group, a few more getting on. "They think you're dangerous."

I barked an unconvincing laugh. "They're right."

She nodded and then started toward the front to see what she could do to speed the process, but then stopped to look at me as I gathered up the jack and some of the tools. "It must be terrible."

"What's that?"

"To have the ability to do things like that inside you."

Placing the air gun, hoses, tools, and jack in the side compartment, I stood there with my hands feeling the cool, corrugated metal surface of the Blue Bird. "It's an acquired talent. You learn restraint and work hard to refine your sense of right and wrong."

"What's that mean?"

"It means I wasn't going to let him kill anybody else."

I picked up the wrench, dismantled it, and put it in its compartment before closing the panel and securing it. When I'd finished, I saw her still studying the gunman's body.

"What are you going to do about him?"

Standing there for a moment, I walked over and slipped off the robe I was still wearing, wiping my bloody hands on it and then draping it over the dead man. I then went past her toward the front of the bus. "Try not to run over him when I pull the bus out."

When I got to the front, Holt attempted to hand me the Colt Peacemaker I'd left on the steps.

"You want to keep it?"

He considered it, but then gently caressed the bridge of his swollen and bruised nose and held it out to me. "No, I don't think I'd be as handy with it as you."

"You served; you've had training."

"Maybe, but I don't think I've had the amount of practical experience that you have."

Unable to argue any further, I took the .45 and turned to the others, who remained rooted to the ground and were not making eye contact with me. "You can stay here, but they're going to kill you; know that." I swung around, looking at the dozen or so who were left. "They've been lying to you all along, and every time they said somebody had found salvation and were moving on, they walked them out there into that desert and shot them in the back of the head just like that one over there did to Mister Espinoza—remember him?"

They were all looking at me now.

"I'm sorry, I'm busted up and tired and I guess I'm losing my patience, but that doesn't change the fact that that bus is pulling out of here in a minute and if you stay here, you'll be on your own and likely dead."

I climbed onto the bus and turned toward them, but couldn't think of a single appropriate thing to say. Giving up, I turned around and made my way up the steps and could see Mrs. Wasserstein sitting in her usual seat, looking out the window, her expression unreadable.

I wanted to say something to her, anything, but once again the words just weren't there. Maybe it was just that I was exhausted or that I'd used up all the words I had, so I continued to the driver's seat where I was confronted with a small, threadbare bouquet of wildflowers on the worn red vinyl.

Along with a very large rock.

16

Almost everybody got on, and I didn't even have to use the rock.

Almost everybody.

Walking over to the parking area near the Forest Service sign, I adjusted my hat and shoved my hands in the pockets of my jeans and took a quick look around. "Mister Ackerman, you need to get on the bus."

He sat on one of the logs in the parking area, arranging his robe in the dust and sand and picking at his toes in his sandals. "Young man, I'm not going."

I glanced back at the idling Blue Bird and the faces pressed against the windows, thinking about how I didn't have time for this. "You're the only one. Do you mind if I ask why?"

He laughed and shook his head. "What in the world does it matter if I get on that bus?"

"It means you won't die."

"In the greater scheme of things, who cares?"

"Well, I do, for one."

"Why? You don't even know me."

I bent my knee, giving it a little relief from the ache that was nagging me there. "You're kind of my responsibility, Mister Ackerman."

"No, I don't believe I am." He looked off toward the mountains to the north, lit handsomely by the low angle sun. "My wife is dead, children are dead . . . Hell, I think everybody I've known in my life is dead." He laughed again. "I believe for the first time in a very long time, I'm my own responsibility and I'm just going to sit."

I stood there, looking at him.

"I've lived a good life and I've done a lot of things; I just think I'm done, so why don't you just run along."

"You say you've lived a good life; what leads you to believe that you can't continue to? You know as well as I do that there's a lot of bad in the world and the only thing you're doing is ushering it in by rolling over and playing dead." I turned and looked at the mountains he continued to gaze upon. "I've worn a badge most of my life, but things are changing and I may be hanging it up for a good cause, and I'm okay with that. Change is the nature of all living things. I don't think that's too much to pay for such a priceless gift."

He continued to look at the mountains, ignoring me.

"But I'm not retired—yet." I moved to his left, shifting between him and the rising sun. "Ever been arrested, Mister Ackerman?"

He looked up at me through a thick pair of glasses, the right lens cracked, shielding his eyes with a hand. "Excuse me?"

"Have you ever been arrested?"

"Young man, I spent forty-three years as a lawyer . . ."

"So, you have been arrested."

He chuckled at my joke. "No . . ."

"Well, you are now."

"What?"

"I'm taking you into protective custody."

He looked more than startled. "You wouldn't dare."

"You're under arrest, Mister Ackerman. As per Wyoming statute 14-3-405, I am placing you under arrest and temporary protective custody with a reasonable cause of imminent danger to the individual's life, health, or safety unless said individual is taken into custody without time or convenience to apply for a court order."

"Sheriff, that statute is for underage children."

"Which is how you're behaving. Now get up and get on that bus before I pick you up and tie you to the hood and tell everybody that a deer shot you."

Ignoring me, he turned back to the cliffs. "You're bluffing."

I pointed toward the robe-covered body, now drawing flies in the dust. "Does that look like a bluff to you?"

Attempting not to, his eyes were drawn in the direction of the dead man. "I still say you're bluffing."

"I don't have time for this." In two steps I was on him and grabbed the front of his robe, pulling him from the ground and lifting him onto my shoulder, whereupon I turned and started toward the bus with him kicking and screaming. "You have the right to remain silent. Anything you say can and will be used against you in a court of law. You have the right to speak with a lawyer for advice before I ask you any questions. You have the right to have a lawyer with you during questioning. If you cannot afford a lawyer, one will be appointed for you . . ."

Approaching the bus, I raised my head to find Freebee seated on the steps, toying with my Colt semiautomatic. "Whoever speaks the truth give honest evidence, but a false witness utters deceit." He stood, grimacing and stepping to the side. "You know, I figured you were bluffing too . . ." He laughed. "But you don't bluff, do you?"

I stopped, staring at him as Ackerman continued to struggle.

He sat up and moved from the opening and through his open shirt I could see the gunman's entire abdomen was bandaged. "Is that all you do, pick people up and carry them around?"

Ackerman struggled some more before I finally walked over, setting his feet on the steps in the opening. He started to say something, but then saw the gunman and scrambled up the stairs and into the bus, I guess deciding his life had value after all.

"Sometimes I shoot them too."

Stepping back, I turned my face toward the ground and half watched as Freebee circled around to the left, wincing after he glanced over at Lowell. "You shoot him, or fire a cannon through him?"

"I didn't have a gun at the time."

"You got one now, I see?"

"Yep."

"Two of them?"

"I do."

He raised the muzzle of my .45. "Give 'em to me."

I turned my head, draping my right hand behind me. "No, I don't think I will."

He cocked his head to one side and breathed another laugh. "Is this it, Sheriff? Is this that moment between us that we've been waiting for?"

I didn't say anything.

"It's been a long time comin', huh?"

Relaxing my hand, I let it drape on the handle of his Colt revolver. "A soft answer turneth away wrath, but a harsh word stirs up anger."

Squaring off about ten feet away, he continued to smile. "Better to be patient than a warrior."

"Better to have self-control than to capture a city." We both stood there for what seemed like a very long time. "You know, I'd be more comfortable if we traded guns, wouldn't you?"

"The thought had crossed my mind, any ideas?"

"A square trade—I toss you yours and you toss me mine?"

"Who goes first?"

I shrugged. "Same time?"

"Sure."

"You might want to lower the hammer on that .45 before you throw it." Showing my hands, I carefully pulled the Colt from my belt with two fingers, turning it around and making to throw it to him. "Be careful, because it can go off."

"I know what I'm doing."

He struggled with the hammer on the semiautomatic, and I waited, knowing the action was a dicey proposition at best. He had the weapon pointed to the side so I wasn't worried about getting shot, just hoped it wouldn't go off.

It didn't, and he looked at me, wincing in pain and a little embarrassed at how long it had taken him to do it. "When?"

"On three?"

We counted together. "One, two, three—"

My 1911 flew through the air, and I caught it, turning it in my hand and aiming it at him. "Sorry."

He stood there looking at me, not moving. "What do you mean, 'sorry'?"

"Freebee, I'm not throwing you your gun."

His eyes darted around. "But that was the deal."

"Yep." I returned the six-shooter to my belt, still keeping my semiautomatic pointed at him. "I broke it."

"You can't do that."

"Yep, I can. This is not some shitty movie—it's real life, and I'm through killing people for the day."

He took a step toward me. "Gimme my gun."

"No. Now, where's your partner Carruthers?"

"I'm not telling you until you give me my gun."

"That's not going to happen."

He swung around, throwing an arm toward the main road. "Hey, he's old and slow and he was hurt, so I left him in the truck, okay?" He took another step toward me. "Look, I'm not getting on that bus."

"Yep, you are, even if I have to pick you up and put you on it."

He took another step. "You're not going to shoot me, you just said so."

"No, I said I was through killing people, and that's two different things." I aimed the semiautomatic at his left boot. "I know you've never been shot in the foot because until I hit you in the side, you'd never been shot before, period. It's kind of like a wasp sting, in that the more meat there is the less it hurts. You'd think it would work the other way with more flesh and nerve endings involved, but I guess there's less space to absorb the pain. There are twenty-six bones in the human foot, but more important thirty-three joints—generally if you get shot in the foot you never walk right again."

He studied me.

I slowly pulled the hammer back. "Like you just said, I don't bluff."

I tightened the cuffs around one of his wrists and attached the other to the chrome railing at the rear, above the emergency exit, as he looked up at me. "I really have to ride back here, like this?"

"Hey, I cuffed your unwounded side." I straightened and looked up the aisle at the collection of hooded individuals, some of them now looking out the windows. "Besides, it's less than an hour back to Rock Springs."

Starting back down the length of the bus, I passed Blair in the front seat with Penelope as she kept her head down and cooed at the child.

I sat in the driver's seat, closed the front door, and glanced at the gas gauge. It was still holding at about a quarter of a tank, which should've been plenty enough to get us into town. I hit the starter switch and the big Blue Bird coughed and sputtered to life as I shifted into first, popping the emergency brake and pulling out.

About a mile from the turnout, I could see something in the road ahead.

As I slowed the bus at a slight rise, I could now make out it was the International sitting sideways in the road, the front of it on fire and billowing out an enormous amount of black smoke.

I slowed to a stop and parked about fifty yards from the thing, looking at it as Blair joined me. "What is it?"

"Sorry, it's your truck—and it's burning." I called back to the gunman. "Hey, Freebee, you said you left Carruthers back at the Travelall?"

"Yeah?"

"Well, it's setting up here burning."

It was a moment before he responded. "Maybe he got it running and back on the road . . . And then who knows, I guess it caught on fire."

Blair leaned forward, peering through the windshield. "Can we get around it?"

I studied the partially flaming hulk, still belching out black smoke. "Possibly, but I'd hate to ram that thing with that crappy tire on the right rear, who knows if it'll hold."

"Can we push it out of the way?"

"Maybe."

"You'll need help." She turned, looking toward the rear of the bus. "Mister Holt, Mister Ackerman?"

Both stood and came forward along with a few others.

"I think we need to push that thing out of the way, gentlemen." I switched off the motor and opened the door without waiting for a response, making my way down the stairwell and onto the roadway.

The smoke was horrible, but the flames weren't too bad. They seemed to be exclusively in and around the engine compartment, giving credence to Freebee's assumption that Carruthers had got it going, but from the damage of being rammed it had caught fire.

But if that was the case, then where was Carruthers?

It was a slight downgrade into the ditch on the right side of the road, and because most of the flames were coming from the front we could easily push it in that direction if the emergency brake was off and it wasn't in park. Otherwise, we were going to have to climb in the thing and break it free.

I looked back at the other men. "Are you guys game?"

Ackerman was, of course, the first to speak. "What if it explodes?"

"Very rare. It'll just sit there and burn until it goes out, maybe blowing out the windows."

They nodded and followed me as we approached the International. I could see a pool of motor oil underneath the thing, which wasn't likely to catch fire but might explain why it had stopped.

I pulled my .45 from the holster. We were now close enough that, unless Carruthers was slumped in the seat or had fallen to the floor, he wasn't in the vehicle.

I couldn't see him anywhere, and with all the smoke it looked as if the thing had been burning for a while. "You men stay back here to the rear. I'll check and see if it'll roll."

I moved up to the driver's side and could see the thing was, indeed, empty. Seeing no immediate threats, I re-holstered my Colt. The window was open, and the majority of the flames and smoke were blowing in the other direction, but a lot of the interior was smoking, and I was hoping that I wouldn't have to climb inside.

Fortunately, the window was open and I could reach in and flip the warm metal of the selector lever on the steering column down and into neutral. The interior was breathtakingly hot and, though most of the billowing smoke wasn't inside, there were a lot of fumes.

I reached down and burned my armpit getting to the emergency brake release, then jumped back as the thing rolled a couple of inches. "Get to the sides in the back and let's push!"

They did as I said, then I joined them, and we watched as the thing slowly rolled forward into the ditch where it sat, smoking like a sinking ship.

I took out my Colt and scanned the area. "It was in park, and the emergency brake was on."

Holt wiped the sweat from his face, avoiding his busted nose. "Meaning?"

"Carruthers must've stopped the thing and gotten out, and then set it on fire."

The group of them began looking around. "Do you think he saw you with Freebee and decided to hide?"

"Possibly. Either way, the authorities will find him out here—at least he better hope so."

We started back for the bus as I checked the position of the International, but it looked like it was far enough from the bushes and stunted trees that it wouldn't start a fire. Hell, for what it was worth, we should've been able to just sit here and wait until the smoke brought in the Forest Service, CIA, FBI, INTERPOL, or the sheriff or fire departments.

Following the others back onto the bus, I jumped in the driver's seat, placing my Colt on the dash and starting the Blue Bird up again.

"Hey, Sheriff?"

I looked back at Freebee in the very rear, still cuffed to the railing. "What is it?"

"My bandages are bleeding."

I started to turn away. "We'll be in town in forty minutes."

He called out again. "It's pretty bad."

"Well, you're going to have to tough it out."

"I don't think I can, I could really use some help here."

I half turned and called to the entire group. "Can somebody go back there and help him?"

Nobody moved, so I looked to my left and the front row for my strongest ally. "Blair?"

She wasn't there.

I switched off the bus and stood, turning and retrieving my .45 from the dash, and looking up and down through the rows of seats. The men who had moved the truck with me were seated and looking around as confused as I was.

Holt spoke up. "You want me to go take a look at him?"

"No, stay where you are." I moved down the aisle and studied all of the hooded individuals, seeing some I recognized and some I didn't, none of them moving.

The gunman called out again. "I think I must've pulled the bandages loose or something."

I studied Freebee, still cuffed to the railing. "Well, you're just going to have to live with it."

"I'm telling you, Sheriff, I'm bleeding to death back here."

Sighing, I started down the aisle, still looking around me. When I got to him, he looked very much like when I'd cuffed him. "Where are you bleeding?"

He looked down at his abdomen, taped and immaculately clean, his eyes coming back up to mine as he grinned. "Maybe it wasn't as bad as I thought."

Shaking my head, I started back toward the front only to see one of the robed figures now standing in the middle of the aisle in muck boots with the jerry can of gasoline, the cap turned with the spout extended as he poured the contents out on the floor of the bus.

I took a step toward him with the .45 aimed at his chest and he threw the can down, the remainder of the fuel pouring out as he lifted his head and dropped the hood onto his shoulders, smoking one of his signature Cuban cigars.

He pulled the smoldering thing from his mouth and blew on the embers at the other end as we both watched them glow, his movie-star eyes finally coming back to me. "Hello, Sheriff." He brought the cigar to his lips, stopping just before it got there. "Care for a cigar?"

"No." I noticed when he turned his head a bit that there was dry blood there. "Hurt yourself?"

He placed the cigar back in his mouth and took a puff, blowing the smoke toward the ceiling as the gasoline wept down the rubber mat of the bus toward me. "No, I'm afraid you did this."

"Sorry about that. This bus is a little unmanageable."

He looked around. "Lowell?"

"Dead."

He puffed on his cigar, considering. "I suppose you did that too?"

"He didn't give me much choice."

I took another step toward him. "Carruthers, what do you think you're doing?"

He plucked the stogie from his mouth again, blowing on it and holding it out at arm's length toward the ceiling of the vehicle as he backed up the aisle. "Purging the world with fire."

"Why?"

"Why not?" He gestured with the cigar toward my sidearm. "I might also point out that if you pull the trigger on that firearm it's possible it will have the same effect as me dropping this Robusto."

Raising the Colt, I lifted both arms. "You were saying?"

He gestured to the area around him. "One quick flick of ash and all my enemies and evidence go up in smoke."

"These people aren't your enemies. They believed in you . . ."

"Alas, I do not think such is the case any longer." He cocked his head to one side. "But what about you, Sheriff? Are you my enemy?"

"If you're about to burn an entire bus full of people alive, then yep, I'd say I'm about to be your worst nightmare" I took another step forward. "Where's your daughter and granddaughter?"

"Out of harm's way."

"This is the only operable vehicle out here; you destroy it and there's no way out for you or them."

"I've made arrangements for that."

"Arrangements?"

"Nothing to worry about, Sheriff, everything is going to be fine."

"For you."

He brought the cigar down and took another puff. "Well, for me perhaps not so much."

"You're dying."

He shrugged. "So it would appear."

"There's no sense in taking all these people with you."

He gestured around at the hooded group. "You don't seem to understand. They're my followers, they want to go with me."

"First, let's get them completely off the horse tranquilizers and see if they do."

He puffed his cigar. "Simply a precautionary measure. They weren't on xylazine when they first began following me, but it provides them with a solace they desperately need in this hectic and godless world." He placed a hand on his hip and struck a philosophical pose I was sure he'd used in one of his small-screen roles. "We're all going to the stars; I'm just helping them along."

I gestured toward Freebee in the back. "Him too?"

"One of my most devoted servants . . ."

The gunman's voice called from the back. "Wait, what?"

I spoke over my shoulder. "In case you haven't figured it out yet, Freebee. You're about to be incinerated along with the rest of us."

I listened as he rattled the handcuffs. "Hey, that wasn't part of the deal."

Carruthers peeked around me. "The deal has changed, my friend."

"Now, just a minute—"

"I'm afraid both you and Lowell have become something of a liability since you began taking these poor people out into the desert and killing them, you bad boy."

"You told us to do it!"

He shook his head almost as if in pity. "Now is not the time to desecrate your mortal soul, but better to repent and accept your lot in this life and the next."

Freebee rattled the cuffs some more. "Sheriff, it was his idea all along!"

"You know, I believe you, but I don't think that's going to help our situation. When he says that with a flick of that cigar he's going to cleanse the world of all of his enemies and evidence, I'm afraid that includes you."

"I'm not going to die like this."

I casually stepped toward Carruthers again, now only about twelve feet from him. "Well, none of us are particularly crazy about the idea."

It was about then that someone seated beside Carruthers suddenly leaned out and smashed something on the man's rubber-booted foot, something very large and heavy. The matinee idol scream was high enough to break glass, but all I could see was the cigar flying from his hand and bouncing off the shoulder of one of the hooded brethren before rolling off the back of one of the seats and falling toward the floor.

No matter how fast I was, I wasn't going to make it, but I had to try.

Leaping forward several feet, I snatched off my hat and thudded onto the rubber mat, stretching out my arm in hopes that the cigar might fall into the crown, but could see I was going to be a foot short.

Galumphing forward like a flipperless seal, I watched in slow-motion horror as the cigar continued to fall, only to be snatched out of the air by a marvelous pair of dexterous fingers.

I found myself now within striking distance of Carruthers. Lurching up so that the madman wouldn't have a second chance to ignite us all, I surged forward and placed my shoulder into his midriff and carried him backward, tripping over something as we both crashed into the instrument panel of the bus. The air left his body as he slumped to the ground, unconscious.

Lying there, I felt as if the gasoline fumes were beginning to overtake me. I finally rolled over, pushing Carruthers's bloody foot off my hip to see a large stone sitting in the middle of the aisle.

Mrs. Wasserstein was in the seat beside the rock, her legs crossed, bobbing a sandaled foot and smoking the Cohiba. "I told you, young man, I don't think you know what I'm capable of if properly motivated."

EPILOGUE

Mike Thurman shook his head as we sat there on the wall of the parking lot of the Sweetwater County Sheriff's Department with Dog at our feet. "You got your partner back, I see."

I drank from my bottle of iced tea. "Yep, Rick Scout Traveler picked him up along with Richard Zevin, Keeper of the Light of the Second Quadrant, the Cheyenne Rifle of the Dead, and my other stuff. He'd given the last of the water to Dog just before Ranger Rick showed up."

"Is he going to be okay?"

"Yep, they've got him and a couple of the others over at Memorial Hospital of Sweetwater County, most of them for the lesions from the xylazine they were injecting some of the more resistant members with."

"Good to hear." He slipped off the wall and stooped to pet Dog, who took the opportunity to roll over and offer his belly, something he rarely did. "And they got Luis Diaz?"

"Jim Thomas did out on 80. I guess Doctor Diaz was hauling Blair and Penelope back to California and Thomas intercepted them around Green River."

"I've got to ask . . . How did you know the coroner was involved with them?"

"He mentioned having a clinic on the north side, the same one I heard Carruthers mention. Carruthers also said he had a connection for those Cohiba cigars he smoked, and I figured the Cuban doctor was a pretty good bet. I put two and two together, especially after he purposefully botched the autopsy on the woman that was supposed to be Blair."

"And who was she?"

"Joyce Lundgren, another of the brethren who ran out of money."

He exhaled as if punched. "Psychos."

"Yep, so it would appear. Grossnickle's got people out there all over the desert digging up bodies left and right with Richard Zevin's map that blocks the sun as a guide." He stood, walking out to the curb and then turning back toward me. "You want to know something funny?"

I stared at the sun-drenched concrete sidewalk, trying not to think about how tired I was. "I'm dying to know something funny."

"Carruthers is indeed dying of lung cancer, among other things . . ."

"That's funny?"

"Not that part, but you have to admit that with the cigars it's kind of ironic."

"What's the funny part?"

"After all they've been through, Blair, as his daughter and only child, is his living heir, meaning she gets everything he's gotten away with from all these people. The Order of the Red Gate wasn't even set up as a legal charity; it just all went into his bank account. And with him standing trial both here and back in California, and likely not going to make it through that, she's going to get it all."

"How much?"

"Close to four and a half million." He looked up and smiled at me. "You know what she's going to do?"

"Give it back."

He made a face. "How did you know?"

"It just seems like something she would do." I took another sip of my tea, finishing it off. "She should buy herself a new truck. I think the brethren owe her that much." Slipping off the wall myself, I joined him as we looked out into the parched land and rimrock hills.

"You know, I think this place is growing on me. It's not pretty, but it's stark and honest—kind of like a charcoal sketch."

"Blair coming back?"

"No." He laughed to himself. "I don't think she is."

"Maybe she'll surprise you."

"Maybe."

I took a moment to think about how all of this had started. "The longest postal route in the country."

"Three hundred and seven miles." He shifted his head toward me. "You looking for a job?"

"Not particularly."

He finally turned and studied me fully. "Jeez, I'm sorry, Walt . . . I almost got you killed. I wouldn't blame you if you never spoke to me again."

"What're family for?" I looked across the parking lot at my vehicle. "You washed my truck?"

"I did. What're family for?"

I patted my leg and Dog joined me as I started across the parking lot, but then there was that strange sound that I'd heard before, and finally remembered it was the JugBug in my pocket. Hooking a finger, I pulled out the device by the antenna and stared at the incoming call, area code 202, and figured it was Maxim Sidorov. Holding up a finger to Mike, I flipped the thing open. "Let me guess, the Russians are coming, the Russians are coming . . ."

"Excuse me?"

I didn't recognize the voice.

"I'm looking to speak with Sheriff Longmire?"

I cleared my throat, lowering the tailgate on my truck as Dog jumped up and I gestured for Mike to take a seat. "Speaking."

"What was that about Russians?"

"Nothing, just a little inside joke. Um, to whom am I speaking?"

"This is Agent in Charge Blake Foster of the FBI/FAA task force, we're leading the search for Ruth One Heart. Your deputy, the Basque guy with the thirteen-letter name, said this was the number to get in touch with you?"

"Saizarbitoria, yep. Have you got something for me?"

"We found her plane."

I sat on the tailgate, joining the others. "The Husky?"

"Yes, near a golf course in Iowa—an abandoned hangar for Laurens Skyways Charter Rides and Instructions that was shut down in '04."

Glancing around the parking lot, I avoided Mike's eyes. "And?"

"Mint condition, not a mark on it. It's almost out of gas and the batteries are dead, but other than that it looks like she flew it in and landed it yesterday. It doesn't have a fuel leak or any other mechanical issues we can see, and all her charts and personal items are still in it, her purse with her ID, a couple of pieces of luggage, cell phone . . . even her badge and sidearm."

"That doesn't make any sense."

There was a pause. "People do it sometimes, I mean, she's already put in her papers. I'm thinking she just walked away."

"Agent Foster, that just doesn't sound like her."

I listened as he rustled some papers. "Excuse me for asking, but are you family?"

"I am."

He adjusted his phone, probably coming to the conclusion that he wasn't going to get rid of me. "Close?"

"Well, in the last couple of months . . ."

"Does she have any other living relatives?"

"Not that I'm aware of, no."

There was another silence as he composed his thoughts. "In my experience, it happens. Especially in our profession, Sheriff. There's a removed quality here in the bureau and sometimes people get to the end of a career and simply disappear."

"She was participating in an officer-involved shooting investigation . . ."

"Who was the shooter?"

"Me."

He laughed. "Even more of a reason to walk away, rather than spend the next six months of what's left of her retirement in a courtroom?"

"But to leave her ID, cell phone, badge, and sidearm?"

"It happens. I had a section chief who was reaching retirement and went to a beach house down on Oak Island one time, and he just left all his stuff laid out and disappeared and then turned up on an island in Micronesia with a fourteen-year-old bride."

"Well, I'm not buying it, Agent."

"Suit yourself, but we're closing the investigation on our end."

It was my turn to pause as I stood and took a few steps and stopped, looking around for answers and seeing none. "On a missing federal agent?"

"A missing federal *ex*-agent—no harm, no foul, Sheriff." There was yet another pause. "She'll turn up, I can almost promise you."

"Almost." I turned and found Mike studying me as I continued to converse on the phone. "I'm assuming my deputy with the thirteen-letter name has all your information?"

"He does."

"And you'll send me a copy of your report as a professional courtesy?"

"I will."

"Nice talking to you, Agent."

"Nice talking to you, Sheriff."

I closed the phone and just stood there enveloped in professional courtesy as I studied the phone in my hand.

"Anything I can do?" Mike sat there looking at me.

"I'm not sure there's anything anybody can do, but thanks." Walking around, I opened the door for Dog as he leapt off the tailgate and circled around, jumping in the passenger seat as I closed the door behind him.

I met Mike at the driver's side as I attempted to poke the phone in my pocket, but found it blocked by something. Pulling my shirt out, I looked under the flap and sighed. "Hey, Mike, it looks like there is something you can do after all."

"What's that?"

Taking the item still wrapped in the handmade map out, I handed it to him. "Could you run over to the hospital and give Richard Zevin, the Keeper of the Light of the Second Quadrant, his finger back? And try not to lose the wedding ring, would you?"

Somewhat reluctantly, he took it and then watched as I climbed in my truck and started it. I was about to pull it in gear when I paused for a moment and then lowered the window and looked at him.

He laughed and asked. "What?"

"I'm smiling."

He shook his head, glancing off to the rimrock to the northeast. "You know, nobody does that anymore, right?"

"Yeah, I'm trying to start a trend."

Pulling out, I waved goodbye to Mike and turned the corner. I saw what I was looking for near the end of the building alongside a truck dock and drove in that direction. I stopped and paused for a moment, weighing the phone in my hand, and then tossed it into the dumpster and headed due north with the smile still on my face.

100 YEARS of PUBLISHING

Harold K. Guinzburg and George S. Oppenheimer founded Viking in 1925 with the intention of publishing books "with some claim to permanent importance rather than ephemeral popular interest." After merging with B. W. Huebsch, a small publisher with a distinguished catalog, Viking enjoyed almost fifty years of literary and commercial success before merging with Penguin Books in 1975.

Now an imprint of Penguin Random House, Viking specializes in bringing extraordinary works of fiction and nonfiction to a vast readership. In 2025, we celebrate one hundred years of excellence in publishing. Our centennial colophon features the original logo for Viking, created by the renowned American illustrator Rockwell Kent: a Viking ship that evokes enterprise, adventure, and exploration, ideas that inspired the imprint's name at its founding and continue to inspire us.

For more information on Viking's history, authors, and books, please visit penguin.com/viking.